THE KING'S OUTLAWS

HIGHLAND RAIDER

Bestselling & Multi-Award Winning Author

AMY JARECKI

Book Cover Design by: Midnight Muse

Published by Oliver-Heber Books

0 9 8 7 6 5 4 3 2 1

SERIES BIBLIOGRAPHY

Highland Warlord

Highland Raider

Highland Beast

I

THE BATTLE OF LOCH RYAN, 10TH FEBRUARY, THE YEAR OF OUR LORD, 1307

"Retreat!" Angus bellowed above the thunderous tumult of battle. Swords clashed, barbed maces thudded into iron mail while dying men shrieked in a fight no mortal could win. Sidestepping toward the shore, he thrust out his shield, stopping an attacker with the deadly spike jutting from its center. Within his next heartbeat, Angus drove his sword into the gullet of another. "To the boats!"

"They outnumber us ten to one," shouted Raghnall, still fighting like a man crazed.

"Go now," Angus ordered, as he cut down another, creating a gap for his men to escape. "Raghnall, I commanded ye to withdraw!"

The man-at-arms leapt in front of Angus, fending off the army as the gap closed. "Not until ye're aboard, m'lord."

Slinging his targe to his back, Angus grasped the man's plaid and dragged him into the surf. "There are too many of them and I'll not see ye killed this day."

Behind them, MacDonald warriors had already taken up oars in the nearest *birlinn*, its sail billowing with a fierce westerly, thank the gods. His boots filled with water and slowed his progress, though Angus gnashed his teeth and surged ahead with all his strength, defying the tug from murderous kelpies of the deep. He tossed the enormous sword he'd inherited from his father over the side and summoned the dregs of his strength to haul himself into the hull. Raghnall landed with a thud beside him.

Gael MacDonald thrust a helping palm in front of Angus' face. "We feared we'd lost ye, m'lord."

"Never." Taking the offered hand, Angus let his man tug him to his feet, though nothing could have prepared him to face the massacre on the shore behind them. Worse, the two men who'd led the charge were already bound and gagged. All but two of the *birlinns* Angus had provided for this mishappen raid were alight, flames leaping where they moored just shy of the sands.

"My God," growled Raghnall, leaning heavily on the rail as he sucked in deep breaths.

"'Tis amazing anyone survived," said Gael. "I fear the king's brothers are lost."

The man-at-arms pounded his fist on the side of the boat. "Those hapless bastards will be executed for certain."

Gulping against his urge to wretch, Angus turned away and headed for the tiller. Before they set out, he had told Robert the Bruce this was a stargazer's plan, but the king chose to ignore his warning. Regardless of what Angus predicted, he had already given his word—committed sixty men and five of his fleet to Scotland's cause, which set the bile to churning in his gullet. 'Twas a foolish risk, though one he'd recklessly hoped was worth taking if it meant ridding the Hebridean Isles of the Lord of Lorn and his clan of MacDougall scourge. Those feuding bastards sided with Longshanks. They'd killed his brother, the man who ought to still hold the title of Lord of Islay. Come what may, Angus would pledge his soul to any king who promised to help him in his quest to claim vengeance.

Raghnall sat on the bench in front of the tiller and took up an oar. "Robert never should have divided our forces."

Angus ground his molars. He'd argued the same to no avail. From the outset there'd been nary a choice—side with Bruce or side with Longshanks, even though at one time they'd all pledged fealty to the English crown. 'Twas difficult to believe an alliance with the man who claimed himself overlord of Scotland once seemed the right thing to do—until the bastard had become a tyrant.

Nonetheless, Scotland had been embattled for nearly a score of years and her sons were not yet ready to take on the fiercest army in Christendom. Aye, the newly crowned King of Scots had spent most of the winter in hiding. Now His Grace had only begun to raise an army and the damn mutton-head decided to split his forces—attack the northern and southern borders of his ancestral lands. Although, if Angus wore the man's cloak, he'd thirst for retribution as well. But before he sent his kin into battle, he would have made certain they had the numbers needed to face Edward's army.

As the *birlinn* sailed into the North Sea, Angus bore down on the tiller and pointed her westward. His losses had been heavy, but not as devastating as those of the king. Moreover, Angus should have been the man to lead the charge. He should have been the one the English captured—rather than taking up the rear, no matter how much the Bruce's brothers had argued.

He may have been overruled from the start, but never again. He was Angus Og MacDonald, Lord of Islay, and he intended to protect clan and kin no matter what. As the boat chased the setting sun, the dreaded truth weighed heavily upon his shoulders, yet the hours passed in a blur.

By the time they reached the promontory on the

southern end of the Isle of Islay, Dunyvaig Castle was but a black shadow against the night sky—looming like the murky abyss in Angus' heart.

"It looks as if the king has returned," said Gael, pointing to a row of MacDonald *birlinns* used in the attack on Turnberry. Even if the king had failed, more men must have survived the northern raid for certain.

Ready for a confrontation, Angus disembarked first. Raghnall hastened to catch him and walked at his shoulder as they made their way up the hill and into the great hall of the keep. "What are ye planning to tell the Bruce?" asked Angus' most trusted man.

"The truth."

"Aye? Ye aim to tell the King of Scots he sent his brothers on a fool's errand? 'Cause that's the reality of it. Damnation, Scotland's never going to win this war."

Angus stopped and grabbed his man by the throat. By the gods, he loved Raghnall as a brother, but he'd not tolerate anyone who bleated words of everlasting doom. "We may have lost this battle but, mark me, I'm no' aiming to lose another."

Raghnall threw out his palms. "Forgive me," he croaked. "I spoke out of turn."

Releasing his grip, Angus shook off his ire. "Och, I'm every bit as disappointed as ye are, lad. We've not but to face our failures, pull ourselves together, and persevere."

"I'd be happier about it with you at the helm."

"I'm no king," Angus growled.

"How can ye say that? The blood of Somerled flows through your veins. Besides, ye look as if ye've been kissed by the sun itself."

Rather than reply, Angus continued to trudge along the path. Aye, the great Norse-Gaelic king, Somerled, had formed the Lordship of the Isles and were it not for the marauding MacDougalls, the entirety of the Hebrides would be well and truly under the MacDonalds' banner. If only Alasdair were still alive to claim it. But the burden of the lordship had fallen to Angus, a mere second son.

"Fairhair has returned!" shouted the sentry from atop the baily walls.

Angus snorted. He'd been referred to thus since he was a wee bairn and, at one time, the epithet caused him consternation, even though his ancestor Harald Fairhair had reigned as King of Norway. When they were lads, Alasdair had oft poked fun and thought his younger brother weak, until Angus grew larger and stronger. Now he'd met no man who could best him, though the name Fairhair had stuck. Every time the men called it out, he was reminded of his mishappen youth—and the triumph of besting his elder brother, God rest his soul.

Tonight, the weight of an anvil hung about his neck. Not only had good men lost their lives, Angus had naught but to face the king. As he strode through the sea gate and toward the doors to the Dunyvaig keep, his feet grew sluggish, the fatigue from the battle made facing his duty all the more repugnant.

"Greetings, m'lord," called a pair of sentries as they opened the heavy oaken doors.

Angus gave a tight-lipped nod. No salutations were in order for this day's failure.

Judging by the music and merriment coming from the great hall, the raid to the north had been a success.

To my very bones, I pray they fared better than my sorry lot.

Indeed, the ale was flowing, the piper and fiddler playing, but as soon as Angus stepped inside, the merry-makers took one look at the grim expression he wore upon his face and the hall fell silent.

Upon the dais, King Robert slowly lowered the tankard from his lips. He first looked to Angus, then his gaze trailed beyond. Any joy that may have shone in his eyes turned to black cinders.

Steeling himself, Angus removed his helm, strode to the dais, and climbed the steps. At the top, he dropped to one knee, bowing his head. "My Lord King."

"What news from Loch Ryan?"

"We were ambushed, Your Grace. Upon our approach, it first appeared there were no more than a handful of soldiers guarding the bay. However, after we disembarked, Edward's army set upon us like ghosts descending from the trees."

As the silence swelled through the air, Angus didn't move. He barely breathed. He focused on the floor, his knee grinding into the unforgiving hardwood in front of the high table where most days he presided as Lord of Islay. There he knelt as time stopped, his helm tucked in his arm, his fair head bent to a king whose next act might be to sever it from his body.

"Where are the others? Did ye not return together?"

"All dead." Angus looked up and met Robert's hard stare. "Your brothers Lord Alexander and Lord Thomas led the charge as agreed. They were captured early on. We were outnumbered ten to one—out-armed and out-armored as well. Five *birlinns* set sail. Only two returned."

"And yet ye sailed for home in one of the fortunate two?" asked the king, the same question Angus had grappled with ever since catching sight of the Bruce's brothers being bound and gagged as his *birlinn* made its escape.

He must offer no excuses. "I was, sire."

Robert pounded his fist on the table with such force, goblets and tankards teetered, their contents sloshing. "Fie!"

Angus stood and approached. "I swear on my brother's grave, I would trade places with your kin here and now."

"Aye?" the Bruce scoffed. "Yet there ye stand, mayhap bloodied, but alive and otherwise unscathed whilst my brothers will doubtless suffer the same fate as Niall and William Wallace. Am I to have no family remaining when the time comes to march on Stirling?"

Angus could provide no answer. The king was aware of their plans—Alexander and Thomas were eager to lead the charge, eager to claim accolades for a victory while the MacDonald forces were ordered to take up the rear and attack with a second wave.

"What of Turnberry?" he dared to ask.

"We captured the village and Lord Percy has fled. I've left the task of seizing the castle in Sir Douglas' *capable* hands."

The news posed as much of a relief as it did a slap to the face.

"Perhaps if I had sent the Black Douglas in your stead, matters would have been different at Loch Ryan," the king added, the jibe hitting its mark. Angus deserved such a retort and more.

"Only two ships returned?" asked Sir Arthur Campbell, sitting at the king's right. "How many men lost?"

"As I said, two *birlinns* returned. The rest were set afire." Angus gripped the hilt of his sword. Good God, the bitterness of his next words might slay him. "Two and ninety lives lost."

"But not your kin," groused the Bruce.

Angus scowled. His clan alone had lost twoscore of good fighting men but saying so would only further incite the king's ire. If only he had insisted on leading the charge, at least one of the Bruce's brothers may have returned to tell the tale.

"Losing so many boats and soldiers will cripple us," said Sir Robbie Boyd, a young knight who sat on the king's left. In truth, had Angus the use of the skill of Douglas, Campbell, and Boyd this day, their losses might have been far less.

The king's expression grew even darker. But no matter how much the man would like to heft the blame of this day's tragedy upon Angus' shoulders, the burden was the Bruce's to bear. Though the truth gave Angus no comfort. Not only were lives lost, clan MacDonald was now seen as unworthy in His Grace's eyes, a fact that stung more bitterly than a hive of angry bees.

Just as Angus steeled himself to be seized by the guard and hung in his own tower's gibbet, the king leaned forward, resting his forehead in his palms. "I've no choice but to appeal to Ulster."

Campbell reached for a pewter ewer of ale. "With all due respect, Lord King, he is aligned with Edward."

"Mayhap, but Longshanks is the same bastard who has captured his daughter, my wife, mind ye. The miserable sop has imprisoned her in some frigid dungeon in Wales for all we ken. Elizabeth is of Ulster's blood. The earl must have some sense of decency, some sense of justice."

"I reckon 'tis worth pursuing," Boyd agreed. "But we go in ready for a fight."

"Nay." The Bruce grabbed his eating knife and pointed it toward Angus' heart. "We go in bearing the flag of parley—*and* a well-fortified retinue."

"Aye," Angus agreed. "And this time I'm no' staying with the bloody boats."

"WHERE ARE YE OFF TO NOW?" ASKED FINOVOLA. "I thought the countess said you were to have the embroidery completed for your gift to Lord O'Doherty afore Saint Valentine's Day."

"And what if I do not?" Anya loved her sister, but the lass had no sense of adventure. "His Lordship will be none the wiser and I can present the linens to him on our wedding day." If there was to be a marriage. She had been not quite betrothed, and more or less promised, to the man for two years, yet the date still had not been set. Unfortunately, however, it seemed Anya wasn't destined to be waiting for the rest of her days. Lord O'Doherty was due to arrive for the Saint Valentine's feast two days hence, when he planned to finalize the details of the marriage contracts with her guardian, the Earl of Ulster.

Anya cringed every time she thought of marrying O'Doherty. In truth, she'd been reticent about the idea ever since her guardian had proposed it. Why was it only men were allowed adventure? Would it be too much to ask to see a bit of the world before she married? Goodness, even a jaunt to Dublin or London might be welcome.

Finovola twirled across the floor of the bedchamber the two sisters shared. "If I were you, I'd be over the moon with glee. Imagine it, oh, sister mine. Ye are to be wed to a fine Irish lord. Ye'll have your own keep to run, and servants aplenty."

"Mayhap." Yes, Chahir O'Doherty was a lord, though an underling of the Earl of Ulster, who had assumed guardianship of Anya and her sister after their father's untimely death. Her intended was fine-enough looking, she supposed, though a bit dull. Months ago, they had strolled atop the wall-walk together and after they'd spanned the distance between the first two towers, they had absolutely naught to say. At first, Anya had tried to find some activity they both might enjoy, but they may as well have been on opposite shores of Ireland for all they had in common.

The notion of marriage filled her with more dread than warmth and no matter what Finovola said, the longer it took to finalize the contracts and the terms of her dowry, the better. "Lord O'Doherty may come to Carrickfergus on the morrow and tell the earl he has had a change of heart."

Finovola stopped dancing and dropped her hands to her sides. "Whyever would he do such a thing?"

"Perhaps he has fallen in love with another."

"Nay!" Stamping her foot, the lass turned as red as the scarlet thread Anya used to make the roses on her godawful embroidery. Her sister was such a dear—thoughtful of others, always dutiful. If only Finovola were the elder of the two girls, she could marry His Lordship. "Lord O'Doherty would never renege on his word. Heavens, defy the Earl of Ulster? It simply is not done."

And there was Anya's conundrum. No one ever defied their guardian. Even if Chahir O'Doherty loved another, he would still proceed with the marriage. If only Anya were able to ask him if he found her appealing, or clever, or interesting. In truth, Finovola was far prettier with golden hair and flawless skin. The two sisters couldn't be more opposite. Anya had dark brown hair and a splay of freckles across the bridge of her nose. She was shorter than the withers of a wee pony and stout to boot, while willowy Finovola was tall, thin, and graceful.

But neither Anya's adventurous spirit nor Finovola's beauty would ever prevent them from walking down the aisles of their fates. They were the daughters of Lord Guy O'Cahan and destined to wed for the benefit of augmenting their future husbands' lands, riches, and power. Alas, if only she could meet someone, fall in love with him, and sail into the sunset on a journey of new beginnings and fascinating discoveries.

Why was it love matches abounded throughout Ireland for everyone except the highborn?

Anya tied her cloak and slung her satchel over her shoulder. "I'm nearly finished with my drawing and Lord only knows how much longer I'll have the freedom to slip outside the castle walls."

"Ye hardly have the freedom now."

She kissed her sister's cheek. "I must complete it

today whilst the weather is fine. This is the last time—at least afore the feast, I give ye my word."

Without further argument, Anya slipped out the door and hastened through the corridor until she reached the narrow stairs leading to the cellars. She stopped and listened for a moment. Though the keep consisted of five stories, Anya could detect a guard's heavy footsteps all the way down to the bottom of the stairwell. After hearing nothing, she tiptoed around and around until she reached the dark cellars. She'd been using this route for seven years and needed no light to show her the way. Besides, torches were dangerous. They brought too much attention. If her guardian ever heard how often Anya left the castle to steal coveted time alone, she'd be disciplined for certain.

She ran her fingers along the damp walls, turning left, then right, then left again until daylight shone through the bars of the forgotten old cellar gate. Anya dug in her satchel, pulled out a key, and slipped it into the rusty lock. Shortly after she'd arrived, she found the key hidden behind a loose stone near the hearth in her chamber. A slip of velum was attached to the loop with a bit of twine. Upon the note was written two words: *vinariam porta*, the Latin for cellar gate. Of course, having been tutored in Latin as well as being a bit of an adventurer, Anya immediately went searching for the mysterious lock to fit the key.

She let herself out of the captive tower, locked the gate for good measure, and returned the key to her satchel. Pulling the hood of her sealskin cloak low over her brow to ensure she wouldn't be recognized, Anya quickly skirted the shore, ever so careful to stay away from the prying gazes of villagers who tended the earl's livestock and whatnot. She hastened up the hill to a small outcropping where she'd be sheltered from winter's bitter wind—straight to her own little alcove.

By the saints, it was good to be alone in her secluded hideaway. With her warm cloak wrapped snuggly about her person, she sat in the comfort of the grass and pulled out her scroll of velum and charcoal. Generally, Anya drew flowers and animals, but because she was soon to be taken away from Carrickfergus, she'd been working on a drawing of the castle and the cottages in the foreground. Aye, on any given day she'd be able to draw the keep with her eyes closed, but this work was different. She painstakingly detailed the masonry, the merlons and crenels, three feet in depth, no less. She used the minutest of strokes to etch the thatch on the cottage roofs, making it look as if it were real. Most of all, she paid particular attention to the animals —the thick sheep's wool, a workhorse who was old and stooped, the dairy cows with their black and white spots.

Over and over again she sharpened her charcoal and painstakingly added the finer details, while in the bay, ships came and went, bringing their cargoes of grain and stores for the castle, all none the wiser that Anya sat in her little alcove concealed between the stones, taking in every detail. She even captured the seabirds in flight.

Lost in her work, she didn't notice when the sun sank low in the western sky, but she jolted upright when a drop of rain splattered the toe of her shoe. Quickly rolling up her work, she looked to the clouds. When she'd ventured out, the sky had been clear, and now it looked as if a storm were brewing. She shoved her scroll and charcoal into her satchel and grabbed the strap. In her rush to keep the drawing dry, the bag caught on a craggy stone and upended, spilling everything into the grass.

"Curses!" she swore, shoving her things back inside, then hastened down the hill.

2

By the time the two *birlinns* arrived, ferrying King Bruce to Carrickfergus Castle, there wasn't much daylight remaining, not that days offered many hours of sunshine this time of year. Moreover, the wind had brought in a squall, the rain already misting atop their helms. Before they set out, His Grace almost insisted Angus remain behind, but these were MacDonald boats and the few soldiers they'd brought along were MacDonald kin. They took orders from Angus.

Dammit all, the failure at Loch Ryan had not been his fault, though by the jeers the king had spewed at him, anyone would have thought Angus was solely to blame. In hindsight, he should have refused to supply the men from the outset. He should have refused to provide the ships. Except that would have done nothing to further the MacDonald cause. He had naught but to take his lumps and persevere. He'd thrown down his gauntlet and committed to support Robert the Bruce. And that decision had not been made lightly. Angus was a Scot, and a Highlander to boot. Sooner or later an opportunity to redeem himself would arise and he fully intended to stay the course until it did. He would gain the king's favor if it bloody killed him.

"Taking up the rear again," growled Raghnall under his breath as they marched toward the sea gate.

Angus shot the man-at-arms a glare from beneath his helm. "Wheesht."

"Och, let us pray the weather doesn't worsen, especially if we're forced to make a hasty exit."

Angus slowed his pace as he examined the deadly teeth of the iron portcullis tucked into the archway above. The cogs of the wheel sat just inside on ground level rather than atop the guard's walk. A sledgehammer and an old shovel rested against the masonry nearby. Nudging his man-at-arms with his elbow, he inclined his head toward the gate's guard. "Distract him."

Raghnall knew better than to ask why. He strode directly toward the man and pointed to the top of the curtain across the courtyard. "How many archers have their arrows trained on us at the moment?"

As Angus upended the shovel and jammed its shaft into the rear side of the cogs, the man laughed. "And ye reckon I'd tell ye if I knew?"

"We've come in peace," Raghnall persisted. "Robert the Bruce is Ulster's son-in-law."

Pushing down on the handle, Angus ensured the shovel's scoop was wedged good and tight against the stone wall. It just might save the king's neck, and those of the men, should the earl's hospitality be found lacking.

"Ye follow a fool king who knows not his arse from his eye." The guard glanced Angus' way. "Move along, ye oaf."

Angus yawned and ambled beside his man, ever so happy to have his bonny face hidden beneath the nose guard of his helm. "Where can a fella take a piss around here?"

"Tie a knot in it," growled the buffoon, giving Angus' shoulder a shove.

Raghnall's fingers skimmed his hilt, but Angus

stilled the man's hand with a sharp hiss. "We're nay here to make war."

The man-at-arms snorted. "At least no' today."

As the retinue filed into the courtyard, Robert held aloft the black flag of parley and moved into the center with Boyd and Campbell on his flanks. A tic twitched at the corner of Angus' eye. He ought to be beside the king rather than among the soldiers who encircled the bailey walls.

From the mammoth tower doors, Ulster's guardsmen approached in diamond formation—not a good sign for a greeting with kin. The earl's purple robes flapped with the wind, though he was mostly hidden by a wall of soldiers.

"I haven't a good feeling about this," grumbled Raghnall under his breath.

"No man can ignore a request for parley, nor can he raise a hand against us," Angus whispered, though if he acted on the prickles that had been firing across the nape of his neck since they'd set sail, he never would have stepped beneath the chilly, razor-sharp teeth of the sea gate's portcullis. "Be on your guard."

Before Raghnall had a chance to mumble another prediction of doom, the King of Scotland bowed to his father-in-law, the Earl of Ulster. "I come in peace to beg your forgiveness and your favor."

With the light rain, a fog rolled in, making Ulster appear as if he were standing behind a shroud. "Do ye now?"

"As ye are aware, not only has your daughter Elizabeth been taken by the hands of Edward's men, my only daughter has been captured as well. My brother Nigel, hanged, drawn, and quartered in Berwick-upon-Tweed merely for the crime of protecting my wife and daughter. And now it seems Lord Percy is leading my brothers Alexander and Thomas to the same fate."

"And ye wish me to stop the delivery of justice? I'd be outlawed with the stroke of Edward's quill."

"I need men. 'Tis all I ask."

"Ye disappoint me, Robert. Not only have ye turned my daughter against me, ye believe me fool enough to absolve ye of your crimes?"

The king thrust out his hands. "What crimes are they, compared to the Scottish blood spilled?"

Ulster smoothed his fingers along the earl's chain atop his chest. "Ye want to stop the senseless bleeding? Throw down your arms and bow to Edward."

"Scotland's subjects tried to do so and were treated worse than chattel. Our sons were forced to fight England's wars, our daughters were raped and murdered by those who called themselves Edward's own."

"And ye think more fighting will make the King of England acquiesce and kiss your filthy feet? The man will not stop until your head is on a spike on the Tower of London. Did ye learn nothing from Wallace's demise? When I gave my daughter to ye in marriage, I thought ye to be a savvy man, but I was grievously mistaken." Ulster took a step away. "Look at ye come begging for men—a sheep on a fool's errand, backing a cause ye can never win."

Robert drew a hand down his beard and, as he glanced over his shoulder, the look in his eye was as deadly as nightshade. Any other man might have been defeated by such a tongue-lashing, but the tripe spewing from Ulster's mouth appeared to embolden the Scottish king.

Angus gripped his fingers around the hilt of his sword as the Bruce backed away from the man he'd come to ask for help. "I see the quarrel between us is too great for the strength of kin and clan to assuage," said the king, his voice deep and resonating between the courtyard walls.

"Ye're no kin of mine." With a flourish of purple robes, the earl thrust his finger at Robert. "Seize him!"

The order to apprehend the Bruce hadn't left Ulster's lips before Angus and his soldiers drew their weapons and readied for battle.

"Protect the king!" Angus bellowed, racing ahead as he and his soldiers surrounded His Grace. Taking the lead, he eyed Ulster from behind the mask of his helm. "We wish no bloodshed here!"

Hesitating, the earl squinted at Angus before two pikemen crossed their weapons in front of His Lordship's body.

Not about to wait for a reply, Angus and his retinue backed the king toward the sea gate, sidestepping while eyeing every venomous cur in the courtyard. They hadn't attacked yet, but the surrounding enemy encroached, pikes leveled and weapons drawn.

"I said seize him!" roared Ulster.

Within a blink of an eye, the battle came from all sides. Angus and Raghnall stood shoulder to shoulder, fending off the brunt of it. Angus ducked beneath the strike of a lance. As he straightened, he deflected a thrust from a sword, slamming the spike of his targe through the attacker's throat.

"Run for the boats!" he shouted, urging his retinue of fighting men to move faster.

As they approached the portcullis, the brutish guard lunged for Raghnall, swinging a ball and chain over his head. Before the bastard thrust forward with a killing strike, Angus bellowed his war cry and hacked through the man's arm.

Raghnall didn't even flinch as he fended off three. Angus smashed the broadside of his blade atop one's head, sending him to the cobbles while the man-at-arms dispatched the others.

"Archers!" bellowed an order from above.

"God's stones," Angus cursed, raising his targe as an

arrow hissed past his ear.

"Haste!" shouted Raghnall, darting through the gate. "The king has escaped."

Backing into the gate's narrow archway, Angus overturned a barrel and kicked it toward the onslaught of attackers, purchasing enough time to issue a chop through the shovel's handle. Above, the deadly portcullis groaned and screeched as he launched himself beyond her savage teeth. His feet barely touched the dirt as the iron gate thundered closed behind him, shaking the ground as he ran.

But he wasn't safe yet.

Arrows darted through the air on all sides. Forcing his legs to pump harder, Angus crouched, holding his targe over his head, praying for nearsighted bowmen. Only when he was out of range and had reached his *birlinn* did he realize a storm had rolled in, bringing with it driving rain and a hellacious wind.

NOT LONG AFTER A SCORE OF MEN FILED INTO THE courtyard via the sea entrance, Anya stood at the cellar gate, fishing in her satchel for her key. "Curses, where is it?"

When a gust of icy wind cut through her cloak, she glanced back to the hills and her hiding place. Dread pulsed through her blood. The key must have fallen out when her satchel contents dumped onto the ground. Blast her rotten luck. And dashing back to retrieve it wasn't an option. Not only was she late to dress for the evening meal, at this time of year, it would be dark before she reached the outcropping.

The fishermen had all returned for the day, their boats moored alongside the pier. Most likely, the sea gate was still open. Anya didn't dare head for the main entry, else she'd be flayed by her guardian. If not the earl, the countess would be happy to issue discipline in his stead.

Making her decision, Anya headed aft, her feet slipping on the wet stones. Goodness, she missed Dunseverick Castle where she'd been raised until the Earl of Ulster had arrived with news of her father's passing at the hand of Alasdair MacDonald. It was of no consequence that the miscreant had been killed in the same battle by the MacDougall Lord of Lorn. No matter who issued the killing strike, her father was gone. Anya and her sister had been taken away from their home to spend the next seven years as wards, serving the Countess of Ulster's every whim.

As she neared the gate, the wind carried her guardian's voice over the walls. "I said seize him!"

Sliding to a stop, she froze in place. The sounds of battle resounded from the courtyard. Men shrieked, weapons clanged.

Clenching her fists beneath her chin, Anya shot a glance toward her cellar gate—perhaps she ought to double back and try her chances with the main. Except a horde of Ulster's guards were racing her way along the narrow path, with pikes at the ready.

"Blessed Mother, have mercy!"

With nowhere to run but to the pier, Anya hastened for the ramp. A sentry bellowed for the archers while heinous cries came from beyond the gates. One thing consumed her mind as she ran the length of the pier.

Hide!

Rain pelted her face as she turned in place, her mind racing. Just as footsteps pounded the planks of the pier, she climbed into the bow of a sea galley, pulled an oiled tarpaulin over her head, and curled into a ball. As she shivered, something sharp and hard grazed her hip. Anya reached down and wrapped her fingers around a shaft as the footsteps grew louder and more numerous, rattling the old wharf's timbers.

3

"Cast off!" bellowed Angus, removing his helmet and leaping into the hull of his *birlinn* while a half-dozen men took up the oars. Thank God they were finally out of range of the archers' arrows.

"Where are the others?" he demanded, unfurling the sail.

The sinews in Raghnall's neck strained as the man-at-arms pulled on an oar to the cadence of "heave" by the lead oarsman. "Those who survived are in Robert's vessel."

As the sail flapped and filled with air, Angus peered through rain and darkness, out toward the open sea. Well underway, the Bruce's *birlinn* sailed low in the water on an eastward heading—the fastest escape. Angus let the wind take them eastward as well, at least until they were leagues clear of Carrickfergus. He secured the sail's boom and headed aft to the tiller.

After he took control of the steering, his breath stopped in his chest. Clouds as black as coal bore down from the north, carried by a tempestuous wind. Not long later, when the *birlinn* cruised farther away from the protection of the bay into the open sea, enormous, white-capped swells sloshed over the sides of the boat.

"She's taking on water!" shouted the lead oarsman.

"Oars up," Angus commanded, no longer able to see the king's ship. "Start bailing unless ye want to bed down on the bottom of the icy sea this night!"

The relentless wind violently rocked the ship, tilting her from starboard to port with the anger of each furious wave. "Tack northward and set a course for home!" Angus shouted while the sting of freezing water spray stung his face and salted his mouth. Besieged on all sides, there was no other option. A retreat to Ireland would end in certain death at the hands of Ulster's army. Turning south and attempting to outrun this wrath of God would deliver them into the arms of Edward the Longshanks with a surefire meeting with a headsman's axe.

Angus and his men had faced many tempests before. MacDonalds were born seafarers, afraid of nothing. By the grace of God, they would see the shores of Islay this very eve.

TACK NORTHWARD? TO SCOTLAND?

The only Scots Anya knew who would dare pay a visit to Carrickfergus were the MacDougalls.

Has the Lord of Lorn fallen out of favor with Ulster?

She'd taken a glimpse out from under the tarpaulin and seen the sky. A winter's storm was upon them for certain. To establish a northward heading was akin to inviting Satan to release hellfire and damnation. Already chilled to the bone, a tremor as frigid as ice pulsed through Anya's blood. She was no stranger to the sea, and sailing directly into a squall was as foolish as it was reckless.

Who were these men and where did they hail from? Judging by soldiers she'd seen running toward the sea gate, and the way the galley was so hastily put to sea, they were clearly no allies of the Earl of Ulster.

What if they discovered her?

Dear God in heaven, help!

The boat pitched from side to side, taking on water by the bucketful. Soaking wet, Anya clutched the tarpaulin and dared to again rise up high enough to peer over the top of the hull. Storm clouds touched the water while the wind whipped and flapped the oiled cloth. An enormous frothy wave crashed over the bow, deluging her entire body.

There wasn't a speck of land in sight, though she could see no farther than a few yards.

Everyone knew winter tempests were the deadliest. The sea would swallow her whole if she tried to swim. If she stayed put, she might succumb to the cold. Her teeth chattered as another wave doused her, filling her mouth with seawater.

"Gael, take the tiller!" boomed the man who gave the orders in a thick Scottish brogue.

Trying not to cough, Anya quickly ducked down, her knee knocking against the axe she'd found after it had poked her in the hip. The blasted thing thudded. Still clutching the tarpaulin, she sucked in a sharp breath. What if they found her? What would she do? If these Scots had fallen out of favor with her guardian, they wouldn't be likely to turn the galley around and head back to the sanctity of the bay.

As water washed over her legs, her teeth chattered.

"The wind has changed!" shouted a man.

"Prepare to tack!" bellowed the leader. He was right beside her now, his bucket ladling only inches from Anya's toes.

Bless it, she should have jumped onto the pier when she'd had the chance. If only she'd leapt out of the ship as soon as she'd heard footsteps, she most likely would have survived any tongue-lashing from the earl. Now, chances were they'd all perish.

The galley turned and sailed directly into the surf.

Like a jolting ride on an unbroken horse, over and over they sailed up the enormous swells and plunged downward, the bow repeatedly submerging and dousing her with icy seawater. Anya shivered, her teeth still rattling in her head.

"She's not going to make it!" shouted a sailor.

"Bloody oath, I'll be sitting by Dunyvaig's hearth afore dawn or I'm nay Angus Og MacDonald!"

Holy Mary, Mother of God! There was no doubt. The men sailing this boat were the loathsome MacDonalds, and the man leading the crew was none other than Fairhair himself. Clutching her fists to her face, she squeezed her eyes shut.

Oh my, oh my, oh my God!

These were the vilest miscreants on the seas. Would they slit her throat and cast her into the angry swells? Would they take her captive and throw her in a pit prison?

What if they discovered she was the daughter of Lord Guy O'Cahan?

"Achoo!"

Oh no!

Every muscle in Anya's body tensed as she curled tighter into a ball, the ship rocking mercilessly. How in heaven's name could she have allowed herself to sneeze? But it had come on so fast. And her sneeze wasn't a polite little squeak like Finovola's sneezes. It was an unladylike, earth-shatteringly thunderous roar.

The man bailing beside her grew oddly silent.

Not daring to breathe, Anya wrapped her fingers around the axe's handle and prepared for battle.

THOUGH ANGUS' HEARING WAS ACUTE, THE SNEEZE that came from beneath the tarpaulin was barely discernable over the howling wind. He studied the oiled cloth as he stilled his hands. Had some lad stowed aboard? If so, the wee fellow must be soaked to the bone.

Angus grabbed the tarp and pulled it away. Rather than a terrified lad, a screaming banshee sprang up, wielding a battle axe, the blade bearing straight for his face. Stumbling backward and falling onto the bench behind, he barely blocked the weapon's strike with his pail. The axe hacked through the timbers while Angus rolled aside, taking a glancing blow to the shoulder.

With a shrieking war cry, the imp recoiled. Taking advantage of the weapon's backswing, Angus lunged forward and seized the demon's wrist, wrenching the axe from her grasp.

Her.

'Tis a bloody female?

Angus regained his feet while the skies opened with renewed ferocity, dousing them with a torrent so heavy, the lass' face blurred into a surreal nightmare. No taller than the middle of his chest, she reminded him of a drenched hedgehog.

Or an angry badger with piercing emerald-green eyes.

He hovered over her with the axe in his fist while a fissure of ire shot up the back of his neck. How dare anyone stow away on his ship and then launch an attack like a hellion from Sparta? "What the blazes are ye doing on *my birlinn*...in the midst of a squall, ye hellacious rapscallion?"

Lips blue, teeth chattering, the lass tipped up a saucy chin. "This was supposed to be a fishing vessel, moored for the night!"

"Bloody hell," groaned Raghnall from behind.

Angus glanced over his throbbing shoulder. Bless it, there wasn't a dry piece of cloth on the boat, including the sealskin cloak hanging from the woman's shoulders. Against his better judgement, he offered his hand. "Nay, 'tis no fishing boat," he growled. What the devil was he going to do with an Irish waif in the midst of a winter storm? "Come, ye'd best move back to the tiller."

Not budging, a ferocious spark flashed in her eyes.

"I'll no' hurt ye, lass. But if ye remain here in the bow, ye'll catch your death for certain." Angus extended his palm a bit farther just as a wave crashed over the prow, slammed her in the back and sent the shivering waif careening into his chest. Instinctively, he wrapped his arms around her, stopping her fall. Good God, the woman was trembling like a sapling in the wind.

"Come now," he said a bit more gently, while swiftly rubbing his palm around her back to warm her.

Saying nothing, she went limp against him. Angus lifted the lass into his arms and headed aft, stepping over benches and ducking beneath the boom. "Bail faster, men!"

"Land ho!" shouted Gael, pointing.

Angus searched in the direction of the man's finger but saw naught but a wave as tall as his keep bearing down upon the port side. He tightened his hold around the lass in a feeble attempt to protect her from what could only be the wrath of God.

As if a monster from the deep had come to feast, the wave picked up the hull, tilting the *birlinn* to the starboard side until her sail touched the sea. "All hands to port!" Angus shouted, praying their weight would be enough.

Beneath his feet, the timbers shuddered as the wee boat strained to battle the ravaging wave.

The woman in Angus' arms screamed, pounding her fists against his chest, but he wasn't about to let go. By boarding his boat, she'd placed herself in his care, vixen or nay.

"Prepare to swim!" Angus bellowed, using one hand to release his heavy sword belt and letting it clatter to the timbers. The ire of the tempest sent three overboard while Angus fought to maintain his footing, only to find the fury of the sea was not in their favor this night. The sturdy *birlinn* rolled over as if it were no more than a child's toy.

Flung into the swells, icy water silenced the woman's screams as together they plunged into the bitter North Sea. The undertow pulled them downward, tumbling around and around.

Kicking with all his strength, Angus had no sense of up or down. The only thing consuming his mind was God-given air. If he did not break the surface soon, both he and the lass would expire before they succumbed to the cold. But fight as he may, the woman's sodden cloak was enough to drown them both. Angus brutally tore open the ties at her throat. With the release of the weight, the water buoyed them enough for him to gain a sense of up from down.

Knives of pain drove through his flesh as he kicked, all too aware the lass had already lost her fight. Angus dared to release one of his hands, fighting for the surface, swimming toward the faintest modicum of light. His lungs seared with the need to breathe. His throat closed. His vision blurred.

All at once, his head broke through as he gasped, sucking in a gulp of air, only to be assailed by another wave and again pushed to the deep.

Still clutching the woman in his arms, Angus kicked, refusing to give up.

Not today.

Not ever!

❧ 4 ❧

Sapped of strength, Angus ground his molars, summoning his last vestiges of fortitude as he dragged the woman ashore. "Ye'll nay die this day!" he growled, panting and sucking in gasps of air. The pain in his shoulder had long since gone numb, as had his fingers, his toes, and every other bloody extremity of his body.

The lassie's legs cut trenches through the sand as he hauled her away from the foaming surf and onto the smooth stones lining the shore. Her face and lips were blue, a swath of wet, dark hair wrapped around her throat. Fighting his exhaustion, Angus tugged her into his chest while his backside plummeted to the ground. "Live, damn you!" he cursed, repeatedly slamming his palm against her back.

With a violent cough, seawater spewed from the woman's lips.

"Again," he shouted, hitting her hard and making her sputter.

"Thank God," he mumbled, dropping his forehead against her back.

The woman's shivering commenced anew while an icy wind cut through the weave of Angus' brechan. Bless it, both their teeth were chattering loud enough to wake the dead. Holding her steady, he rose to his knees and searched beyond the shore. Ballocks, they'd landed on the wee skerry of Nave. 'Twas but a half-day's sailing from Dunyvaig. Hell, if it weren't dark, he'd be able to see the Isle of Islay from this very spot.

"M'lord!"

Angus turned toward the sound, his heart skipping a beat. "Raghnall, thank God!"

The man-at-arms stumbled toward them before collapsing at Agnus' side. A stream of blood dribbled from his temple, staining his shoulder red.

"Where are the other survivors?" Angus asked.

"Ye pair are the only souls I've seen." Shaking, he rubbed his arms against the frigid cold. "With luck, they drifted farther east than we did."

Angus looked to the skies. Still raining, black clouds hung ominously low. "We'll no' survive the night unless we can warm our bones. Let us away to the chapel."

The wee lassie in his arms had barely survived, yet it was all he could do to push to his feet and lift her into his arms. She was a fighter, that was for certain. A less-robust woman would have succumbed to the ravages of the sea.

Though the little church Angus' grandfather had built overlooking the North Sea was only about a hundred paces away, by the ache of every sinew, he felt as if he were starting at the base of Ben Nevis on an uphill climb.

"Would ye like me to carry her?" asked Raghnall. "Your shoulder needs tending."

"I can manage," Angus grunted as he trudged forward.

Once they made their way inside, Angus sighed at the relief to be out of the wind, though it was still bitterly cold. The chapel had been used annually for the Lammas Day feast and bonfire. The clan always began by giving thanks and praying for a successful harvest.

The nave had but a small altar with a brass cross and a vaulted ceiling, which made their footsteps echo.

"Start a fire," Angus said, gently resting the woman on the only strip of carpet, which was near the altar. She was barely conscious, shivering and gripping her fists beneath her chin.

"With what?" asked Raghnall, rubbing his hands. "Everything that might take a spark is soaked."

Angus looked to the altar, carved with a scene from Christ's last supper. Though it was priceless, he'd set the entire block of mahogany alight if it meant their survival. As he panned his gaze across the nave, the wooden chairs, their seats woven with wicker, caught his eye. "We'll start with the chairs. Then we'll bring in rushes to dry."

While Raghnall set to work, smashing a few chairs into burnable bits, Angus pulled the tapestry from the wall. "We must remove our sodden clothes afore we're chilled all the more."

With flicks of his fingers, Angus took off his belt and the brooch at his shoulder, only now realizing he'd lost his father's sword. Aye, with the prospect of a swim in the North Sea, he'd needed to release the buckle and drop the weight, but Da's great sword with its bejeweled hilt was gone. His dirk and *sgian dubh* remained secure in their scabbards, thank heavens for small mercies.

After Raghnall had a fire crackling in the brazier, the man-at-arms stripped to his shirt as well, their cloaks long gone. He nodded toward the stowaway. "What about her?"

"She's come this far. I'm no' about to lose her now."

The man-at-arms stooped to retrieve his dirk. "I'll fetch the rushes."

Angus kicked off his sodden boots and peeled away his hose, draping them over the back of a chair. Releasing a deep breath, he faced his charge. "Ye'll nay survive if ye remain in that heavy woolen gown."

On the boat she'd worn a sealskin cloak—a sign she might be highly born—but had he not ripped it from her person, they would be dead for certain.

When she didn't respond, he touched her shoulder. "Come, lass."

With a bat of her hand, her eyes flashed open as she startled. Angus' breath caught. Either those deep pools of emerald green were as mesmerizing as a silkie's spell or he was teetering at the edge of his endurance. Though he was weary and his shoulder throbbed, truth be told, those intoxicating greens caught him off guard. Thick chestnut lashes made them ever so intense, though they filled with ire and stared at him as if he were Satan incarnate. "Do not touch me!"

It was nary a wonder the woman was confused. After all, she'd been through a harrowing ordeal. Angus snapped his hand away and raked his fingers through his mop of dripping hair. "Och, with all due respect, miss, ye've been in my arms whilst we battled a tempest from hell. Ye cannot possibly think I would lift a finger to harm ye."

Scooting away, she clutched her hand atop the ties at the front of her kirtle. "Nay!"

"Just strip down to your shift, lass. I promise to avert my eyes." He placed his palm over her fingers. "What is your name?"

A resounding chatter of teeth was her only reply. While the spark in her expression told him she wanted to fight, he had no difficulty pulling her fingers away and untying the laces of her kirtle. As he worked, she closed her eyes, her tremorous shivers resuming.

"There's a good lass," Angus said, trying not to look, but unable to avert his gaze from magnificence.

Her linen shift clung to ideal feminine proportions. Ample breasts tipped by taut rosebuds swelled beneath, leading to a slim waist and full, voluptuous hips. Even her thighs were sculpted like a Greek goddess'. At their apex nestled a dark triangle that stirred his blood far more than it ought.

"We shall have ye warm and dry in no time," he croaked, unable to mask the longing in his voice. With the Bruce occupying his keep, Angus hadn't enjoyed the pleasure of a woman for months.

Though he was no stranger to the temptation of the fairer sex, Angus had never—and would never—taken advantage of an unwilling lass. He'd given his word and he'd stand by it. "This will set ye to rights." He continued to ease her troubles, pulling her onto his lap.

But as he tried to wrap the tapestry around them, she pushed away. "Nay!"

"Bless it," he growled, clutching his arms around her like a vise. "I'm trying to save ye from dying of exposure. I swear on my father's grave, your virtue is safe, lass. Just stop fighting me."

With his words, the woman collapsed against him, allowing him to finish. Together with the heat from their bodies, trapped by the thick woven cloth, in moments it already felt warmer. Angus stretched his feet closer to the brazier and sighed while the fire set to thawing his toes. In no time, the stowaway's breathing became deep, indicating she'd dropped into the sanctity of sleep.

Raghnall returned with his arms full of rushes. "I'll just spread these..." He stopped and gaped, giving a licentious waggle of his eyebrows. "The pair of ye look mighty cozy, m'lord."

"Wheesht. Mark me, the lass would sooner dirk me in the back than allow me to revive her with my warmth. I've seen it in her eyes."

The man-at-arms kicked the rushes to spread them out. "Then ye'd best sleep with one of your eyes open, m'lord."

AWARE HER SHOULDER WAS DRIVING INTO STONE, Anya stirred. The goo in her arid mouth tasted like salt. She ached everywhere, yet she was absolutely ravenous.

She wriggled out from the wraps of a heavy cloth and sat up, expecting to see Angus Og MacDonald or his henchman standing over her with a dagger in his fist. After they'd plunged into the sea, she'd prepared to meet her end, losing consciousness and only regaining it once or twice since the big Highlander had pulled her ashore.

Surely, he was nowhere near as shockingly handsome as she'd first imagined. After all, she'd been frightened half to death. Without a doubt, Fairhair was the barbarian he was reputed to be. Though on the ship when he'd pulled the tarpaulin away and she'd tried to kill him, barbarian was the absolute last word that had come to mind.

One day, God might strike her dead for letting the vile Lord of Islay help her. If only she'd had the strength to fight, but in her hour of need, her body had failed her. It was a miracle she was still alive.

Anya glanced about the small chapel and breathed a sigh of relief to find herself alone. Within her grasp was a silver chalice filled with crabmeat and beside it was another filled with water. Using her fingers, she shoveled the food into her mouth faster than she could chew. Juice ran down her chin as she rolled her eyes to the rafters and swallowed.

Mm.

It took her no time at all to devour the remainder of the crab and guzzle the water. Only then did she glance downward and realize she wore nothing but her shift. Reminded of last eve's struggle, she buried her face in her hands. She never should have allowed that man to touch her. Aye, she'd tried to fight, but half drowned and colder than she'd ever been in all her days, Anya had barely been able to hold her head upright, let alone defend herself.

She slid her hands over her shift, then pushed to her feet. Though she couldn't be completely certain, she was nearly positive Angus Og MacDonald had kept his word. After all, he was an important lord, even if he was an enemy. Perhaps the man's mother had taught him a modicum of chivalry. Regardless, Anya had no doubt that if Islay knew she was the daughter of Lord Guy O'Cahan, he would have let her drown. And irrespective of whether he'd saved her or not, the Highlander was a pirate, renowned for pillaging along the western isles of Scotland and beyond. He'd even threatened her father's very own Dunseverick Castle—at least, Fairhair's brother had done so. And now rumors had spread that the MacDonalds had taken up arms with Robert the Bruce, the outlaw who'd proclaimed himself King of Scots. Worse, the Bruce had married the Earl of Ulster's daughter, Anya's dear friend, Elizabeth.

The poor dear. She must be suffering so.

After their mishappen coronation, the false king had sent his wife to Kildrummy Castle for safe harbor, where Elizabeth was captured by King Edward's army. Not even the Earl of Ulster was privy to her whereabouts.

Heavens, if it weren't for Elizabeth's kindness, Anya's move to Carrickfergus Castle would have been unbearable.

And now she had capsized somewhere with yet another Scot who was about as trustworthy as a weasel. Anya quickly slipped into her dry kirtle and tied the laces. She found her boots but the leather had grown stiff from salt and the sea, making it difficult to shove her feet inside. As she tied the laces, she wriggled her toes and worked them in. It didn't matter where they may have washed ashore, she fully intended to escape

His Lordship's clutches and find a way back to Carrickfergus forthwith.

Surely her guardian would pay any fare owing once she was safely home.

Anya smacked her forehead with her palm. By now they would know she'd gone missing. Finovola must be distraught with worry. And Lord Chahir O'Doherty was expecting to see her at the Saint Valentine's Day feast on the morrow.

Ulster is going to flay me for certain!

With no time to waste, she listened at the door. Hearing nothing but the howling of the wind, she cracked it open and peered outside. The shore was only paces away while north and south seagrass bent with a strong westerly.

Had the men left her alone?

"Good morn. 'Tis nice to see ye're awake," called Islay, marching from the south. "We've been scavenging for—"

Not listening to another word, Anya took off at a run—northward. Yes, she knew Ireland was to the south, but there was no chance she'd risk running within the Lord of Islay's grasp. Besides, she needed to find a boat, she needed to find allies, or flag the English fleet.

Her mind raced as she struggled to navigate through the thick grass and the sharp stones hidden betwixt and beneath.

When I return to Carrickfergus, I will never again doubt the sensibility of a marriage to Lord O'Doherty. He's a good man. He's a sane man. He is not a marauding pirate and I doubt he would lift a finger to harm me. 'Tis a good match. I never should have doubted my guardian's sensibilities. I never should have slipped out of the castle. Not once. Blast that stupid key and blast my adventuresome spirit. The countess always said it would send me to ruin!

A stich in Anya's side ached, but she didn't dare

slow down. As she charged up an incline, she chanced a look over her shoulder. Islay was following, but not at a run.

As soon as she reached the crest, Anya realized why. Water surrounded her as far as the eye could see. For the love of God, they were stranded on a worthless little isle.

Panting for air, she wrapped her arms across her waist and girded herself to face the brother of the man who had killed her father.

Oh, by the saints, the man in the boat had not been an apparition. Now dry, Fairhair was even handsomer than when he'd faced her in the midst of the driving rain.

The wind whipped his blond hair sideways and he had a dastardly swagger to his gait, made far too beguiling by his plaid draped over one very broad shoulder and belted low around his hips. His shockingly blue eyes focused on her, the full lips of his mouth giving nothing away, neither smiling nor frowning. Lord save her, the man's reputation had not been an exaggeration. There was a good reason Angus Og MacDonald was called Fairhair. Never in all her days had Anya seen a man so beautiful. He was prettier than her, perhaps more beautiful than Finovola, and as brawny as Ulster's most prized knight for certain.

But the rumors about Islay were nothing short of sinister. This man might be as appealing to the eye as foxglove, but everyone knew him to be as ruthlessly noxious as the toxin within her blooms.

Suddenly very self-aware, Anya tucked a lock of hair behind her ear. She already knew he was taller than a warhorse, but when he stopped in front of her, she felt incredibly small and vulnerable.

He gestured with outstretched arms. "Och, there's no place to run on this wee isle."

Anya didn't dare look him in the eye. Instead, she

stared at his feet and two muscular, hairy legs. "I-I must return to Carrickfergus forthwith."

"Is that so?" He folded those powerful arms across a broad chest. "I'd like nothing better than to ferry ye home in one of my *birlinns*, but presently that poses a wee problem. Not only are we shipwrecked, we're stranded. At least until we can piece together enough wood from the wreckage for Raghnall to sail across to Islay and seek help."

Anya didn't respond, though she followed his upturned palm, gesturing toward a dark strip of land in the distance.

"I'm afraid we weren't properly introduced." The scoundrel took a step back and bowed. "I'm Angus Og MacDonald, Lord of Islay—the island just yonder. Unfortunately, my keep sits on the southern end and we've been shipwrecked to the north, where nary a soul can see us."

Anya licked her lips and dipped into a hasty curtsey. "I'm...ah..."

"Can ye no' remember your name, lass?"

"Anya," she clipped. Her given name was common enough.

"An-y-a..." he said, drawing out the word as if trying to place it. "And who might your father be?"

"I-I'm an orphan." At least that was not a lie.

His eyebrow quirked in disbelief. "Most orphans I ken, do no' go traipsing about in sealskin cloaks."

Anya gulped while heat rushed to her cheeks. Well, she wasn't about to tell him she was the ward of the Earl of Ulster and most definitely did not want Islay to know she was the eldest daughter of Lord Guy O'Cahan. Instead, she squared her shoulders and tipped up her chin. "That matters not. What is of foremost importance is I must return to Carrickfergus for the Saint Valentine's Day feast."

"Or what, pray tell?"

"Or...or the man to whom I am to be betrothed will most likely withdraw his offer of marriage, which absolutely must not happen."

"Withdraw, will he?" Angus rested his hand on the pommel of his dirk. "Well, I reckon any fellow worth his salt will wait for a woman as bonny as ye. A lass who has won his heart...*unless*..."

Anya pursed her lips. Blast, blast, blast! She knew what he was thinking. Any man would wait for a woman unless it wasn't a love match, unless it was an arrangement that included her dowry, which was very sizeable, indeed.

5

It was late afternoon by the time Angus and Raghnall had pieced together enough scraps from the wreckage to make a raft. They'd scavenged for bits of rope to secure the broken planks of wood together, but it hadn't been enough. Fortunately, Anya made herself useful and found a priest's stole in the chapel and, though it may have been sacrilegious to use it, Angus refused to believe God would smite him for trying to save their lives.

Among the wreckage, they'd found a few useful things, including an intact oar and a half-cask of wine.

As they worked, the lass sat off by herself, using a charcoal to draw on a piece of vellum. Evidently, she'd found more than a stole in the wee chapel. And from the few glimpses Angus stole of her work, she had a bit of talent.

Raghnall stood knee-deep in the frigid surf and tested the buoyancy of their craft. "I reckon she's seaworthy."

"Mayhap on a glassy loch." Angus looked to the skies. "Ye'd best go now whilst the weather is calm. The only thing we can count on is it will not last. She'll be blowing a gale by the witching hour, mark me."

Raghnall held his thumb to the sun, low in the

western sky. "I'll make it all right. Providing I don't freeze my ballocks, I'll have a *birlinn* here to fetch ye and the lass afore dark on the morrow."

"If only we could go with you."

Raghnall swung his leg over the raft, straddling it. "This jumble of oak will barely support me, let alone three of us."

Angus handed his man the oar. "We'll be fine, providing no English patrols come snooping."

"Or the lassie over there tries to slit your throat whilst ye're sleeping."

"She's harmless."

"She's from the enemy's camp, and that makes her lethal." Raghnall placed the oar across his lap. "What do ye intend to do with her?"

Angus scratched the itchy stubble growing along his jaw. "I suppose I'll find a way to send her home."

"Aye, without getting your head severed in the process."

"Or my arse filled with Ulster's arrows."

"Mayhap the Bruce will have an idea."

"Ye reckon so?" Angus picked up a smooth stone and skipped it across the surf. "As a result of the king's brilliant plans of late, I've lost a quarter of my fleet and a number of good fighting men. With luck, the storm carried the king past Islay and he is seeking safe harbor elsewhere."

"In such a hurry to be rid of His Grace?" Raghnall teased. "I thought ye wanted to secure the Lordship of the Isles."

"I do, and 'tis the reason we're in this mess." Angus gave the raft a push. "Ye'd best dip that oar in the water unless ye want to spend another night sleeping on cold stone."

He stood for a time watching his friend head for the swells of the North Sea, the raft riding low in the water. So many things weighed on Angus' mind. Yes, he'd thrown in his lot with Robert the Bruce and now that he'd committed, he must see it through to the end. In England's eyes, he and Clan MacDonald were now outlaws, and he had no intention of being captured, tortured, and put to death by Edward, Hammer of the Scots. Angus must do everything in his power to ensure King Robert's success.

Tucked away in the isles during Wallace's rise, the MacDonald clan had not been subject to as much tyranny as those on the mainland. But now with the increase in English patrols, Angus had seen enough to know if Longshanks wasn't stopped, his clan and kin would suffer. Perhaps he might even lose his lands. It would slay him to watch the MacDougalls muscle into Islay, Skye, and Jura. Ruination had befallen many mainland lords, and it didn't seem likely Edward would stop there.

The Scots may have been forced to eat crow for the past decade, but as Angus stood on that godforsaken shore, he made a silent vow to vanquish the enemy and drive them from Scotland once and for all.

"When do ye think he'll return?" asked Anya, coming up from behind.

"This time on the morrow, God willing."

"And then ye'll take me back to Ireland?" she asked, as if it were more of a directive than a question.

"Aye." He gave her a sideways glance, then mumbled, "When 'tis safe to do so."

"Safe? Why do ye not hand me over to the English anon? Are they not patrolling these waters?"

He studied her wide eyes, beautiful, innocent emeralds. He hadn't known Anya for long, but as plain as the nose on his face, she'd been sheltered and cosseted. Clearly, the lass had no idea what the English would do to him. Moreover, she was without a clue as to what they might do to her. "Ye do not want to climb aboard an English cog without an escort."

"Whyever not?"

"Because ye're female."

"Do ye think they'd harm me?"

"I do not think. I ken. One look at a wee wisp of a lass such as you and they'll be queuing up to sample your wares."

"Ye are vile. No one—"

"Men are vile." He started toward the makeshift oven he'd fashioned of sand and stone. Hours ago, he'd set the coals and added the brown crabs they'd harvested that morn. They were about the only thing to eat on the isle, barring the seals, and, when it came right down to it, crabs were far easier to catch and prepare. "Come, the food ought to be ready to eat."

He used a stick to push away the stones and uncovered their meal. "I reckon these are ready." He flicked them onto one of the chapel's pewter alms platters. "It isn't much, but it will keep us alive."

Anya gave a nod, though she hadn't said much since their encounter this morning. Regardless, there were things Angus needed to know before he took her to Dunyvaig and allowed her a free rein. Thus far, she had yet to earn his trust and she most certainly hadn't earned Raghnall's. Who, exactly, was this orphan and what was she hiding?

Angus held up the platter and gave her a grin, one that hadn't failed him in all his years. Though God had cursed him with the face of an angel, he'd learned at a young age to use it to his advantage, at least where women were concerned. Not even his mother was able to resist his smiles.

However, he seemed to have no effect on this Irish woman whatsoever. As soon as he showed his teeth, she averted her gaze and headed for the chapel.

Huffing, Angus followed, unable not to notice the way her shapely hips swung beneath the folds of her woolen kirtle.

"Come, lass," he said when they stepped inside. "These wee beasties are best whilst they're warm."

They sat on a pair of the remaining chairs and used another as a table. Angus poured her a healthy spot of wine and helped himself to a chalice as well, then held his aloft. "To Raghnall and a safe crossing."

"And to his swift return," she added.

"*Slàinte mhath*," he said before taking a sip.

Anya drank as well, then made a sour face.

Doing his best to restrain the grimace playing on his lips, he set his cup on the makeshift table. "The one good thing about vinegary wine is the second sip always tastes better." After all, what did they expect from a cask washed up on the shore? At least it wasn't full of salt water.

"Have ye any siblings at Carrickfergus?" he asked.

"A sister."

"Younger, older?"

"Two years younger."

"I'll wager she's nay as bonny as you."

Anya's shoulders shook with her snort. "I assure ye, Finovola is everything I am not. Golden tresses, willowy limbs, and she's as graceful as an eagle in flight."

Angus used his *sgian dubh* to cut into a leg's hard outer shell and dig out the meat within. "Why is it lassies always want to look different?"

"I don't recall saying I was unhappy with my appearance. I merely said my sister is a beauty."

He tapped the crabmeat toward her and started working on another morsel. "Mayhap she is fair, though I say ye do yourself no credit. Och, your eyes alone are enough to take the wind out of a man's sails." And Lord knew last eve it was all Angus could do to ignore the soft curve of her bottom nestling against his cock. If Anya's sister was long and willowy, there was no chance she'd be as plush a bed partner.

"Am I to thank ye for your observation, sir?" she asked with an edge to her voice.

For a moment, he watched as she savored the crab, following her bite with a drink of wine—sans the sour face this time. "There's no need for false congeniality," he said. "If ye do no' wish to offer thanks, then do no'." The woman still saw him as an enemy, a fact he intended to rectify by the night's end.

They ate in silence for a time and Angus filled their chalices twice more. Only when Anya swayed a bit, her eyes a tad glassy, did he test the waters. "Tell me, why were ye hiding in my *birlinn?*"

The lady's dainty throat bobbed as her face flushed. "Ah...I thought it was a fishing boat, moored for the night."

"Aye, we've already established that, but ye haven't told me why ye were there in the first place."

"I was walking along the southern side of the barbican on my way to the sea gate when I heard the scuffle. I turned to go toward the main gate but there were soldiers running along the path." She swiped a hand across her mouth, her eyes shifting aside as if there might be far more to the story. "The path skirting the castle is quite narrow, I'll have ye know."

Angus sucked the remaining meat from a crab leg and licked his lips. "And then what happened?"

"Well, not wanting to be trampled, and not wanting to head into a skirmish, I did the only reasonable thing I could think of at the time. I ran to the end of the pier and hid."

"In my boat."

"It appears so."

"Why were ye approaching the sea gate? It seems ye could have used the main gate in the first place."

The lass turned three shades of scarlet before she took a healthy gulp of wine. "I'd rather not say."

Such an admission made her story all the more intriguing. Though Anya may be an orphan, she was no servant, nor was she a waif. It was obvious she had secreted out of the castle, or at least she had been attempting to secret inside. Earlier, she'd admitted that she was to be betrothed, which meant she wasn't already promised. But someone of import must be negotiating on her behalf. Who?

One thing at a time.

"Since the daylight hours were fading," he hedged, "I believe it is safe to assume ye were returning from somewhere."

Though her shoulders shrugged, the lass nodded.

"A tryst, perchance?" he mused. "One last moment in a lover's arms afore your hand was to be given to another?"

Anya's jaw dropped as outrage filled her eyes. "I beg your pardon, sir, but never in all my days would I entertain such...such...doing something so *wicked*. I may be a tad adventuresome, but I certainly am no harlot."

Now Angus was getting somewhere. "Forgive me. Without knowing what happened, I fear I jumped to an untoward conclusion." Regardless if his smiles had any effect on the lass, he grinned all the same. Doing so certainly couldn't make matters worse. "Tell me, why were ye beyond the castle walls alone?"

Again, Anya averted her eyes. Was she trying not to allow him to charm her? This time, her gaze settled on the roll of vellum she'd been etching with the bit of charcoal. "'Tis the only time I can be alone to..."

Angus leaned forward. "To?"

"Draw."

He tapped the scroll. "May I see?"

Anya's color remained flushed as she scraped her teeth over her bottom lip. "'Tis not yet complete."

"Come." He picked it up. "May I?"

"Naaaaaaaay."

She reached for it, but he was faster. Taking an edge,

he held out the vellum, making it unroll before she could snatch it back. As the lass yanked the drawing from his fingertips, his heart took to flight, stuttering in his chest until it dove south and fluttered somewhere it had no business flapping its wings.

Of all things, she had drawn a picture of *him*.

"Ye let it unravel on purpose."

Angus thrust out his palm and beckoned with his fingers. "Let me see that."

Shaking her head, Anya hugged the damn drawing against her breasts. "What else was I supposed to draw? We're stranded on an island with nothing but a crumbling old chapel, craggy rocks, and seagrass."

"Just allow me another wee peek." Not giving in, he shook his hand. "Please?"

With a tsk of her tongue, Anya placed the scroll in his palm. "Remember, the work is not complete, not by half."

"Thank you." He turned the vellum over and studied it. She had captured him as if he'd been looking in a mirror—his hair tousled by the wind, his shirt the worse for wear, his plaid belted low, a dirk in one hand and the chapel's stole in the other. "My word, this is quite a good rendering."

"Do ye really think so?"

He grinned again, this time without forethought. "Ye have a talent for certain."

Anya released a long sigh. "Ye're not angry with me?"

"Why would I be angry?" He chuckled as he rolled the scroll and returned it. "Though I reckon, the man to whom ye're *to be* betrothed may take exception."

"Aye, Lord O'Doherty," she said, with a distinct lack of enthusiasm. Then she cringed. "I must return to Carrickfergus. I simply must."

Angus bristled. He knew the name and O'Doherty was no ally, but he was a lord and that confirmed Anya was no mere orphan. "Not to worry, lass. When ye reach Ireland's shores, something tells me your sweetheart will still be waiting. I certainly would no' give up on a lass as bonny as you."

Anya turned away, hiding her expression.

"I reckon the man must be travelling for the feast, mustn't he?" Angus continued.

She nodded.

"And I'll wager, aside from this O'Doherty, there are a great many people who are worried about ye."

"I'm certain Finovola is beside herself with worry."

"And who else?"

"Just my sister."

"Och, lass. I may be a simple Scot, but I ken a high-born woman when I meet one. And a lord doesn't travel across the Isle of Ireland for a mere orphan."

Anya pursed her lips, proving Angus right. "I-I am a ward of...of Ulster's steward, as is my sister."

Perhaps she was telling the truth. Stewards held lofty positions and usually had dwellings within the walls of their lords' fortresses. Perhaps she was the daughter of a learned man—mayhap an illegitimate daughter of a holy man. Perhaps that explained her desire for secrecy.

Angus sat back and crossed his ankles while he made another attempt at savoring the mediocre wine. "Something tells me this betrothal is one of duty."

"What marriage is not one of duty? All her life, a woman looks forward to her wedding day—the time when she can wed and run her own cast—*ah*, I mean a home of her own."

Through the smoke-filled air, he regarded her from over the rim of his chalice, and Angus chuckled. "I'll wager the steward's wife is a woman to be reckoned with."

"Why do ye say that?"

"No reason." He filled his glass. Aye, he had plenty

of reasons. Firstly, Anya slipped out of Carrickfergus to be alone and draw pictures But, most of all, the tripe she just spewed about the duty of marriage obviously had been put there by a wizened old crone, and Angus wagered the steward's wife fit the bill.

ANYA WAVED A HAND OVER HER CHALICE. "PLEASE, NO more."

The big Highlander stood straight, balancing the cask in the palm of his hand as if it weighed nothing. "Nay? Then I suppose there's naught to do but to turn in."

He was right, even though the thought of sleeping made Anya's insides squirm. But the candle had nearly burned to a nub. Biting her bottom lip, she glanced at the folded tapestry—the one they had shared last eve. The one she must never share with him again. "Are ye intending to make up your pallet in here, my lord?"

As she spoke the words, the wind howled, making the rafters shudder and creak.

Setting the cask aside without refilling his own cup, he glanced to the door. "'Tis February and blowing a gale. I was rather hoping to survive the night without succumbing to exposure. Unless ye have a better idea?"

She rubbed the back of her neck. "Would you be using the tapestry, then?"

"What sort of gentleman would I be if I did so?" He pushed to his feet. "I'll sleep near the door and keep the banshees at bay for your ladyship."

"I'd best step outside first, then." As soon as Anya stood, her head swam, making her stumble, falling against the man's chest. Good heavens, his chest was like a wall of stone, yet it was warm and far too inviting. "Forgive me. I'm so clumsy!"

Those powerful arms encircled her. "Easy, lass. Mayhap we drank a bit too much wine."

No matter how much she ought to push away, Anya couldn't bring herself to do so. After all, it was February and the brazier hardly removed the chill from the air. She dared to raise her chin and meet his gaze. "My goodness, your eyes are so blue, they look like a clear midwinter sky."

The corner of his mouth ticked up. "Not a summer sky?"

"Definitely midwinter—the blue is a bit deeper in winter."

Islay's devilish grin grew wider. "Spoken like an artist."

"The countess would say I'm more of a dreamer."

A pinch formed between his brows. "Countess...of Ulster?"

By the rood, I'm daft.

Realizing she was willingly pressing her body against a vile pirate's chest, Anya twisted out of his embrace and took a few steps backward. Had she truly mentioned the countess? She ought to have said the steward's wife. "Well, she is the lady of the keep and she oft chides me for my daydreaming."

"Does she now?"

"Ye are nothing like what I expected," Anya said, hoping to turn the subject away from her.

His brow arched with a hint of disbelief as he tapped his foot. "Now ye cannot tell me ye planned to stow away in my *birlinn*."

"No, of course not. But everyone at Carrickfergus Castle has heard of Angus Og MacDonald. Fairhair—a ruthless pirate, plunderer on the high seas with a face like an angel yet the heart of a devil."

Those intense blue eyes narrowed. "Ruthless? Plunderer? Where in all of Christendom have you arrived at such an ill-begotten judgement?"

"Do ye deny it?"

Rolling his shoulder, the man grimaced—the same shoulder she'd clipped with the axe. "I steadfastly reject every accusation that just spewed from your lips."

"Then why did ye flee?" she asked, worried that she might have truly hurt him. "Why were Ulster's soldiers firing arrows upon ye?"

"It seems your beloved Ulster is not as fond of his daughter as Robert the Bruce had hoped."

Anya clapped a hand over her heart—the rumors were founded. Islay had joined forces with the Scottish king. "I disagree and will tell ye now, Ulster has only the utmost fatherly love for Elizabeth."

"Ye refer to her quite fondly—almost as if ye were kin."

"We are not kin, though before she married that Scottish fiend, we were friends. Good friends."

Islay sauntered toward her, his eyes narrowing as if he were linking together the fragments of Anya's life. Oh, no, she wasn't about to let him bait her into saying more. The more she said, the more likely it was for her to make a blunder. And what would Angus Og MacDonald say when he discovered she was an O'Cahan?

"I'll be but a moment," she said, pushing outside into the blustery wind. At least the chill was sobering. Goodness, if that fair-haired Highlander grinned at her one more time, she'd swoon for certain.

And she didn't need a seer to tell her she had no chance of returning to Carrickfergus in time for the feast. Anya clutched her arms about herself. What if Lord O'Doherty withdrew from the marriage negotiations? Only yesterday, she would have been elated at the notion. But now, she wasn't so certain. What would happen to her if she returned and all was lost?

Good heavens, Ulster might arrange her marriage to some smelly old buffoon. At least Lord O'Doherty was near her age. He most likely wouldn't beat her. Of course, the man was nowhere near as handsome as the Lord of Islay. But Anya had never met anyone as braw as the pirate with whom she was marooned—the man she'd scandalously slept beside last eve.

The man she absolutely must not allow to seduce her. Not even with a smile. If only she could fashion a pair of blinders for herself.

Saints preserve me!

6

True to his word, Islay had spent the night sleeping beside the chapel door while Anya nestled at the far side of the tiny nave. This morning, she busied herself putting away the chapel's things in a drawer hidden in back of the altar, while His Lordship stood on a chair and rehung the tapestry. When he hopped down, he brushed off his hands. "I'd best hunt for some crabs. If the weather grows any worse, Raghnall may be waylaid."

He wasn't wrong. The wind had been blowing a gale all day. "Do ye reckon 'tis safe enough to sail at the moment?" she asked.

"Aye, as long as the boats hug the shore. Though after surviving the storm that stranded us here, I'll nay take any chances. We'll need food afore the day's end." He headed for the door. "I recommend ye stay here, 'tis a mite warmer inside."

Anya listened to his footsteps crunch over the stony shore and fade. Climbing into an enemy boat might not only ruin her, it could mean her end. If she was going to find a way back to Carrickfergus, now was the time to do it. Surely her guardian had sent out all manner of ships and fishing boats to search for her. Though, how would they have any idea to where she'd disappeared? By now, Finovola would have told them Anya had oft slipped out her secret passageway to draw. Mayhap one of the soldiers saw her hasten for the pier? The Earl of Ulster was a shrewd man, he must have pieced together the clues.

Anya cracked open the door and peered out. Fairhair was mostly hidden by the bluff, all but his mane of blond hair whipping with the wind. When he stooped down to where she could no longer see him, she darted out of the chapel and hastened up the hill until she reached the highest point.

Of course, Islay had tried to discourage her from searching for the English fleet, but that was because he'd thrown in his lot with the outlaw Bruce. It didn't take a seer to know if Anya waited for the man to take her back to Carrickfergus, she might be an old maid when she next set eyes on her beloved Ireland. Yes, he'd been kind—far kinder than she would have expected for a vile rogue, but he was not concerned about anything but returning to Islay. She even doubted he gave a wit about her upcoming betrothal.

It didn't take long to spot a cog's square sail on the horizon, but the ship was too far away and heading northward. Anya shivered as icy wind whipped across the skerry and cut through the weave of her woolen kirtle as if it were but a linen shift. She crouched in the grass and wrapped her arms tightly across her body, keeping her gaze trained to the south.

Good heavens, she missed her cloak. She missed the warmth of a hearth and the comforts of the chamber she shared with Finovola. As soon as she arrived home, the first thing she planned to do was linger in a hot bath. Aye, she'd been cold before, but this little isle was miserable, especially without a mere blanket to wrap around her shoulders.

Anya had tolerated about as much misery as she could when she checked over her shoulder. "Thanks be to Mother Mary and Joseph!" The boat that had been heading north had turned and was sailing directly toward Nave, and they were flying King Edward's colors. Springing up, Anya waved her arms, hopping up and down. "Here! Help! Help!"

As the ship neared, a man in the bow waved a hand over his head, then pointed his finger, indicating toward the beach. Of course, the high point was no place to moor a ship with the craggy rocks down below.

Excited out of her mind, Anya headed down the slope at a run. "Islay!" she hollered, spotting him on the shore. "There's a ship!"

He mustn't have heard her above the rush of the wind and surf because he didn't even glance her way. But he did look to the sea when the cog ran aground on the beach. Dropping the crab in his fist, he drew his dirk as at least ten men leapt over the side of the boat with their weapons at the ready.

"No!" Anya yelled, right before her toe caught on a rock, sending her stumbling forward onto her hands. Something jagged sliced into her palm. With no time to fuss with it, she cursed her clumsiness and sprang to her feet, clutching her bleeding hand against her waist.

Ahead, Islay backed in a crouch while the English sailors converged. "No!" she shouted as the big Highlander lunged with his dirk. The men attacked on all sides, blades slicing through the air in a blur. Islay put up a valiant fight, yet he let out a rumbling bellow as he took a blow to his shoulder and dropped to his knees.

Frantic, Anya dashed onto the beach just as a cur leveled his blade across the Lord of Islay's throat. "Stop, I say!"

"Stay back," shouted the leader, thrusting his palm at her face.

She looked on, wrapping her fingers around her throat while they secured a rope around His Lordship's wrists. He was bleeding from his shoulder and the corner of his mouth. Why had she not foreseen this?

"This man saved my life. He does not deserve to be bullied and bound like a criminal."

"This is not your concern, miss. We've not only found ye, we've been waiting for our chance to seize this MacDonald scourge. Fairhair attacked Edward's army at Loch Ryan." The man-at-arms kicked Islay in the belly, making him double over with an oof.

Anya dashed in front of His Lordship, shielding him from the English crew. "Do not harm him, I say. If it hadn't been for the Lord of Islay, I would have drowned."

"Did he not abduct you?" asked the leader, eyeing her. "Ulster has ordered half the northern fleet to patrol these waters."

Dear Lord, what was she to say now? Admit to hiding in His Lordship's *birlinn* like a child? "I was not abducted."

"You willingly went with this man?"

"Not exactly willingly. I happened to be in his boat when they set sail."

"And he didn't stop to allow you to step ashore?"

Clutching his stomach, Islay met her gaze with an anguished furrow to his brow.

"Please," she said, gripping her hands over her heart. "It was not his doing. He-he didn't know I was aboard. I heard the fighting and was afraid. Thinking I'd climbed into a fishing boat, I hid beneath a tarpaulin."

"Well, it matters not." The man sauntered so near, he made her take a step away. "We must take ye back to Carrickfergus and this outlaw will be sent to Carlisle where he'll join the traitors Thomas and Alexander Bruce. I reckon he'll arrive just in time to be executed alongside them."

Executed? The word took the breath from Anya's lungs. "His Lordship acted with chivalry. Not once did he raise a finger to harm me."

"Mayhap not, but this rogue has sided with the

outlaw Bruce. That in itself is an act of treason against a king to whom he swore featly."

"My brother took the oath. Under duress, mind ye," Islay mumbled, earning another kick to the ribs.

Anya panned her gaze across the faces of the English soldiers and spotted not a single compassionate mien. Dear God, it was up to her to do something. Squaring her shoulders, she stretched to her full height. "In that case, I insist we take His Lordship to Carrickfergus and let the Earl of Ulster decide what is to be done with him." If they took Islay to Ireland, she'd at least have a chance to plead for leniency.

The man sneered, looking her from head to toe. "By the way ye speak, I would think ye might have grown fond of this rabble."

Anya raised her chin for good measure. "Not at all. He saved my life."

"He is a miscreant of the highest or—" Suddenly stopped, the cur's eyes popped wide as if in shock, his mouth opened and closed like a fish on dry land, then blood spurted from his throat.

As her gaze focused, she gagged, realizing his neck had been pierced by an arrow.

In the blink of an eye, a barrage of arrows hissed past Anya's ears. Screaming, she covered her head and dropped to her knees. "Stop, stop, stop!" she shouted over and over, certain she would be the next person skewered.

As she took in a deep breath, things grew eerily quiet until the rocks crunched with Islay's footsteps. He grasped her elbow with his bound hands and tugged her up. "'Tis over, miss."

"I leave ye alone for a day and return to find ye under an English knife," said Raghnall, standing in the helm of a sea galley with a bow and arrow in his hands.

A dozen Highlanders pulled the MacDonald *birlinn* beside the English cog while Anya gulped, her gaze trailing to the carnage on the beach. "Lord have mercy," she mumbled, her fingers trembling as she worked lose His Lordship's bindings.

After the rope dropped to the ground, Islay pulled her into a powerful embrace. "Hide your eyes. 'Tis a grisly sight not meant for a lady."

Unable to draw away from him, Anya buried her face against his chest. "But...but they were a-a-alive a moment ago. And I-I thought if they took ye to Ulster, I could plead for leniency and-and he would see that ye have a good heart and—"

"Nay, lass. No matter how good your intentions were, the man spoke true. In King Edward's eyes, I am a traitor, though I fail to see how I can commit treason against a country to which I am no' a subject."

Gooseflesh rose across Anya's skin as she wiped away her tears and searched his eyes. She'd never heard the conflict between the kingdoms explained in such a way. Too many clashing thoughts rifled through her mind. There she stood in the arms of a man whose brother had killed her father in a battle for lands and power—not because of the wars between the kingdoms but in the course of a clan feud. Anya's da had joined with the MacDougall Clan on a promise of Scottish lands, except her father had never returned and the lands promised remained in the hands of the MacDonalds. She'd been raised to hate the Lord of Islay and his kin, as well as to believe any Scot who did not pay fealty to King Edward was evil.

Can there be an exception?

She'd lived her entire life under the belief that MacDonalds were violent, pillaging murderers. And the proof was right here before her. Yet Edward's men were about to lead an innocent man to a heinous death. A man who had saved Anya from drowning. A man who had warmed her when she was on the verge of succumbing to icy exposure.

When she placed her hand on his chest, hot blood oozed through her fingers. "Ye're hurt."

"'Tis but a scratch."

It wasn't, but presently, Anya had no bandages with which to tend him.

He took her palm and turned it up. "You've injured your hand as well."

"I'd say this is more of a scratch than the gash to your shoulder."

"Nay, miss. This wee cut evens out the axe blow ye delivered on the other side." He blew on her tender flesh, relieving the ache. Then he gave her a wink with one of those grins steamy enough to melt a heart of ice, while he tore off a piece of his shirt and wrapped it around her palm. "This will help staunch the bleeding until Lilas can tend you."

"Lilas?"

"Our healer."

Angus turned to Raghnall as he came up beside them. "Och, ye are gifted with impeccable timing, friend."

The man-at-arms chuckled. "One of us has a gift and I doubt it is me, m'lord."

"What news of the others in our boat?"

"Gael washed ashore on Islay—made his way back to the keep about the same time as I."

Angus' shoulders dropped as he bowed his head and crossed himself. "We've incurred too many losses of late."

Raghnall made the sign of the cross as well. "I wish there was time to head into the chapel and pray for their souls, but there are more patrols sailing these waters than I've ever seen. Unless we want to join our fallen kinsmen, we'd best hide the English boat and be on our way."

"Nay, we shall remove her colors and add this cog to my fleet. I need half the crew to help me sail her to

Dunyvaig." Angus pointed to Raghnall as he grasped Anya's elbow and tugged her toward the English ship. "Bury the dead, then haste for home."

Once they were under way and the sail was full, Anya sat the tiller beside Angus. "I kent ye were no commoner," he said. "Are ye kin to Ulster?"

She scrunched her nose. "Not exactly. I am his ward."

"Explain."

"I withheld my identity from ye because at first I feared for my life. Ye see, my father was killed by Alasdair MacDonald." She looked him square in the eyes. "Your brother."

With her words, everything turned icy.

THE SIGHT OF DUNYVAIG'S WALLS ALIGHT WITH THE reflection of the afternoon sun, made the pent-up tension in Angus' body blow away with a gust of wind. Except for the roiling in his chest. He had been forthright with Miss Anya from the outset, but because she knew of the rumors smearing his name, she'd hid her identity from him. And then he'd trusted her.

The gashes in his shoulders throbbed as he thought about how daft he'd been, leaving her in the chapel while he went off to collect crabs. He should have tied her up, or at least kept her under a watchful eye. The bloody daughter of Lord Guy O'Cahan, ally of John MacDougall, the bedamned Lord of Lorn? The woman had nearly caused his undoing. If it hadn't been for Raghnall arriving when he did, Angus would be heading for his execution on the Carlisle gallows, alongside his allies.

Wouldn't that have made the King Robert's heart rosy?

Ever since she had confessed her true identity, Miss Anya had moved to the bow of the ship. Regardless of the sea spray up there, she'd chosen to remain as far away from him as possible, sitting as rigid as a statue. And so be it. He hadn't uttered a word to the woman during the voyage, either. Aye, the sooner he arranged for her return to Carrickfergus, the better.

Thank heavens it didn't take long to sail around the southern end of Islay and into the bay that protected Dunyvaig Castle. After the men pulled the *birlinn* onto the shore, he ordered them to help the lady alight while he hopped over the side and headed for the keep.

"Good tidings for a blessed Saint Valentine's Day, m'lord," said Friar Jo. The man's name was Jonas, but ever since the Benedictine monk had arrived on the island, he'd been dubbed Jo. He was one of the few people Angus confided in. After all, he'd known the cleric all his life.

"'Tis good to be home at last."

"I heard about your wee stowaway."

"Aye." Angus glanced over his shoulder and frowned. Flanked by two guards, Anya was following. "She's the daughter of Lord Guy O'Cahan."

Huffing, the old friar waddled beside him as they made their way through the sea gate. "My heavens, no."

"Ye'd best believe it, do no' let her out of your sight or she may very well dirk your back. I'll be arranging transport for the lass just as soon as I've had a bath and a change of clothes."

"Ye might want to rethink your priorities, m'lord."

"Oh? And why, pray tell? I've just spent two nights sleeping on an icy stone floor in the wee chapel on Nave. I'm in sore need of a bath and a change of bloody clothes." He also wouldn't mind a blanket or two to stave off the bitter wind.

"King Bruce wants to see ye straightaway. The lass as well."

Angus groaned. Damnation, he'd forgotten about the king. And why the hell hadn't Raghnall mentioned the Bruce was still here? Bless it, Robert the Bruce had taken over the lord's chamber, which meant Angus would again be relegated above stairs to the small room he'd occupied as a lad.

He stopped and beckoned Anya forward. "We're to have an audience with King Bruce, then I'll see to it the servants draw ye a bath and find some suitable clothes. After all, we heathens do feast on Saint Valentine's as well."

"My thanks." Pursing her lips, the lass grasped his elbow, the sensation of her lithe fingers making tingles skitter all the way up to the back of his neck. "I'm sorry."

"For what?" he growled, not proud of the gruff tone in his voice. He knew why she had apologized. He just wasn't ready to accept it.

"I'm Friar Jo," said the cleric, smiling as if he weren't facing the daughter of one of their most hated adversaries. "Welcome to Dunyvaig, miss."

She cringed. "I'm not quite certain of your welcome."

Angus led the way up the ramp leading to the keep. "The friar kens who ye are, and he'd welcome ye even if ye were married to Satan. This man hasn't a grudgeful bone in his body."

Friar Jo chuckled and rubbed his belly. "Aye, the good Lord says love thy neighbor. I reckon he means the Irish as well as the English, no matter which king to whom ye happen to pay fealty."

Inside, the smells of roasting venison and baking bread wafted through the air, making Angus' mouth water. His last decent meal had been when he'd broken his fast three days past. And though the clan would be assembling soon to enjoy a grand feast, a feeling of tension in the air weighed upon him. And Angus knew why. The king had wintered at Dunyvaig and the MacDonald servants were on edge.

"Islay," said Robbie Boyd, bowing at the entry to the great hall. "'Tis good to see ye survived the storm, my friend."

Angus greeted the knight, clasping his forearm and squeezing. "I'm glad ye were able to spirit the king away afore Ulster's archers honed their skills."

"Between us, I reckon the earl gave orders for near misses. After all, the queen would have never spoken to her father again had the bastard murdered her husband."

"MacDonald," bellowed the Bruce, sitting in Angus' chair at the head table upon the dais where he had taken to holding court these past few months. "Come forward."

Angus didn't consider himself a prideful man. But, nonetheless, he'd had a gutful of being a pawn in his own castle. Beckoning Anya to follow, he inclined his lips toward her ear. "This will no' take long, then I shall see to your comfort."

As they processed, Angus nodded to his mother who was also seated at the high table along with Arthur Campbell and a number of the king's confidants. As a courtesy, Angus grasped Anya's elbow to climb the dais steps. After reaching the top, he bowed, noting the lass beside him was savvy enough to dip into a respectful curtsey. "Good tidings, Your Grace. Please allow me to introduce Miss Anya O'Cahan of Dunseverick."

Mither gasped, clapping a hand to her chest.

Robert the Bruce arched a thick eyebrow, his eyes widening. "Ah, yeeees, I remember ye, Miss Anya. Ye stood with my wife at our wedding. She spoke highly of ye and your sister."

"My thanks, Your Grace. Elizabeth is...*ah*...was my closest friend. If it had not been for her kindness when I arrived at Carrickfergus, I would have suffered greatly."

The king's gaze flickered to Angus before he dipped

his quill and signed the document on the table before him, which was then taken and sealed by his cleric. "I understand Ulster claimed guardianship after your father was killed." Robert looked up from his work and tapped the feather to his chin. "He joined with MacDougall against the MacDonald, did he not?"

Anya blushed as bright as a blood rose. "Aye."

"Unfortunate turn of events that, what with two dead lords and nothing gained."

Angus cleared his throat, dislodging a lump that had suddenly formed. Beside the king, his mother had gone terribly pale, her eyes boring through him with the anguish of a woman who'd lost her firstborn. It wasn't easy for Angus to grant hospitality to the offspring of Lord Guy O'Cahan and, most likely, it was doubly as distasteful for Mither. "I plan to arrange transport to return Miss Anya to Carrickfergus on the morrow."

The king whipped his quill through the air while a pinch formed between his brows. "Ye will do no such thing. This woman is now my political prisoner just as my wife is held captive by Edward of England. Miss Anya O'Cahan has worth and will be a useful pawn when the time comes to negotiate the exchange of prisoners. I've a monastery in mind where the monks provide our captives with meaningful labor—somewhere Edward will never find them, ye ken the one."

Anya clasped her hands over her heart. "But I must return—"

"May I be so bold as to make a suggestion, sire?" asked Mither.

Rarely did Angus' mother interrupt, though she was as shrewd as any man, Her Ladyship was very calculated and careful about everything she said, especially when in the king's company.

The king set his quill in the holder. "By all means."

"I am in need of a lady-in-waiting and, as ye are aware, Dunyvaig is impenetrable. Why not allow the lass to remain here, under my watchful eye and tutelage, of course."

"Hmm." Robert slid the velum he'd signed toward the cleric. "Interesting that ye would be willing to take on such a task, given the feud between your kin."

"Which is exactly why I thought of it. Miss Anya's younger brother assumed the Lordship of Keenaght, did he not? What better time to repair relations than when youth assume an ancestral seat?"

Angus tried to read Anya's expression, but she stood emotionless. Nonetheless, she had been planning to wed Lord O'Doherty or at least accept his offer of marriage this very night. What panic must she be feeling inside with all her dreams being brushed aside with a wave of the king's hand? Did Mither honestly believe she could win the lass over?

One thing was for certain, Miss Anya would live in far more comfort at Dunyvaig than she would at Eynhallow Monastery on the Isle of Orkney where Angus had ferried Robert's highborn prisoners before, though the location was a closely guarded secret and only known by a handful of men. The place was not only desolate and cold, the wind blew constantly while the monks survived by tilling rocky land and raising a flock of feeble-looking sheep. The king had grossly overstated the comfort she might find up there. 'Twas akin to the misery they'd shared on Nave.

"What say you, Angus?" asked Robert. "This is your domain. Are ye willing to harbor the lass until she's needed for negotiations? Mind ye, it could be years afore I see my Elizabeth again."

Beside him, Anya released a stuttered breath. Aye, she was roiling on the inside, for certain.

"I agree with the Dowager Lady Islay. The lass will enjoy far more comfort here than at a monastery. Furthermore, if my mother is willing to take on such a responsibility, then I shall see to it Miss Anya remains safely within Dunyvaig's walls." Angus made a point of looking the lass in the eye. "After all, we will destroy any enemy ship that comes too near our shores."

"'Tis settled, then." The king reached for a tankard while he nodded to Miss Anya. "Consider yourself fortunate. I only pray my wife is receiving similar consideration in regard to her station." Robert shifted his gaze to the rafters. "Dear Lord, watch over her."

7

Anya wanted nothing more than to languish in the wooden tub and pretend she was in her bedchamber at Carrickfergus, preparing to meet the man who had been negotiating for her hand. Unfortunately, the Dowager Lady Islay had given the servants strict instructions to assist Anya to dress for the feast as swiftly as possible. As soon as she had been shown to a small bedchamber, two sentries had brought in a wooden tub, followed by a line of servants carrying pails filled with steamy water.

Even more surprising, a dress awaited her with a crisp linen shift, as if Her Ladyship were expecting a new lady-in-waiting. Anya raised the rose-scented soap to her nose and inhaled. What might the woman's expectations be? At Carrickfergus, the Countess of Ulster required Anya and Finovola to help her dress in the morning, assist her to change for any outings, as well as change for every evening meal. They provided companionship while the countess had given the two girls an education, preparing them to become wives of well-born gentlemen. In short, they were more or less treated as family, as daughters or, at least, nieces of the earldom.

Anya's limbs felt ever so heavy as she bathed away

the stench of the sea and the smell of the heady smoke from the chapel's brazier. Robert the Bruce had said it might be years before he used her as a pawn to trade for Elizabeth's freedom. In truth, Anya would gladly volunteer to do anything to help her dearest friend, but such an option was not presented as a request. Rather, she was forced to remain at Dunyvaig with no care given to her feelings on the matter.

Would she ever again find an opportunity to escape? It did not seem likely—not when she was being guarded by a man reputed to be the vilest scourge in the Western Isles, his fortresses impenetrable, housing soldiers who fought like demons.

After rinsing her hair, she sat immobile, staring at the water, now a tad murky from the lye in the soap. She was actually missing the Saint Valentine's Day feast at Carrickfergus. Just a few days ago, she'd been a bit melancholy about the idea of marrying, though never again. If Lord Chahir O'Doherty wanted her for his wife, then so be it. And by the rood, she missed Finovola. If only Anya could send her sister a message and let her know she was well.

Of course, over the next few to several years, Lord O'Doherty would find another woman to wed.

Though Anya rued the day she'd hidden in Fairhair's *birlinn*, oddly, the idea of her intended marrying another didn't bother her in the slightest. Why had she never warmed to him? They'd met but once when he'd visited the earl. Lord O'Doherty was of average height and, aside from crooked teeth, was pleasant enough to the eye. During that brief stroll atop the wall-walk, he spoke of duty and the need to produce an heir. He told her about his keep and how his mother had managed the servants with an iron fist. But not once had he commented about affection, or tried to kiss her hand, or complimented Anya aside from mentioning that her sister was quite lovely and ought to make a good match.

Anya knew full well she was not the beauty in the family. But she was the eldest and, according to Islay, was not entirely unpleasing to the eye. Even if Angus Og MacDonald was an abhorrent pirate, the way he looked at her made her insides inflame like never before. Were all rogues scandalously attractive? Heaven's stars, she must never allow herself to look upon the man with any semblance of affection.

Alas, she was a prisoner in a stone fortress, with a mammoth guard posted outside her door. She would grow old here, destined to be a spinster for the rest of her days. Aye, she may not have loved Chahir O'Doherty, but he would have provided her with a home and the opportunity to raise children of her own.

A knock came at the door.

Startling, Anya dropped the soap. "I am in the bath."

"'Tis just Freya, miss." The door opened and a middle-aged woman stepped inside. She wore an apron over a plaid kirtle, and a linen mob cap atop her head. "I'm the lady's maid the dowager sent to help ye dress for the feast."

Anya slipped lower in the bath and fished out the cake of soap. "Wonderful."

"Are ye not feeling well, miss?" asked Freya, moving to the stack of drying cloths.

The gash on Anya's hand stung a bit and she blew on it. "A tad melancholy, I suppose, seeing I am now a political prisoner."

The maid shook out one of the cloths and held it up, her smile friendly. "I can think of far more despicable places in which to serve your term. Her Ladyship is fair and thoughtful, and her son is far kinder and more compassionate than his brother, I'll say."

Such a comment piqued Anya's interest. "Oh? Was Alasdair a cruel man?" she asked, his name bitter on her tongue.

"Not cruel, but perhaps a wee bit severe. He wasn't one to allow second chances."

"And Angus is? He seems rather commanding to me."

"Och, His Lordship is very commanding, but I reckon he inherited a bit of his mother's kindhearted nature. I say, if a crofter is unable to pay his rents, Angus will work with him to improve his lot, where Alasdair would have demanded payment and given a very short time for the man to make amends."

"Is that so?"

"Aye. Ye ought to be comfortable here, if not happy." Freya waved the drying cloth. "Come now, ye must hasten to dress. There will no' be time to dry your tresses, but I'll make plaits and roll them into caul nets and ye'll be the bonniest woman in the great hall, mark me."

Anya sniggered as she stood and took the cloth, quickly hiding her nudity. "I rather doubt it."

It didn't take long to don the new clothes, and the maid proved quite efficient tending her hair. By the time Freya rubbed a salve into her palm and wrapped it in a fresh dressing, Anya had almost run out of excuses to avoid the feast—except for one. She peered down at her hem, kicking out a foot. "My sister would wear this gown far better than I. I'm afraid 'tis too long for me."

"Not to worry, I'll fetch a needle and thread straightaway. It won't take me but a moment." The maid hastened to her sewing basket. "Her Ladyship will see to it ye visit the tailor to be measured for new clothes on the morrow."

Anya nodded, realizing the MacDonalds would be providing her clothing for years to come. "My thanks," she whispered, her shoulders sagging.

"Come, lass, ye've not but to make the best if it. I ken it will take time, but if ye let us, we will prove we are not an evil clan." Freya kneeled and started hemming. "And ye look radiant. The plaits coiled about your ears are lovely, even if I do say so myself. Might I add that the Dowager Lady Islay chose well. The green in your gown makes your eyes sparkle like jewels."

Anya patted the netting covering the braids. She hadn't ever worn caul nets before, but they did hold her hair secure, and the style made no difference if her tresses were wet or dry.

"There ye are, 'tisn't my best work but it will set ye to rights for the evening," said Freya, standing back and examining her work.

Taking a few steps, Anya tested the length. "That's better. At least if I trip, it shouldn't be because of my hem."

The maid laughed as another knock sounded at the door. "'Tis time to head for the hall, miss," came the gruff voice of the guard. "Her Ladyship requires your presence."

"Go on," urged Freya. "Ye must be famished."

Taking in a deep breath, Anya wrung her hands as the maid opened the door. Aye, she was off to the Saint Valentine's Day feast, but this meal was in the wrong castle, among a clan she'd considered enemies only two days past.

The old guard led the way down the wheeled stairway, the sounds from a busy hall echoing off the stone walls and the rich scent of roasted meat making her mouth water. When she'd first arrived at the fortress, Anya was so nervous, she'd forgotten her hunger, but now her mouth watered in anticipation of a meal. She intended to eat her fill, keep her eyes lowered, and escape to her chamber as quickly as possible.

As they entered the great hall, the rumble from the crowd reduced to a low hum. Stopping for a moment, she glanced across the faces—all gaping at her. She could swear the low mummers were about the daughter of Lord Guy O'Cahan, who would be held at Dunyvaig until the king could make a trade for her and who knew how many others in exchange for Elizabeth.

"Follow me, miss," said the guard, leading her into an aisle separating numerous tables, filled with dozens of MacDonalds, doubtless waiting for her to stumble.

Anya's face burned as she kept her gaze focused on the guard's feet, his boots clomping on the stone floor. About halfway along, he stopped and stepped aside. She swept her gaze across the people crowded shoulder to shoulder onto the benches and wondered if they might be able to make room, at least long enough for her to eat.

"Miss Anya."

Startling, she recognized Islay's voice before she saw him. And when she turned, the braw lord took her breath away. She'd thought him beautiful on the Isle of Nave, but now that he'd bathed, he looked like a golden god. He was clean-shaven and wore a crisp shirt and plaid, belted low across his hips and drawn over his shoulder in the Scottish way.

Fairhair.

Lord in heaven, she wanted to hate this man, but any ice she'd harbored in her heart melted with his easy smile. He took her hand. "Ye are as bonny as a rose this eve." He bowed and kissed the back of her hand. It wasn't a mere courteous peck, but he seemed to linger, his warm lips almost tasting her, his breath scorching her flesh seductively.

Anya's heart fluttered as if it had grown wings. Biting down on her lip, she vowed to herself never to allow such feelings to be revealed. She may find him charming and handsome, but he must never know her true thoughts. Revealing them would be akin to betraying her father's honor.

When he straightened, he didn't release her hand, but placed it in the crook of his arm and started toward the dais. "Come."

She glanced back at the table where the guard still stood. "But am I not to sit there?"

"You will sit beside me."

"Does the king invite all political prisoners to the high table?"

"I've no idea." He gave her a wink and started up the steps. "I have never been host to a political prisoner before."

"I thought ye might lock me in a tiny tower room or worse," she said, taking in the grandeur of the table alit with dozens of beeswax candles and set with fine silver. Robert the Bruce sat in the lord's chair, flanked by knights and nobles.

At one end of the board, Angus held a chair for her. "Would ye like to be at the top of the tower? There is a wee chamber up there that I believe is unoccupied at the moment, aside from a few pigeons."

After she sat, he joined her while a servant immediately filled her goblet. "Truly, the chamber I've been assigned will do. I am looking forward to sleeping in a bed this eve."

"I am as well." He raised his cup and she followed, the fruity wine delicious on her tongue—much more pleasant than the awful vintage from Nave. "Ye must be bereft," he continued. "I ken how important it was for ye to return to Ireland. Contrary to what ye may believe, I honestly intended to see ye home as soon as I could arrange secure passage."

"Then it seems King Bruce surprised us all."

Enormous platters of venison, chicken, and bread arrived. Islay speared a juicy portion of meat and held it up. "My lady?"

She chuckled to herself at the use of lady. Had she married Lord O'Doherty, she would have become a lady, but now she was destined to be unwed for the rest of her days. "My thanks."

"Perhaps the war will be over soon," he said, selecting a joint for himself.

Anya took a slice of bread, slathered it with butter, and took a bite. It was all she could do not to roll her eyes back as she savored the taste. She washed it down with a hasty sip of wine. "I love Elizabeth de Burgh like a sister. Had I been asked to stay here to help her husband negotiate Her Grace's return, I would have agreed without hesitation."

Islay's hand stilled midair as those intense blue eyes raked down and up her face. "Ye would willingly give up your own happiness for a friend?"

There was no way in all of Christendom Anya would say that only moments before she had hidden in Fairhair's *birlinn* did she perseverate over her reservations about her betrothal. Besides, if she were put on a ship bound for Carrickfergus at this very moment, she would go tell the Earl of Ulster she desired a hasty marriage. "For Elizabeth, yes. I'd do the same for my sister as well."

His Lordship grasped his goblet and took a long drink, though his eyes never shifted away from Anya's face. "Well then," he said, lowering his drink and leaning closer. "There are more complex layers to the daughter of Lord Guy O'Cahan than I ever would have guessed."

Heavens, when he looked at her with those unnaturally alluring blue eyes and made such a judgement, she had no chance of hiding a smile. "I hope I haven't disappointed."

8

Disappointed? He mightn't completely trust Miss Anya, but how could he remain disappointed in a woman with such mettle? Their mishappen shipwreck aside, Angus had never met a lass so selfless that she would turn her back on a chance to become the esteemed wife of a lord to help a friend, especially since the friend happened to be married to a man she most likely considered to be the vilest outlaw since William Wallace.

Though he must never forget how Anya had disappointed him when she'd flagged the English ship. Nonetheless, if he had been in her shoes, shipwrecked on an isle with a man she considered an enemy, he would have done everything in his power to be rescued by someone he trusted—which certainly wasn't the Scots and most definitely wasn't anyone allied with Clan MacDonald. Aye, he had to admit the lass had all but ripped his heart out of his chest when she admitted to being the daughter of Lord Guy O'Cahan. Angus still hadn't recovered from that wee disclosure.

But at the moment, he supposed it mattered not who had sired the lass. What mattered was that she was now under his protection and Robert expected him to watch over her until she was needed by the crown.

Though he could not deny his attraction to Anya, it would be a political blunder of the highest order to woo her.

With the feast spread out in front of him, Angus' mouth watered while the claws of hunger gripped his belly. He took an enormous bite from his joint of venison, moaning with pleasure and savoring the juice as it burst in his mouth.

On his left, Mither leaned forward and regarded his new ward. "Raghnall told us ye were anxious to return to Carrickfergus."

Stopping mid-chew, Anya drew in a ragged breath. "Aye," she whispered, lowering her gaze and not explaining further.

Angus knew very well his mother would have squeezed every last detail she could out of the man-at-arms and most likely knew about the marriage contract negotiations, albeit between Ulster and O'Doherty rather than Anya's concocted story about the earl's steward.

"I am sorry for this state of affairs, truly," said Mither, her tone warm and sincere. "We will endeavor to make your stay here memorable."

Angus nearly snorted. The poor lassie's experience was already a catastrophe she'd never forget.

Anya craned her neck, looking directly at his mother. "This is a fine keep, I'm certain, but I do pray to return home anon."

Sobering, Angus returned his attention to the venison on his plate, eating in silence for a time. When Anya leaned aside to allow a servant to remove a trencher, the lass' knee brushed Angus' thigh. As their gazes met, Angus could have sworn her breath caught in unison with his. Was there a hint of attraction on her part?

If only he were able to find out. But the moment passed soon enough, with Anya shifting again, though the folds of her dress still brushed his knee. Every time she moved, the caress of fabric reminded him of how closely she sat.

At the center of the table, the king and the knights around him burst forth with raucous laughter. Robert raised his goblet and stood. "Let us make merry and dance, for God only kens what the morrow will bring!"

After an uproarious cheer, the servants began moving the tables aside to make way for music and dancing. A lutists, a drummer and a flautist took their positions upon the gallery.

"Do ye like to dance?" Angus asked.

"Very much so, though I'm not as graceful as—"

"Finovola?" he ventured.

The lass turned as red as the scarlet background on the tapestry behind them. "She's quite accomplished at most everything."

He moved his knee ever so slightly to see if he could touch her leg again but only managed another wee brush of woolen skirts. "Ye have put your sister on a pedestal, have ye not?"

While a servant placed a dish of stewed apples in front of her, Anya leaned away, though she seemed to be careful not to brush his thigh this time. "She's everyone's favorite."

Angus found that difficult to believe. "Why do ye reckon so?"

"First of all, where I am short and squat, she is long and lithe. She enjoys embroidery and will sit endlessly with the countess while they work their needlepoint, discussing menus, the servants, and the latest fashions."

"I take it ye don't care for needlepoint or idle chat?"

"Neither, really. I prefer to be outdoors. I like a spirited steed beneath me, with the wind in my hair. I like to hide away and draw everything I observe. I find so many new and astonishing things, I cannot see how anyone would prefer to be shut in the lady's solar with needle and thread."

"What have ye found that has surprised you?"

"So many things." She drummed her fingers on the stem of her goblet. "One of my most treasured discoveries is a blue crystal stone—not blue like the sky but blue like a shallow sea laced with green kale. 'Tis iridescent in the sunlight and nearly as large as the palm of my hand."

Angus enjoyed watching the animation on her face, the bonny splay of freckles that seemed to dance when she spoke. "The way ye describe the stone makes it sound priceless."

"It is. Though I..." She sipped her wine, her expression turning sad.

"You what, pray tell?"

"I doubt I'll ever see it again. After all, Ulster couldn't possibly know what has become of me. I fear soon he'll be preparing for my wake."

"That does sound a wee bit grim. I ken ye expected the terms of your betrothal to be final this eve."

Anya replaced her goblet as music swelled through the hall. "I suppose Lord O'Doherty will be setting his sights elsewhere now I've vanished."

Unable to think of a consoling response that didn't sound indifferent or trite, Angus bit the inside of his cheek. Poor lass, all her dreams had been dashed with one unlucky guess. Had she chosen a boat closer to the gate, her fate never would have changed.

Sir Arthur Campbell slid his chair away from the table and strode directly to Anya's side and bowed. "Will you dance with me, miss?"

Cracking his knuckles beneath the table, Angus scowled at the knight. The dancers hadn't even begun taking their places. And though the men outnumbered the women three to one, he should have been the first one to accompany her on a turn around the floor.

The lass glanced up. "Does King Robert allow his prisoners to dance?"

Campbell's jaw slackened with his shrug. "Ye are a guest at his table, why not enjoy the merriment of the feast day?"

Angus cracked his knuckles again. *This is my damned table*.

Anya took the knight's hand. "Well then, shall we?"

"Bloody hell," Angus mumbled under his breath while Campbell led her away. Did the knight not know better than to interrupt? And who did he think he was, barging over and asking Anya for the first dance? The Highlander might be favored by the king at the moment, but this was not his keep, nor was he charged with the protection of the O'Cahan lass for Lord only knew how long.

The dancers moved into their places, assembling in two lines. When the music began, Anya curtseyed while a smile blossomed on her face. She skipped and turned as if well practiced, her movement like that of a doe in the forest. That the woman thought she was stout and ungraceful was utter folly. She was delightfully adorable. Though Finovola might be statuesque, Angus could wager she had nowhere near the character of her elder sister.

"Ye have an eye for the O'Cahan woman," said Mither, nudging him with her elbow.

His mother's meddling always set him on edge, especially this eve. Worse, it made the gashes on his shoulders ache. "Nay. I have a great deal on my mind, is all." Angus reached for the ewer of wine and filled her glass before he topped up his own. "And at the forefront is what the devil were ye thinking when ye suggested we hold Miss Anya at Dunyvaig?"

"Humph. I'm surprised ye must ask." Mither traced her finger along his cheek. "My fair son."

He batted her hand away. "I'm a man of thirty. Please answer me."

"Alas, ye are in a sour mood. If ye must ken, I reckon we MacDonalds have far too many enemies."

"On that we are agreed."

"It might be of benefit to make an alliance with the House of O'Cahan. 'Tis an ancient, well-respected Irish name. They have strong influence over a number of our adversaries and—"

"Lord O'Cahan is but a lad of fifteen, I reckon." Angus pointed to the lass locking arms with Campbell. "The brother of our new charge."

"Perhaps so, but he will no' be a child forever. And the wee woman out there dancing with Sir Arthur most likely has a dowry large enough to pay for fifty sea galleys with coin to spare."

Angus batted his hand through the air. "Now ye are dreaming. Ye ken she is expecting a betrothal from that dim-witted maggot, Lord Chahir O'Doherty."

"That may well be but do ye think His Lordship will wait years for the return of his bonny bride? If O'Doherty is anything like his father, he has his sights set on her purse, not those beguiling emerald eyes."

Saying nothing, Angus drained his goblet. He didn't want to think of anyone taking advantage of Anya for her wealth. Or anyone taking advantage of the lass for any reason whatsoever. Most of all, he didn't care to have his mother meddling in his affairs.

"'Tis time you cast away the resentment ye harbor for Ella and find a woman to marry—bless the House of MacDonald with an heir afore something, God forbid, happens to ye."

The mention of Ella's name cut a slice through his gut. Angus hadn't thought of *her* in ages, nor did he ever care to hear her name. Angus had given his heart but once in his lifetime. He'd been a foolish youth and she a deceiving wench as it were. They'd met at a *ceilidh* on the Isle of Skye and she'd stolen his heart with a mere kiss. In the end, the vixen had rejected his offer of marriage and wed a MacLeod laird. At the time, Angus had been a lowly second son and lord of nothing but the sea and his *birlinn*.

"Did ye hear me?" asked Mither.

"Aye."

"Ha." His mother thumped his arm with a backhand. "The question is, did ye listen?"

As the dance ended and Campbell led Anya back toward the dais, Angus pushed back his chair. "I bid ye remember I am Lord of Islay, and I will decide when and to whom I will marry."

When he stood, his mother grasped his hand. "Just do no' bed the lass and cast her aside when ye are finished. And don't gape at me with an astonished air. I ken of the long line of wenches who've sampled your wiles. God gave ye the face of an angel but the only time he saw fit to open your heart was when ye were too young to use it wisely."

Snapping his hand away, he turned on his heel. Damnation, if that woman weren't his mother, he'd tell her where to put her opinion.

As soon as Sir Arthur and Miss Anya reached the steps to the dais, Angus pattered down, grasped her hand, and tugged her back toward the dancers. "I should have asked ye for the first dance," he growled, leering at Sir Arthur for his interference.

She squeezed his palm—such a subtle gesture, why had it knocked his heart out of rhythm? "I'm certain there will be many dances this eve."

Angus brushed his lips over the back of her hand, stopped at the ladies' line, and bowed. "Aye."

Without another word, he joined the men's line. Too many emotions roiled inside for him to make sense of them. He abhorred his mother's meddling, yet could not fathom why he felt like slamming his fist into

Arthur Campbell's nose. On top of it all, Angus had spent two sleepless nights on Nave, which ought to turn most anyone into an angry bear. But, more than that, Angus wanted control of his keep. He'd had enough of politics, fighting, and royal court for the moment. Och, he longed to hear supplications and settle the petty grievances of his crofters, to sail the seas and cast his nets, bringing in a harvest of haddock to feed the multitudes.

Anya gazed across the open space between them, her eyes alive with anticipation and fixedly focused on him. Good God, that woman could melt the ice atop the mount of *Beinn an Oir* in winter with the intensity of her stare.

The music began, cuing Angus to skip forward, and grasp her hands in his—small hands, soft, yet with long, artistic fingers he'd noticed when she had drawn the picture...*of him*.

If she liked to draw the treasures she found, why had she bothered to draw his face when she had suffered the loss of her father due to the feud between their clans?

When he'd drawn the tarpaulin away, she'd attacked as if she were terrified out of her wits. But now they were dancing together. The lass was even smiling. Mayhap she didn't detest him as much as she'd let on?

Distracted by his thoughts, Angus almost stumbled over his feet, even though Anya didn't seem to miss a step. She followed his lead easily, responding to every twist of his wrist and turn of his foot. When hand in hand, they sashayed in a circle, her skirts brushed his calves, the friction igniting sparks of awareness, making them flicker throughout his entire body. When Anya's gaze slid up to meet his, he gulped. Dear God, this woman thought herself plain? Why did she not see her own beauty? The music demanded they return to their lines and a hollowness spread through his chest, replacing the frissons of energy gripping him only moments before.

He took the corner woman by the elbow, turning and sashaying until Anya again stood across from him, her cheeks rosy. The dance demanded they move sideways until he beheld another face, friendly, but not intoxicating like that of the Irish lass. He locked arms with Lilis and spun in a circle while Anya mirrored them with the Highlander behind. Angus watched her out of the corner of his eye until she joined him once again.

He grasped her hands possessively, wishing they were alone, wishing they were back on Nave, yet with all the comforts of Dunyvaig. And then she gifted him with a radiant smile—a woman who ought to hate him clear to the depths of her soul, smiled like she hadn't a care and danced like a nymph. The music dimmed while Angus' breath rushed loudly in his ears. Seeing only her face, he pulled her closer for the spin, the sweet bouquet rose soap and Anya's uniquely feminine scent washing over his senses. Breathless, he stopped, standing motionless, the lass but inches from his body.

A concerned expression furrowed her brow. "Are ye well, my lord?"

The music came to an end and Angus released a breath he hadn't realized he'd been holding. "I think I need to take in some air and head for my pillow. Truth be told, I've never been one to function well without a good night's sleep."

She patted her lips as she yawned. "I'm afraid I'm a tad sleepy myself. Would ye mind having a bit of company on your stroll?"

Angus looked to the dais, where the men were drinking and laughing. In fact, the only person who seemed to notice him was Mither. "The wall-walk is hauntingly beautiful at night." He really ought to dissuade the lass.

Her eyes grew round as her lips formed a delicate O. "Hauntingly? Such a sight, I cannot miss."

But then again, it would be nice to take a wee stroll with Anya, especially now that she seemed more at ease with her state of affairs. "The wind bites up there, especially this time of year."

"I believe your mother was so kind as to send up a cloak."

"Was she?" He led her toward the wall while dancers prepared for the next set. "It would be—ah—advantageous to avoid gossip. Would ye mind terribly if I joined ye above stairs?"

"The last thing I would want to do is cause undue rumors. How about if we avoid the gossipmongers all together and I meet you on the wall-walk?"

"Do you ken where it is?"

She gave him a saucy smirk and pointed upward. "Where they all are, at the top of the stairs, I surmise."

He chuckled. "Aye. I'll make your apologies to the king and explain that I've had enough merriment as well, then I shall show you the beauty of Dunyvaig after dark."

9

Anya opened the door to her bedchamber, noting her guard as he stepped out of the stairwell. Of course, he'd been following. He was past his prime with streaks of grey in his beard, taller than average with a girth the size of the hind end of a horse, and she had yet to see him smile. No one needed to tell her the man was to be a permanent shadow during her stay.

Grumbling under her breath, Anya dashed inside and hastened to collect the cloak she'd been given. Before heading out, she took a moment to check her reflection in the polished brass mirror. Patting the caul nets secured at her ears, she decided they looked entirely too frumpish for a stroll atop the wall-walk, and removed the netting, pins, and unraveled her plaits. Her hair was still damp, but the cloak's hood ought to keep her head warm enough.

She gave the guard a frown as she headed out. He followed, the clap of his footsteps making Anya's skin crawl. Stopping before the stairs, she whirled on him and pushed her hood away from her crown. "There is no need to tail me like a puppy dog. I'm only going for a stroll atop the curtain walls."

The man arched his hedgerow of eyebrows. "Forgive

me, miss, but my orders are to keep ye within my sights at all times."

"Humph. I suppose if ye're going to act as my gargantuan shadow, I ought to know your name."

He slid his foot forward and gave a right royal bow. "I'm Rory, miss. At yer service."

She studied him for a moment. Perhaps there was a personality under all that grizzled hair. "Very well, Rory. I hope ye do not die from utter boredom following me about this dreary keep. I can think of dozens of things more interesting for a soldier than watching over the likes of me."

Not even a hint of a smile touched his lips. "Yes, miss."

Rolling her eyes, Anya turned on her heel and proceeded to climb past not two, but three landings before she reached the top. A gust of frigid air immediately blew her hood off. "Oof!" she exclaimed, it was every bit as chilly as Angus had indicated.

"There ye are." His Lordship stepped forward and offered his hand.

Islay's palm was surprisingly warm, though his touch made a shiver skitter up Anya's arm. "'Tis me and my new appendage, Rory, I'm afraid."

Chuckling, Fairhair eyed the guard. "I'll watch over Miss Anya whilst we're taking a wee stroll."

Rory bowed his head. "Very well, m'lord."

Angus placed her hand in the crook of his arm. "I will see to it you receive a pair of fur-lined gloves on the morrow."

"Thank you." Together they started traversing the narrow path around the top of the donjon. "Are there no guards up here?"

"Are ye curious, or are ye plotting?"

"Plotting?" She feigned innocence. "Whatever do ye mean?"

"Do not peg me as a fool, lass. On Nave ye flagged

an English ship against my orders. I'll wager escaping this fortress has crossed your mind more than once since arriving."

"With an oaf the size of Rory following me about, I doubt I'll be going anywhere I am not allowed. I'm curious is all. Ye have so many soldiers. Why none up here?"

"If ye must know, I dismissed the guards for a wee bit of respite. I'm certain it goes without saying, guards are posted atop the barbican walls surrounding the castle as well."

"I would have thought no less." They stopped at the southwesterly corner with an endless view out over the fortress curtain to the inky sea. A relatively calm night lit by a full moon, the tips of the waves glistened with luminous blue.

Islay leaned forward, resting his elbows on a merlon. "Dunyvaig is impenetrable, fortified with the latest defenses and situated atop rock through which no one can tunnel. The English ken better than to lay siege to her. Besides, there's nowhere level enough within her surrounds to stage a catapult."

"Have they ever tried?"

"Not since her walls were reinforced by my great-grandfather."

"If the castle is so secure, then why must a guard be posted outside my bedchamber?"

"This fortress was built to keep enemies out, not to imprison clan and kin. As ye recall, I did no' see fit to lock ye in the tower, or toss ye into the pit for that matter. And as ye explained, ye were quite adept at slipping out of Carrickfergus unawares. Since the king has entrusted me with your care, I am not inclined to sit idle whilst ye brew up ideas for an escape."

Anya pursed her lips. She never should have told him about slipping away to her private outcropping.

His Lordship drummed his fingers on top of the merlon. "I see I've made ye unhappy."

Sighing, she reverted her attention to the sea. Of course she was unhappy. She was a political prisoner for heaven's sake. "Can a person see Ireland from here?"

"Nay. Though it is closer than one might expect—a half-day's sailing at most. And the first bit of land ye'll spy along the voyage is Rathlin Island."

"Oh my. I can see Rathlin from atop Dunseverick, where I was born—where my young brother reigns as lord now."

"I ken of your kin's keep. 'Tis no' so far away, lass. Do ye miss home?"

"Aye, though as a female, I've been destined to leave my family's seat since birth. I only didn't think I would be forced to leave at the age of thirteen."

"War has a way of changing one's plans. It happened to me as well, though I had already passed my majority. I lost my elder brother in the same battle where you lost your father." Though the light was dim, there was enough glow from the moon to see Islay's Adam's apple bob. "'Twas an ugly skirmish, fought just across the sound at Southend, near the Mull of Kintyre, only a mile or so from Dunaverty, the castle where I was born. I'll tell ye true, there were heavy losses on both sides that day."

The awfulness of it made her throat thicken and she pulled her cloak more tightly about her body. "They brought my da's corpse home wrapped in death linen."

"My brother's as well. I carried his body," Angus said with more feeling in his voice than she would have expected.

Anya sighed. "We both suffered."

"You more than me, I'd reckon."

"Why do ye say that?"

"Though I would have preferred to continue living as the second son, without the responsibility of the lordship upon my shoulders, I did no' have to leave my lands. I wasn't appointed with a guardian earl to watch over me or to arrange my marriage to someone I hardly knew."

Anya shivered and moved nearer the Highlander. How perceptive he was. Who would have believed Fairhair, the man reputed to possess the heart of a devil, was actually compassionate? "Come, my lord. Ye cannot possibly know how well acquainted I am with Lord O'-Doherty."

He chuckled. "Believe me, lass, I'm no seer, but I ken in my bones, ye've met the man but once if that."

"Do ye know him?"

"We've crossed paths. Long ago, when Balliol sat on the throne and we were summoned to a gathering to pay fealty to Edward."

"Fealty ye did not give."

His shoulder ticked up. "Scotland is a sovereign nation. Balliol was our king. The MacDonald pledged fealty to *him*."

"The man was appointed by Longshanks, mind ye."

"A great folly that." Islay brushed her cheek with a coarse knuckle. "But politics is not why I invited ye up here, lass."

Anya's heart seemed to stop, then pounded like she'd dashed up past four landings in a stairwell. Every time they chatted, she discovered something new about His Lordship. And discoveries always countered everything she had been led to believe about the man. Was it wrong to admire one's captor? To admire someone who ought to be an enemy?

Heaven help me, I am ever so confused.

The Highlander pointed southward. "On a clear night such as this, ye can sometimes see the spray from the backs of whales. And the waves glisten as if selkies are dancing just beneath the water." He panned his finger to the southwest. "Across the wee bay, ye can see the outline of the village of Lagavulin, where MacDonald crofters raise meat for our table and grow oats, barley, and hops." He shifted a bit, crouching down and inclining his lips toward her ear. "And that big stone building in the dark shadows is the brewhouse. Beside it is the fishing hall. I do no' recommend paying a visit on account of its foul smell. Yonder we boast a tannery, which doesn't smell much better, and the MacDonald smithy is the best in Scotland, if ye ask me."

"Ye sound proud."

"I suppose I am. Our forefathers settled this land, dating back to the reign of Somerled, the warrior who carved out the Kingdom of the Isles."

"I know of his legend. He was born in Ireland in the House of Appin, his mother a Norse noblewoman."

"Aye."

"Imagine that. Our ancestry is not so different, yours and mine." Anya strolled to the next corner while Islay followed, the soft tapping of his footsteps making her ever so self-aware. Even gooseflesh peppered her nape as if she could feel his breath there. "What makes this place *hauntingly* beautiful at night?"

"Aside from ye?" He gave her an audacious wink. "'Tis the eerie quiet amplified by the rush of the sea, has always made me feel as if..."

"What?"

He batted his hand through the air with a dismissive wave. "Ye'll think me daft."

She faced him, craning her neck to peer into his eyes, now dark as the night sky. "Nay. Besides, ye've already started. I must know."

He again leaned on a merlon and looked out into the darkness. "It is as if the spirits of my ancestors lurk here. If I stand very still, they call to me."

A forceful shiver coursed through Anya's body akin to something touching her soul.

"Ye've a chill," he said. "We ought to retire."

"I'm not cold," she whispered, resting her hip on the crenel notch beside him. "I just never thought ye..."

He straightened, cupping her cheek, his fingers rough like a man who worked with his hands or practiced a great deal wielding a sword. "Och, lass, earlier ye insisted I bear my soul. Ye cannot just stop mid-thought."

She huffed. Why not say it? "It is just everything I have been led to believe about, about *Fairhair* is nothing like the man ye are. Ye're not black-hearted, nor are ye a brutish fiend."

One corner of his mouth turned up in a devilishly wicked grin. "Ye have not seen me in battle, lass."

Had he stepped nearer? Anya couldn't be sure, but he seemed closer. "Nay," she replied, a tad breathless. "But aren't most men savage when fighting for life or death?"

"They are." Angus dipped his chin, his breath skimming her forehead. "There is one thing I must set to rights, lass."

She dared meet his dark stare while butterflies set to flight inside her. "To rights, did ye say?" she asked, trying to sound completely unaffected.

He inched even closer, cupping her cheek with a gentle hand. "Ye may be a wee bit petite in stature, but I never again want to hear ye refer to yourself as squat."

"Oh."

There was no doubt in Anya's mind as to his intention. Licking her lips, she tilted up her face, while a maelstrom of desire swirled inside her breast. Oh, how she wanted a kiss—only one while they were alone and unguarded. Aye, she desperately wanted to know what kissing a man was like.

The moment their lips met, her knees turned boneless. His mouth was warm and soothing while his fingers traced along the sensitive skin just below her jaw. Not wanting it to end, she moved a hand to his waist.

With her touch, he sighed, his tongue sweeping across her lips.

Startled, Anya began to withdraw, but as if he'd anticipated her reaction, his fingers slipped to the back of her head while he increased the pressure, his tongue demanding that she part her mouth for him.

Oh, God in heaven, warm cream flowed through her like nectar as the Lord of Islay showed her how to kiss—how to truly kiss. Unable to resist, she wrapped her arms around him and held on for dear life while together their mouths joined in a dance nothing like the merry reels below stairs.

He pulled her into his embrace as his lips moved across to her cheeks, her jaw, and down her neck. Never in her life had Anya felt the powerful pull of seduction in a man's arms. Never had she dreamed kissing would consume her so extraordinarily.

As Islay drew his lips away, a sudden chill coursed across her skin. She gasped, not able to meet his gaze. She'd just kissed the devil and it felt inexplicably wonderful. Yet she must not possibly have feelings for this man.

"Forgive me," he whispered, lifting her chin with the crook of his finger.

She scooted away, her eyes wide, her head spinning. "Y-y-ye must *never* do that again!"

Not waiting for a reply, Anya spun and dashed for the stairs.

"Wait!" he called after her.

But she was not about to stop. As fast as she could, she hastened down past three landings until she reached her floor. Fleeing into the passageway, she spotted Rory.

He opened the door. "Good evening, miss."

Anya didn't dare look at him either, lest he know exactly what she had been up to. "Good evening."

She moved inside and stood in the center of her

chamber until the door closed, then she slid the bolt across, just to ensure no one tried to enter. God save her, where had she landed, and how was she to resist the Lord of Islay? Perhaps he was indeed the devil he was reputed to be.

Anya paced and paced, rubbing away his kiss, yet her lips still tingled. She plopped on the bed and stared at the ceiling. No matter how tired she might be, her mind spun with too many thoughts for rest to come.

She absolutely must never think about kissing Fairhair again.

No. No. No!

In the corridor, the guard stirred, making a bit of a racket. Was he planning to sleep out there?

Sitting up, Anya took note of her pillows—two ornate and two covered by linen cases. Atop her bed was a feather-down coverlet, which would be ample to keep her warm. She didn't need the blanket folded across the base.

Huffing, she took a pillow and the blanket, unlocked the bolt, and threw open the door.

With a rattle of weapons and an old man's grunt, Rory lumbered to his feet. "Forgive me, miss. I assumed ye had turned in for the night."

"I have." She glanced up and down the corridor. "Will ye be sleeping out here?"

"Aye, 'tis expected."

She thrust the bedding into his arms. "Well, then, I'll nay have ye catching your death with no comfort whatsoever."

Rory smiled for the first time since they'd met. Even with one tooth missing in front, his smile made him appear less overbearing. "My thanks, miss. Ye are very kind."

She harrumphed. "I'd offer one of the earl's wolfhounds as much courtesy." She ducked back inside, took one of the wooden chairs from the table and returned to the doorway. "If ye ask me, there's no need for ye to stand at attention like one of the king's guards whilst I'm within. Ye may as well rest your withered old legs."

He took the chair and set it beside the door. "Withered? Old?"

Chuckling, she gripped the latch. "I was wondering when I'd ferret a rise out of ye. Good night, Wolfie."

The guard's jaw dropped, looking doubly stumped. "Wolfie?"

"I meant Rory," she said, closing the door and heading directly for her bed.

❧ 10 ❧

After being summoned to the high table, it appeared Angus had been the last to be notified of today's court session, a fact that chapped him to no end. This was his castle and everyone on the dais was *his* guest, not the bloody other way around. "Ye asked to see me, Your Grace?"

Surrounded by knights, Robert gestured to a chair across the board. "Good morn, Islay, we were just discussing Turnberry."

"Good news, I pray." Angus slid into the seat while his heart sank to his toes. Obviously, the king still held him responsible for the disaster at Loch Ryan. Possibly even for his failure to gain support from Ulster, though the blame sat squarely on Robert's shoulders.

"I've received word from Sir James Douglas that my lands surrounding the keep are secure and impenetrable. Lord Percy has tucked tail and taken his army back to Northumberland."

"That is good news, indeed. The Black Douglas is gaining quite a reputation."

"He saved my life at the coronation and has proved himself many times since."

Angus shifted uncomfortably. One day he hoped to impress the king half as much.

"I'm certain ye will be happy to hear I will be leaving Dunyvaig on the morrow. An army of men will establish a perimeter in Turnberry to ensure she is not recaptured, and I will be heading north with Campbell and Boyd to recruit more men."

Forcing himself not to smile, Angus tightened his fists beneath the table. Not only were his shoulders healing, after three months of hosting the king, he would be lord and master of his keep once again. "So soon? Shall I prepare my army to follow?"

"Nay. Ye are my muscle as well as my eyes in the isles, and I need ye here. Though hold fast, lord. With the confrontations I have planned, I will be calling upon ye soon."

"I would think no less. Clan MacDonald will be at the ready whenever the time is nigh."

Robert narrowed his gaze while giving a thin-lipped nod. No matter how much the king might want to berate and punish Angus for Loch Ryan, he was as shrewd a man as had ever lived. The Bruce needed allies far more than enemies and, though Clan MacDonald may have failed in his eyes, they'd also proved their worth in many ways. Angus had given the king safe harbor throughout the winter, he'd provided ships for both the attack on Turnberry and Loch Ryan and, had the English army been laying not in ambush, expecting the battle led by Robert's brothers, the king very well might have failed to the north where it was more imperative that he succeed.

The Bruce stood. "We shall feast to our good fortune this eve, then depart come dawn."

All men stood and bowed, though Angus sprang up faster, with far more enthusiasm. "I'll see to it we have a feast as grand as last evening's to celebrate your success."

He waited as Robert took his leave, the knights following in a procession of obedient minions. Robbie

Boyd held back and clapped Angus' shoulder. "Ye've been a fine host, m'lord. I ken it has not been easy to play the underling whilst His Grace assumed your place at the high table."

Angus could have danced a jig, but only offered a smile. "It has been a lesson in humility, for certain. Add to it the failure at Loch Ryan and I'm surprised my cods haven't shriveled into prunes. Robert blames me." Angus shook his head. "If only I'd insisted upon leading the charge."

"Och, I was there at the planning, ye ken. Ye did hold forth. As I recall, ye even went so far as to tell Robert's brothers they were daft for insisting the MacDonald take up the rear."

"I appreciate your acute memory, sir. If only the king were thus gifted."

"He kens what happened. He's hurting is all. The man has now lost everyone dear to his heart. Thank God the bastards have not executed Elizabeth and Marjorie, else I fear Robert would have gone mad by now."

"Then we'd best ensure no one ever repeats your words, lest the English catch wind of it."

"My lips are sealed." Boyd tapped a finger to his mouth, then glanced toward the entry. "I've been trapped indoors for too long and am off to ride for a bit—feel the wind in my face. Would ye like to accompany me?"

"Most days I would; however, I lost my father's sword in the shipwreck and must pay the smithy a visit forthwith. I say, the Lord of Islay without a sword is no lord at all."

"Another time then?"

"Aye." Angus gripped the man's arm in a brotherly gesture before they headed down the dais steps. "Ye are a worthy knight, the king is lucky to have ye. I only wish he regarded me in such a light."

Boyd clapped him on the shoulder. "I'm nay so certain of that. He has entrusted ye with the care of Anya O'Cahan."

Angus chuckled. "And now I am to play the warden of an Irish lordling's daughter, who stowed away on my *birlinn*."

"She's a bonny lass, though. I wouldn't complain if she were adorning my keep—if I possessed a keep."

Angus knew all too well Boyd had lost home and hearth during the wars. "Och, she's a spitfire if ye ask me."

"Who is a spitfire?" asked Anya as she stepped out from the stairwell, with a bit of ice in her gaze. She wore her cloak and her guard followed in her wake. Bless Rory for accepting his post and carrying out his duty without a word of complaint.

But when Angus looked at the lassie's inquisitive face, his tongue tied. Who else at Dunyvaig would be referred to as a spitfire?

While Robbie strode away with a deep belly laugh, Angus closed his eyes, and groaned. After she'd run from him last eve, he'd been kicking himself. Why the devil had he asked her to meet him on the wall-walk in the first place? A moonlight stroll was not an appropriate activity to encourage diffidence. His mother had been right. Anya was his ward now, and he must never take advantage of the lass, no matter how tempting she might be.

Recovering swiftly, he gave her a pointed frown. "Ye, that's who."

Her angry expression shifted into a cringe. "Oh." Without another word, she headed for the door, with Rory following near ten paces behind.

Good God, was this what it was like to be entrusted with the care of a ward—always mending fences? "Anya." Angus hastened beside her. "Where are ye off to?"

A sentry opened the heavy oaken door and she

marched through. "Your mother has directed me to pay a visit to the tailor. Not to worry. Rory, the wolfhound, is accompanying me to the village."

Angus dismissed the guard with a flick of his hand. "I'll escort ye. I was heading into Lagavulin myself."

She sped her pace. "There's no need for ye to be kind to me. Wolfie is a perfectly capable dog...I mean guard. And, and companion."

As they reached the courtyard, Angus grasped her wrist and pulled her to a halt. "I owe ye an apology. Please allow me to explain."

She stared up, those emerald eyes as sympathetic as an eel's.

He raked his fingers through his hair. "I never should have tried to kiss ye. I should not have taken the liberty."

"Then why did ye? To toy with me?"

"Nay. I would never do that." *At least not intentionally*.

Angus looked to the barbican walls, wishing he were up there rather than groveling down below. But, somehow, he'd hurt her even though she'd been the one to rush away. Moreover, Anya had felt something. The woman had turned molten in his arms. Hell, she'd been a wee bit timid at first, but as soon as she parted her lips, she gave herself unlike any lass he'd ever kissed before.

"Ye are my ward," he explained. "I am responsible to protect ye."

"With all due respect, my lord, I already have an overbearing guardian. I do not need another."

As she continued toward the guard's tower, Angus followed. "The point is, ye are in my care and I was wrong to have taken advantage."

She sped her pace, hastening through the archway. "Is that what ye call a wee kiss? Well, at least I can say, 'tis nice to have my first experience over with. Thank ye ever so much for opening my eyes, my lord. Though I now have no idea why a woman ever allows a man to kiss her. The experience is rather vulgar."

Och. Angus clutched a fist over his gut. Who knew the woman was adept at throwing daggers with her tongue? She'd given his heart at least two scathing cuts.

Growling beneath his breath, he waited until they traversed beneath a giant sycamore, well away from any prying ears, then stepped in front of the woman and crossed his arms. "Exactly what did ye like about our kiss?"

"Ah..." Anya's eyes grew wide while she hesitated, winding the cord of her cloak around her finger. "It-it...*ah*...I suppose it was not exactly the doing I found unpleasant."

His foot tapped. "The doing?"

"Aye, the kiss itself was agreeable."

A pinch formed between his brows as he took a step nearer, making her crane her neck. "Merely agreeable?"

"Well...*um*...perhaps a wee bit more than agreeable. But that's where the pleasantries ended." She dropped the cord and stabbed him in the chest with her pointer finger. Good God, she was far too tempting when stirred to anger—red cheeks, sparks in her eyes, standing with her shoulders thrown back and her chin held proud. "Kissing me and then apologizing, no matter how gently whispered, ruined *everything*!"

Angus allowed her to move around him and start off again, lest he grasp her shoulders and give another demonstration. Which he must not do, no matter how tempting her full lips, or the way the breeze picked up wisps of chestnut hair and blew them across her face. Most importantly, no matter how much he desired to kiss her again.

He trailed after her with a grin gradually stretching the corners of his mouth. She enjoyed the doing of it. She'd just told him as much, but he'd also been right to apologize. Besides, she was as good as promised to another. Though Angus would hang by his toenails before he'd let her join in holy matrimony with O'Doherty. Even though he'd only met the man in passing, His Lordship was no match for the likes of Anya. O'Doherty seemed a bit too genteel, definitely not someone able to handle a high-spirited woman. His Lordship struck Angus as a man who enjoyed the finer things of life, who needed a wife who truly liked to embroider and discuss menus.

The clang from the smithy shack grew louder as Angus moved beside Anya and pointed to a row of thatch-roofed stone shops. "The tailor is just yonder on the left."

"Very well." The lass slowed, glancing over her shoulder and batting those feathery eyelashes. "Why do I not pay him a visit whilst you attend the smithy?"

"Because Rory isn't here."

"You are insufferable."

"Thank you."

"Argh!" she exclaimed, clearly irritated. Angus was well aware she had reason to be angry, he truly was. But the fact that she had admitted to enjoying their kiss, trumped everything.

Perhaps in time, Anya might come to like his little corner of Scotland. He chewed the inside of his cheek. What could he do to help change her mind about the MacDonalds, about Scotland and its right to be a sovereign nation? About *him*?

Pondering his last question, Angus shook his head and marched to the tailor's door, opened it, and gestured inside. "After you, miss."

"Hmph." Before stepping inside, she glanced at him for the briefest moment. Had he spotted a bit of mischief in those emerald eyes? What was this Irish imp plotting now? And did he want to know?

He followed her in.

"M'lord," said Master Tailor, coming from the back

room. "What a pleasure it is to see ye out and about this fine day."

"'Tis good to see the sunshine for a change," Angus replied, before he nodded to the lass. "This is Anya from Ireland and she is in need of..."

"A new shift and kirtle, if you please."

"Aye," Angus said. "I would think three shifts would suffice, mayhap three kirtles with arisaids to match, three or four pairs of stockings..."

Master Tailor dipped his quill and started jotting notes. "Very well, three of everything?"

"I would not want ye to spend any more coin than necessary, my lord."

Angus ignored her. "Gloves—fur-lined, of course. And a new mantle."

She gestured to the ill-fitting woolen garment draped from her shoulders. "Your mother lent me a cloak."

"Which is not warm enough." Angus pointed to the slip of velum. "A sealskin cloak to replace the one Miss Anya lost in the shipwreck."

The tailor's quill stopped as he looked up. "Was she on the *birlinn* that was caught in that horrible storm?"

"Aye," Angus said, not about to mention she'd ended up aboard by accident. "And she's a guest of His Grace, Robert the Bruce." He also decided not to mention that the king was sailing for Turnberry come dawn.

Master Tailor's jaw dropped. "A royal guest."

"Oh, I'm not anywhere near—"

"She is of important consequence to the king," Angus interrupted, making it clear that Anya was not to be trifled with. Nearly everyone stopped by the tailor's shop in Lagavulin, by noontime on the morrow, most folk on the isle ought to know of her importance to the crown. If she was important to the king, she was important to the House of MacDonald.

The little man set his quill in the holder and held up

a measuring ribbon. "Hold out your arms please, madam." He hummed while he worked, measuring up, down, around, and every which way. "I have a lovely woolen plaid in green and blue that would be perfect for your coloring—'twill keep ye warm as well."

"That will be very nice. Thank you." Anya blushed as the tailor ran the measuring tape around her breasts, his eyebrows arching as he made a notation.

Angus slid his fingers across his mouth to hide his grin. The lass was not lacking in femininity anywhere, especially when it came to curvaceousness. *And yet she believes herself to be plain and frumpish.*

DAYS LATER, ANYA SAT ALONE IN THE LADY'S SOLAR, wearing one of her new kirtles. Angus had paid the tailor handsomely to ensure the work was made a priority, then he'd taken her to the cobbler for new shoes, a belt, and a purse to wear at her waist. Only then did he visit the smithy to place an order for the sword he'd lost at sea.

The solar was quite spacious, with a weaving loom at one end, a writing table in the middle, and a settee and chairs surrounding a hearth at the other end.

Since the Dowager Lady Islay had ventured below stairs to check on the evening's menu, Anya intended to write to Finovola, even though the letter would never reach her sister. Before she started, she pulled the drawing she'd made of Angus out from the leather purse secured to her belt and spread it open on the table. The likeness made her smile.

"Why are ye so confounding?" She traced her finger over his lips, their evening on the wall-walk fresh in her mind as if their encounter only happened moments ago. "Ye do know it would be far easier for both of us if ye were the dragon-hearted devil you are reputed to be."

But he wasn't. Daily it grew more and more difficult to abhor Fairhair the Terrible.

Fairhair the Charmer is more apt.

Anya dipped her quill in the ink pot and addressed the letter to her sister.

As I sit alone and lonely in Dunyvaig Castle, I close my eyes and imagine what ye are doing at this very moment. Not an hour goes by when I do not wish I could actually dispatch a letter simply to let ye know I am well.

In truth, I am surprisingly well for a person who is being held captive. The king—I cannot believe I just wrote the self-proclaimed title of the outlaw, Robert the Bruce, but the Scots do have a viable argument in that theirs is a sovereign nation. And in truth, the king (as everyone here refers to him) is a most formidable man, one suited to kingship, in my estimation.

He has entrusted my care to Angus Og MacDonald, Lord of Islay. Gasp, say you? I felt the same when I realized I had hidden in his ship. Of all the boats moored along the pier, why I had to choose Fairhair's, I'll never understand. Moreover, I nearly drowned when the ship was assailed by a mammoth wave and smashed to bits.

Anya went on to write about her rescue, ending up on Nave, and attempting to flag an English ship.

I did not want King Edward's men to send Islay to meet his end. He saved my life, after all. Is it wrong to care for a person you were brought up to abhor? I pray it is not, because I am unable to deny a fondness for the man we know as Fairhair.

And if I were tortured, I do not believe I'd be able to withhold the truth from ye, though I do not dare mention it here, even if this letter has nary a chance of reaching ye. Which is why I'm daring to tell ye...

Anya hesitated for a moment, needing to tell someone and having not a soul in whom to confide.

I kissed the very man I am supposed to hate. As I write this, I still cannot believe I suffered such a moment of weakness. I ought to be angry with myself. After all, the earl was in the midst of negotiating my marriage contract. Of course, that was before I hid in the wrong boat. But, alas, Angus Og MacDonald did kiss me. And curse my traitorous heart, I enjoyed it. Oh, aye, it mayhap was the most exhilarating experience of my miserable life.

A clanging racket came from the courtyard below, accompanied by a great deal of shouting. Anya placed her quill in the holder, crossed to the window, and pulled back the fur. As she leaned out, the wind blasted her face with an icy bite, though the chill was soon forgotten as her gaze was drawn to the men below.

One man in particular.

Surrounded by soldiers all clapping and cheering, Islay fended off deadly strikes as Raghnall advanced. Every single thrust of the man-at-arm's sword was aimed to kill, and His Lordship wore merely a shirt and plaid with no mail or armor whatsoever. Sunlight flickered through his golden hair as he ducked and defended, doing naught to strike back.

By the saints, he posed a magnificent form, moving as gracefully as a stag, yet expelling no more energy than needed to protect himself from the vicious onslaught.

Anya gasped and jolted with every single blow while her insides twisted and her face contorted in a grimace.

Nearly backed to the curtain wall, Islay bellowed, plunging into a barbarous attack. Raghnall did not let up. The two men were matched in height and girth as their swords clanged until the blades met in a battle of strength. While the shouts grew more raucous, iron screeched and arms trembled until their hilts collided. With thunderous grunts, the two men pushed apart.

Anya leaned farther out the window. Evidently, the smithy had delivered Islay's new sword because it glistened like a shiny new mirror as he held it level, aiming it at his sparring partner. Puffs of air billowed from their noses as they circled in a deadly dance.

As fast as an asp, the man-at-arms lunged in. Fairhair

hopped aside, deflecting the blow before their blades blurred in an onslaught so loud it made Anya's ears ring. Backing, Angus stumbled on the cobbles. Raghnall took advantage of the lord's slip, attacking with an upward strike, ripping the hilt from Islay's grip. With a grunting roar, His Lordship grabbed his shoulder.

The man-at-arms immediately backed away. "Are ye injured, m'lord?"

"Nay. My damned shoulder has no' completely healed as of yet." He stooped to retrieve his weapon and eyed it. "I reckon the balance is not right."

Raghnall took the sword and swung it in an X. "'Tis never easy to wield a new one. But after a few days of practice, ye will not want to return to the old."

"Time will tell," said Islay, glancing up to the window where Anya was standing. A grin stretched his lips before he slipped a foot forward and bowed to her like a gallant knight.

"Raghnall is the only man who poses a challenge to my son."

"Eep!" Anya leapt away from the window, nearly pulling the fur from its nails. She clutched her hands over her thundering heart. "My lady! Ye gave me a fright."

Fairhair's mother smiled before her gaze trailed to the table. "Forgive me. I thought ye heard me come in."

Anya could have melted where she stood. Right there for all to see was her drawing as well as the letter. "I did not." She moved toward the writing table. "There was quite a racket coming from the courtyard."

"My son trains with his men rigorously." The Dowager Lady Islay slid onto the settee near the hearth. "The view of the courtyard from here is remarkable. I remember watching Angus' father work with the lads when they were young. They provided such good entertainment, I oft neglected my duties."

Sliding the drawing from the table, Anya folded it and slipped it into her purse.

"Come sit with me and warm your toes. 'Tis quite pleasant in front of the fire."

Anya collected her letter and jammed it into her purse as well. Surely, Her Ladyship hadn't the time to read it—especially the last bit about kissing her son.

The lady took her embroidery and tugged on the needle. "Tell me, have ye found a great many differences between my home and Ireland?"

"Things are much the same, I suppose. Though I do miss my sister a great deal."

"Hmm, I imagine ye would miss the kin with whom you are close most of all. But what about the fare, is the food similar?"

"Very much so, though I suppose as the crow flies, we're not really all that far apart."

"So true."

"Even black pudding is the same as at home."

"I find that remarkable." Her Ladyship worked her needle in a feather stich for a time before she paused. "As I recall, my dear, your guardian had commenced negotiations for your hand."

Anya glanced to her lap. "Aye."

"I imagine you were most excited about the prospect of marrying a lord."

"I care not to think on it, what with Robert the Bruce imprisoning me for Lord knows how long," she replied, hoping she sounded distraught.

Her Ladyship leaned forward and patted Anya's hand. "Which is exactly why I volunteered to keep ye here. Things would have been ever so unpleasant at the monastery, especially in winter. Those monks are so frugal, ye'd never be able to warm your wee bones."

"I do appreciate your kindness, my lady."

The woman smiled as she pulled her needle through

the linen. "In time, I pray ye will find we are a friendly clan, much like yours I'd assume."

"But how can ye say that when our clans feud so terribly?"

"The lot of women is a strange thing, is it not?" Her Ladyship reached for her shears and snipped her thread. "We support our men who make the decisions as to where borders are to be drawn and stone fortresses are to be erected. But it is the females who oft find ways to end the disagreements between men."

"The women? But how? How, when the fathers and sons are the ones swinging their swords, making decisions, and using us as pawns?"

"Think, my dear. How many men have changed their minds because of love?"

"Pshaw. Love." Anya batted her hand through the air. "Highborn women are slaves to their sex, I've heard that said enough by both my father and the Earl of Ulster. Our marriages are arranged and we've naught but to accept our lot and make the best of it. Did your da not arrange your marriage?"

"He did, and I admit to being fearful at first. However, I was fortunate to have married a man with whom I found love."

Anya sighed. If only she might have found love, though now she had no chance of doing so.

❧ II ❧

Anya's ever-present wolfhound, Rory, stood guard along the wall while the keep's children sat at her feet as she read from a book of folk tales. The lot of them were sons and daughters of servants or guards at Dunyvaig and were as eager to learn as the children she read to at Carrickfergus. "*...The auld wife took her basket and strode into the house, shutting the door behind her. The silly mutton stood for a time, mulling over whether or not to follow. But in the end, he whistled for his dog and left her be, for if she didn't then, she never would offer a whit of Highland hospitality.*"

"Och, is that the end?" asked Fenn, the most boisterous of the group. "That auld wife is a cranky hen if ye ask me."

"She's a cranky squawker," agreed a wee lass.

"I feel sorry for the silly mutton."

"But he was awfully silly."

"Can ye read us another?" asked Fenn.

"Pleeeeeease?" they all chorused in unison.

"What's this?" Angus strode into the hall and planted his fists on his hips, his expression one of feigned exasperation. "Has not Miss Anya read enough this day?"

Fenn stood and bowed. "Nay, we never hear enough stories, m'lord."

Anya closed the book. "Well, I'll be here for some time, perhaps I can read to ye on Tuesdays and Thursdays, but we ought to make the time later in the day, after your chores are finished."

"That sounds fair to me," Angus agreed. "Now off with the lot of ye, there is work still to be done this morn and I need a word with your storyteller."

Anya stood, wiping her hands on her skirts. "Is all well, my lord?" After all, he hadn't sought her out for a conversation in days. Yes, His Lordship required her to join the party at the high table during the evening meals, but since the king had taken his leave, she hadn't been seated beside Islay. Those two places were always reserved for his mother and Raghnall, and Anya was assigned the end place setting beside Friar Jo, which she felt was for the best, given the way she felt whenever the Highlander was beside her.

Akin to this very moment.

Anya's palms perspired, her skin alive with tingles. Goodness, even her stomach swirled as if the man possessed some sort of hypnotic sorcery in his gaze. If only he weren't such a handsome rogue. Curse her weaknesses.

"I've just come from the stables and whilst I was there, I recalled ye mentioned a fondness for riding."

"Oh, aye. I'd ride every morn if I could."

"Well, Cook's packing our nooning in a satchel and sending it out to the stables with young Fenn, so 'tis a good thing ye finished your story, else, the lad would have had his ears boxed."

"Oh my. And thank heavens I changed the reading time to later in the day after their chores. I wouldn't want to be responsible for any ear-boxing. Besides, I need all the allies I can find, no matter their age."

Angus adjusted his belt. "Has anyone been unkind to ye?"

"No, my lord. I am slow to make friends is all."

"I'm not so certain about that. Mither reports ye are quite amenable. Ye ken her word is gospel—even the friar can attest to that. Not to mention ye've impressed the young ones, even if ye are an O'Cahan." He offered his elbow. "Shall we? One of the servants has already taken our cloaks to the stables."

Anya nearly skipped outside. Not only was it winter, the weather had been foul and, with Rory following her about, she hadn't a chance to slip away from the keep and enjoy some much-needed time to herself. It didn't help matters when, during their time shipwrecked on Nave, she had run at the mouth and told Angus about her own special place at Carrickfergus. The only other person she'd ever told about slipping out of the castle was Finovola, though she imagined the Earl of Ulster had completely excavated the little alcove once she went missing.

"Here we are," he said, leading her toward a filly, saddled and tied to the fence beside a bay stallion.

"Oh, my." Anya ran her hand along the mare's smooth neck. She untied the horse and walked her in a circle to examine her gait. "Ye are a beauty, are ye not? And sorrel, to boot. My favorite color."

"I'm glad ye approve." He leaned forward, lacing his fingers together and making a sling. "May I give ye a leg up?"

She took hold of the reins and placed her knee in Islay's hands. Though she landed in the saddle rather gently, the mare shook her head and sidestepped. "This filly has a bit of mettle."

"That she does—I recall ye said a spirited horse."

"I did." Though the mare clearly wanted to run, Anya held her head low while Angus mounted and took up his reins. "Are ye certain 'tis a good idea to ride a stallion alongside a mare?"

"Aye, she's been covered, and I expect she'll have a wee foal come autumn."

"Then I'd best be careful."

The corner of His Lordship's mouth ticked up while a bit of mischief flickered in his eyes. "If she'll allow it once we reach the moor."

Anya sat taller, ready for a bout of good sport. "How far is it?"

"A good hour's ride or so. 'Tis called the Oa."

"Hmm. What an unusual name. Where is it from?"

"The place was named far before my time. The elders say 'tis from the time of the druids," Islay explained as together they rode beneath the gateway and out toward the open.

"It must be magical."

"Aye, in beauty, I say."

"Then let us not delay."

Tapping her heels, Anya cued the mare for a canter. With a rolling laugh, Angus soon took the lead, riding through Lagavulin, and past the brewhouse on the far end of the village. Once they were well away from the townsfolk and a croft dotted the hills here and there, he slowed to a walk and ran his fingers through his horse's mane. "I love it out here."

"'Tis peaceful."

"Aye, and there are no supplications to hear, no quarrels needing my intervention."

Anya hadn't seen him hear supplications, but by his tenor, he'd done so recently. "Do ye not hear the crofters' pleas in the hall?"

"Nay, 'tis too disruptive. I hear them in my solar, which allows for privacy if need be."

Anya smiled. Any overbearing brute of a lord would hear supplications in his hall for all to hear. But this man thought enough of his clansmen and women to meet with them behind closed doors. How very enterprising of him. And how very much not like the Fairhair monster of lore.

They rode side by side for a time, until fences and crofts were nowhere to be seen, and rugged moorland stretched before them. "Look there," Angus pointed. "'Tis a herd of red deer."

In the distance, the animals looked up from their grazing, posing as if trying to decide whether or not to take flight.

Anya ran her fingers through the mare's mane. "Beautiful."

Islay gestured with a sweep of his arm. "This entire peninsula is covered with birds year-round. Burns cut paths from freshwater lochs and peatland bogs further inland. And on the coast, they empty into waterfalls tumbling from the cliffs of Dùn Athad."

"It sounds like Eden." Anya picked up her reins. "We mustn't delay."

"A wee race is it ye're wanting, lass?"

"A stallion against a mare? Pshaw!"

"Only from here to the outcropping yonder. And I'll allow ye five lengths."

Anya leaned forward and kicked her heels, demanding a gallop. "I'll see you there."

As the wind picked up her veil, she laughed aloud, clapping a hand to her head to keep it from sailing away. Behind, the thunder of the stallion's hooves came closer and closer. "Nay!" she shouted, slapping her reins, and leaning out further over the mare's neck. "Haste, ye!"

"I'm gaining on ye, lassie!" Angus roared above the wind.

By the time they reached the outcropping, they were both laughing so hard, the horses had decided the race wasn't to be taken seriously, falling into step alongside each other as if they were hitched to a cart.

Reining the horse to a halt, Anya threw her head back and howled. "Oh, that felt good."

"Of all my lands, this is one of my favorite places." His gaze shifted her way. "It is not often I allow anyone to come with me when I traverse the Oa."

A number of questions arrested at the tip of her tongue. How many young ladies had he brought riding out here? Anya didn't dare ask, lest he thought her jealous, or prying, or interested in him as a suitor.

Which she definitely was not. Nay, she didn't give a whit about any of her silly questions.

His Lordship tapped his heels. "Come, I have something to show ye."

As they rode through the grassy moorland, terns and gannets took to flight. Angus stopped and gazed out over what seemed to be the end of the earth and the expansive sea beyond. "This is Dùn Athad. From here I oft see dolphins and seals in the surf. In summer, her cliffs are alive with nesting puffins and gulls. And throughout winter, barnacle geese make their home down below on the beach and near the burns and lochs of Islay."

"Are they the geese served for last eve's meal?"

"Aye, thousands of them winter on my island. Ducks as well."

Anya smiled to herself, fully aware this was not the Lord of Islay's only island. Why such a powerful man would choose to spend the day with a prisoner of the crown, she had no idea. Was Elizabeth receiving the same treatment, wherever in England she had been ensconced? Anya rather doubted the Queen of Scotland had received much hospitality at all. After all, King Edward had imprisoned Isabella MacDuff in a cage suspended from the barbican of Berwick Castle to punish the woman for the mere act of placing the crown on Robert the Bruce's head and declaring him King of Scots.

Perhaps, Anya had been truly blessed. She was the first to admit she'd had her reservations about marrying Lord O'Doherty. If she didn't want children so badly, she wouldn't give a fig about marrying anyone. As a spinster, she could return to Dunseverick and live with her brother. Mayhap when the wars came to an end, she would do exactly that.

She returned her attention to the vast expanse of water, the sky above speckled with birds diving for fish. Below, a beach came into view with sea-foam rolling onto the shore. "Can we ride down there?"

"Aye, but the path is not for the faint of heart."

She shifted in the saddle, arching her brows. "Did I ever say I was one to shirk danger?"

The grin spreading across his lips was reminiscent of a cat stalking a mouse. "Follow me."

About halfway down a precariously narrow ridge, Anya jolted as stones crumbled beneath the mare's hooves. She almost squealed, but doing so would not do. She'd accepted His Lordship's challenge and, no matter how slim the path or how steep the cliff, she mustn't complain.

Her perspiring hands slipped inside her fur-lined gloves as she dared a downward glimpse of the rocks below, where, with one misplaced hoof, Anya and the horse would plummet to their deaths.

Have mercy on my soul.

She closed her eyes and didn't open them again until the mare stopped.

"Ye made it, lass, and lived to tell about your courage," Angus said, his voice filled with humor as he dismounted. "I did warn ye."

Anya shook away her dread. "If one doesn't leap into the unknown, one can never claim to have conquered it."

In two strides, he was standing beside her horse's withers. His palm smoothed over Anya's thigh as his gaze shifted to her face. "Allow me to help ye to dismount, then I'll hobble the horses."

"What about your shoulders? Are they both not still causing ye pain?"

His hand slowly swirled as he rolled the injured appendages. "They're coming good—ye ken ye are no' overly vicious with a wee battle axe. Please, allow me to help ye down."

Though a frisson of energy shot from her leg and up through her body, Anya coolly swallowed and placed her hands on his shoulders. "Thank you."

In the blink of an eye, those powerful fingers wrapped around her waist, easily lifting her out of the saddle. Anya's breath caught. "Ye have a firm grip, my lord."

"Am I hurting ye?" He drew her against his body, his grip easing.

"Nay," she said, breathless as she slowly slid down his body until he held her gaze level with his.

Anya stretched her toes downward as he stared into her eyes. Was she floating or had he trapped her in his snare? God in heaven, she'd never been this close to him in daylight. His eyes weren't only as blue as the crystal she'd found when she was a child, but they sparkled as well.

She parted her lips as her tongue grew dry. Though the wind blew a gale, warmth filled her. As she dangled, her gaze slipped to his mouth. He scraped his teeth over a full bottom lip as he tilted his head to the side.

For a moment, she thought he might kiss her. "Och," he growled, while he slowly lowered her to the ground.

Disappointed to have the moment slip by so quickly, yet not surprised, she dropped her gaze to her hands. "Perhaps in the future, I ought to dismount on my own."

He didn't respond as he set to hobbling the horses. "A storm's brewing."

"This time of year, it seems a storm is always brewing." As soon as the words left her lips, a snowflake landed on her nose and in no time, the sky was full of them. "Had we best head back?"

Angus straightened and looked west, the wind blowing his hair away from his face and billowing his mantle. "I've packed along a bit of peat. There's a wee cave up the shore where we can take our nooning, unless ye'd rather haste back."

Her stomach growled. "As long as we don't end up stranded here for two days."

He chuckled, removing the saddlebags. "The snow doesn't tend to stick on the shore, though it is a wee bit unpleasant for riding."

Anya looked to the ridge they'd traversed on the way down, now covered with a sheen of white. "And slippery."

"If that's the case, then we'll take the long route back up."

"How much longer?"

"No' too bad." He slung the bags over his shoulder and started toward a small cave not much larger than her alcove. "Mayhap a mile farther."

Once under cover, Anya busied herself clearing stones and making two comfortable places to sit while Angus struggled to light a fire given the wind. Eventually, the flax tow took a spark and soon two bricks of peat were smoldering just beyond their feet.

"What did Cook send along to eat?" she asked.

Angus unfastened the buckles on the satchel and opened it between them. "A flagon of wine, a brick of cheese, a few slices of mutton, bread, and two apples."

"'Tis a feast."

He pulled out the flagon and rummaged inside the

bag. "It looks as if he forgot to send along a pair of goblets."

She took the wine from his grasp and pulled out the cork. "We shall just have to make do." With a giggle, she tipped up the flagon and took a sip, the ruby liquid escaping out the corner of her mouth. As she dabbed away the mess, she returned the vessel. "Goodness, I didn't expect it to come so fast."

He chuckled. "I like your spirit."

"Why?"

"Because ye are no' afraid to bend the rules."

"That is true, for certain. A consummate rule-bender, though of late, my adventurous nature has provided me with a great deal of bother."

"Is that not what life is made up of? One conundrum after another that challenges us. I think conquering one's woes is what makes men and women accomplished." He drank from the flagon, not spilling a drop, and set it aside. "Look at yourself for example. Had ye not slipped away and found your alcove, ye most likely would no' have become as proficient at drawing."

He thought her a proficient? Anya's heart thumped as she broke the bread and handed him the larger share. "Perhaps not. Men have many more opportunities to perfect their skills," she added. "Take sword fighting. I'm nowhere near strong enough to wield a sword like yours, nor have I had the benefit of instruction."

"Sword fighting takes a lifetime to perfect. But there are other weapons more suited to the fairer sex. The bow and arrow might suit."

"I do enjoy archery."

"See? And I'll wager ye are good at it."

"Fair, I suppose."

"Only fair?" he teased, giving her a chunk of cheese.

She nibbled her food.

"Mayhap we ought to practice together," Islay suggested.

"Oh, aye?" She couldn't help but eye him with a mischievous grin. "Ye'd deign to put a weapon in the hands of an enemy of the crown?"

"Och, lass, if ye wanted to kill me, I reckon I'd already be dead."

Anya washed her bite down with another sip of wine, more carefully this time. She didn't want to kill Islay. She didn't want to kill anyone. In fact, she didn't understand the battles and wars that always seemed to rage around her. "Why do the MacDonalds feud with the MacDougalls?"

His Lordship frowned and tossed a piece of driftwood onto the fire. "If the Lord of Lorn would remain on his lands, there would be no quarrel. But the MacDougalls have a penchant for acquiring lands and riches to which they are not entitled. For three hundred years, my kin have been the Lords of the Isles and we do not intend to allow anyone to take our birthright from us."

"And now the Lord of Lorn has joined with Edward and you with Bruce."

"Aye, that's the way of it."

"But who is right and who is wrong?"

"I've said it afore, and I'll stand by my conviction. Prior to the death of King Alexander, Scotland was at peace with England. Only after the king fell to his death did Longshanks step in and declare himself overlord. But it was the unspeakable carnage at the Battle of Berwick that soured our stomachs for good. Most Scots desire freedom from tyranny, which I do not believe is too much for any man to ask."

Anya sat for a time, staring into the fire. Her father had been a strong man who stood by his convictions just like Islay, yet he had always, and only, paid homage to one king. Since the Norman Invasion, her kin had ruled over Keenaght, though clan feuds had always been rife with her kin's ambition for more power. She supposed it was as Angus said, a yen to acquire lands and riches to which they were not entitled.

"If only there were enough land for all," she mused.

He bit into an apple. "There is, lass. I reckon there is."

"I have another question."

"Aye?"

"How did ye come by the epithet Fairhair?"

He tossed his head, making his tresses sweep across his brow. "First of all, Harald Fairhair was the first King of Norway as well as my ancestor. But it was my brother who dreamed up the name—used it to taunt me." Islay looked to the cave's ceiling and laughed. "I hated the name when I was a lad. But it stuck like a wart on my arse."

Anya covered her mouth and held in a chuckle at the image his words conjured. "If ye didn't like to be called Fairhair, why did ye allow it?"

"Ha! Growing up in my brother's shadow, I was oft used as his proverbial whipping post. The older lads teased me because my face was too bonny. Och, and my hair was as white as the snow still falling out there." Angus stretched out his legs and crossed his ankles. "Alasdair's heckling made me tough. I strove to prove myself at every turn, until I grew taller and stronger than my brother, then I set him to rights."

"How did ye do that?"

"We had a row. I was about twenty at the time. I cannot recall the cause of our argument, but we came to blows." Angus tore a bite of bread with his teeth. "He took the brunt of it. Afterward, he started calling me Fairhair the Terrible."

"With the devil's heart," she mused.

"Aye, that as well."

Here all along she believed His Lordship's enemies had marked him, spreading rumors about his vile temper and ruthlessness, but it had come from his own kin. "If ye ask me, ye have a kind heart."

ANGUS STOPPED MID-CHEW. HAD HE JUST HEARD Anya say she thought him kind? After the shipwreck, and the way his men had dispatched the English sailors? Even the mere fact that she was being held at Dunyvaig against her wishes made such a statement unlikely. Aye, she was there on the king's orders, but Angus was the man responsible for carrying them out. When so many referred to him as a fiend, this curious, charming, imaginative, yet opinionated woman saw the good in his heart despite all the forces working against her.

The lass had most likely missed her chance at wedded bliss because of him. Perhaps not bliss, but if her intended chose to move on, Anya had foregone her opportunity to bear children and raise a family. And after watching her read to the wee ones in the hall this morn, she would make a fine mother.

When Anya cringed, he realized he hadn't acknowledged her compliment.

He swallowed. Hard. "Ye'd best not repeat those words at the keep, else my men will reckon I've gone soft." He meant to intone a bit of humor into his voice, but it came out more like a whisper.

She shifted her gaze away and a cold shiver coursed across Angus' skin. His mind whirred with so many things. First of all, he'd been a fool to bring her out here where they'd be alone together—miles away from any soul.

Yet he'd done it all the same. He'd wanted to show her the beauty of the Oa.

Lord knew he wouldn't tell her about the nights he lay in his bed wondering if she was still awake. Wondering if she had kept the picture she'd drawn of him on

Nave. Though he liked having Anya at Dunyvaig, he abhorred the reason for her presence, at least the reason she had not returned home. If only she were there by her own choosing.

But that would never happen, would it? Sooner or later, she would return to Ireland and would be out of his life—reduced to nothing but a sweet memory.

"Why did ye bring me here?" she asked.

Unable to look into those stunning eyes, he shifted his gaze to her lips. Och, by the flutter of his heart, staring at her lips wasn't the best alternative. But he owed her the truth. "Your captivation on Islay is not your doing. Ye hid in my *birlinn* thinking it was safe, and now ye are away from your sister and all ye hold dear. Worse, I fear your dreams are ruined."

She brushed her fingers over the back of his hand. The mere friction of her touch made his breath hitch, and yet again when she leaned nearer. Though it was snowing and the wind blustering, she smelled as sweet as fresh grass covered with dew on a spring morn. "Mayhap my dreams have changed," she whispered. "In fact, a great deal has changed, but I have not been unhappy here."

He deigned to gaze into those eyes while she tapped her upper lip with her tongue. Angus wanted to kiss her so badly, his mouth grew dry.

But Anya was no meek lass, nor was anything she said or did predictable. Before his next blink, she placed her palm on his cheek and ever so lightly swept her lips across his.

God strike him dead where he sat, he could no sooner resist such a temptation than cease to breathe. His mind filled with an all-consuming desire to return her kiss and show her exactly what she did to his insides. He pulled her onto his lap and sealed his lips over hers. Closing his eyes, Angus claimed her mouth as she sighed and returned his kiss with a fervor as passionate as her lust for adventure. Defying all the voices of logic that had been torturing his mind, he wrapped her in his arms and kissed her thoroughly and possessively.

When breathless, he tapped his forehead to hers. "I pray that was more enjoyable than the last."

She cupped his cheek with a gloved palm made icy by the chill in the air. "Unbelievably enjoyable, but it is I who must apologize this time."

Angus pushed a lock of her hair beneath her veil. "Nay."

"Aye. After all, ye are a sworn enemy of the O'Cahan Clan." With a sigh, she moved off of his lap. "We'd best head back afore the snow begins to stick in earnest."

Angus' heart sank like a stone. ***What the hell am I doing?***

12

Anya completed rolling a newly spun wool into a skein and placed it on the shelf in the solar. "'Tis hard to believe your tapestry is nearly finished, my lady."

Angus' mother sat at her loom and drew the shed stick through the tight rows of thread. "Aye, and it has been a long time in the making."

Anya examined the detail of the three *birlinns* sailing on dark blue waves crested with white. "It is one of the most beautiful works I have ever seen."

"Ye are kind to say so."

"Nay, I am but honest." Anya pointed to the spindle and distaff. "I've finished with the wool. Is there anything else ye need of me?"

Her Ladyship inclined her head toward a linen garment folded on the table. "Angus' new shirt is ready. Would ye mind taking it to him?"

Gulping, Anya quickly turned away so the Dowager Lady Islay wouldn't see the color rushing to her face. "To His Lordship?" she squeaked.

"Please."

Anya moved to the table and traced her finger around the expertly stitched collar. It warmed her to know this shirt would be worn by Angus. If only she could keep it for herself. Then she'd have something she might wear to bed while she dreamed of being in his arms. The problem was every time she was alone in his presence, she did things that were positively audacious and scandalous. Like kissing him or wishing him to kiss her.

"Should I deliver it to his chamber?" she asked.

"Nay, he ought to be in the lord's solar."

Oh, dear. Anya had grown up the daughter of a lord and it had always been unwise to broach anything with Papa when he was within. "But I doubt he'll need a new shirt in there."

"Nay, however, I want him to see it now."

Anya curtseyed. "Yes, my lady. I shall return anon." She collected the shirt, careful not to unfold it, before she hastened out the door. The Dowager Lady Islay was so much different in comparison to Lady Ulster. The former certainly did not need a lady-in-waiting and seemed to dream up things for Anya to do. The countess, on the other hand, always had the two O'Cahan sisters attend her every whim, insisting it was good experience so they would know what would be expected of them when they married into noble families.

The countess would never make a shirt for her husband, or anyone, for that matter. She would either have Finovola or Anya do it, or she would ask the tailor. Neither did Lady Ulster own a loom. At Carrickfergus, the spinning of wool was never done above stairs, either. In truth, Anya had enjoyed the bit of spinning she'd done for the dowager, and weaving looked interesting as well as intricate. That Her Ladyship had acquired such a skill was truly astonishing.

But it was odd that the woman had asked Anya to take the shirt to her son. The Lady Ulster would have assigned the task to a servant, who would have delivered the garment to the lord's bedchamber without interrupting the earl's day. But now here she was on her way to the Lord of Islay's solar.

Rory met her in the corridor, his wiry beard sticking out every which way as if he'd been scratching it. "Where are we off to, miss?"

"Well..." A hundred saucy responses came to mind, though she opted for a completely different tack. "By the state of your whiskers, Wolfie, I reckon ye're looking more like a wolfhound every day. Aside from that, I thought ye might like a change of place, else your old bones might grow so stiff ye'd be stuck against the wall beside Her Ladyship's solar for the rest of your days."

He chuckled, always seeming to enjoy her little jibes. "No need to tell me. I'll just follow along as I always do. Mayhap I'll sprout a tail soon as well."

As they neared His Lordship's solar, Anya's palms started to perspire. Three days had passed since she'd boldly kissed him in the Oa. And though he'd kissed her quite passionately as well, once they returned to the keep, Anya was still so shocked by her behavior, she'd scarcely been able to look him in the eye. And it hadn't been as if he'd flirted with her afterward. In fact, he'd taken less notice of her since.

I'll just mind my own affairs, deliver the shirt, and be on my way.

When she arrived, the door to the lord's solar was slightly ajar. Voices from within spilled into the corridor while Rory stood at a respectable distance.

"I hate to come afore ye with me hat in me hands, m'lord, but the harvest was a wee bit poor last season and we've not a morsel remaining in the sheiling."

"I understand. Is it oats and flour ye are in need of?" asked Angus in an authoritative voice.

Anya peered through the gap. The lord of the castle sat in a large chair while a bent old crofter stood with his back to the door.

"Aye, m'lord."

Angus spotted Anya before he motioned to his factor to make a notation. "Help yourself to what ye need. In return, come summer, I'd like five spools of flax thread. My mother is awfully fond of your wife's spinning."

The man bowed. "Thank ye, thank ye. I'll have Her Ladyship's five spools just as soon as the first stalks are harvested."

"Very good." As the crofter took his leave, Angus shifted his attention to the shirt in Anya's hands. "Have ye a supplication, miss?"

She checked to ensure no one else was waiting. "Nay, my lord. Your mother sent me bearing a gift."

"Since the crofter was my last visitor for the day, it seems ye've arrived at a good time," Islay said, beckoning her inside and giving the factor a dismissive nod.

Anya stepped aside while the man collected his ledgers of accounts and headed out. From across the solar, she presented the shirt. "I say, your mother's needlework is exquisite. Had she not married a nobleman, she would have done well as a tailor's wife."

Laughing, Angus pushed back his chair and stood. "Do not tell her such a thing, she might change her mind about ye."

"Forgive me, I meant it as a compliment. Your mother is ever so skilled with a needle, as well as a loom. I am truly astounded."

As he sauntered toward her and reached for the shirt, the Highlander's fingers brushed hers, the light touch making Anya's breath hitch. He hesitated for a moment, the corner of his mouth ticking up as he met her gaze. She didn't dare inhale while his eyes trailed to her mouth and he scraped his teeth over his bottom lip.

Was he thinking about their kisses? Was he thinking about how forward she'd been? Anya was desperate to ask, but doing so would have been too mortifying, even for a spirited lass like her.

"Let us have a look at Mither's handiwork," he said, stepping back and breaking the spell. He shook out the shirt while the door clicked closed. "It is fine."

"Just fine?"

"Aye, and exactly like all the others she has sewn for me over the years."

"Why does your tailor not make your shirts?"

Angus tossed the garment on the table as casually as if it were a playing card. "It makes my mother happy to sew them herself. It also occupies her time so that she doesn't occupy mine."

"Truly? I find your mother to be quite interesting. Very different from the Countess of Ulster, but in a good way."

"She's not too overbearing?"

"She hasn't been thus far. I say, the countess was overbearing on an hourly basis."

Stepping nearer, Angus tucked a lock of hair behind Anya's ear. "Is that right? Mayhap my mother only is meddlesome when it comes to me."

"Oh? Has she been nosy of late?"

"Aye, though her ways are subtle."

"How so?" Anya asked, a bit breathless. Had Angus grown taller? More imposing? Certainly, he couldn't be better looking than he'd been when she'd seen him at dinner last eve.

"Your presence here is not because of the Bruce, if ye recall. The king would have shipped ye to a frigid monastery."

"Do ye believe your mother meddled to help me?"

"Mm-hmm."

"Why?"

"Mayhap ye ought to ask her." Rather than step away, Angus rested his palm on the wall beside Anya's head. "What schemes are running through that vivid imagination of yours?"

Her stomach fluttered as she glanced to the door. Heavens, did he know what she was thinking? Did he know how much she wanted to kiss him again? Yet every time the idea popped into her thoughts, she chastised herself. Continuing to steal kisses from Fairhair would only serve to cause her torture for the rest of her days.

She affected her most innocent expression, batting her lashes for good measure. "I have no idea what ye mean, my lord."

Chuckling, he brushed a whisper of a kiss across her cheek. "Of course, no'."

"Ye do know, no matter how much I want..." She looked into his eyes and nearly swooned. Goodness, if she didn't make a stand now, she'd lose herself in his enchanting stare. "I...we cannot."

Angus dropped his hand, making a loud slap on his thigh. Then rubbing his neck, his lips disappeared into a thin line. "Ye are right and I've no business trifling with ye. Forgive me."

Good heavens, why had his words sounded so final? And why must Anya feel so inexplicably disappointed?

Clasping her hands, she headed for the door. From the start, she knew visiting his solar was a misbegotten idea. Moreover, they both were playing with fire. She couldn't fall in love with a man like Fairhair, the devil of the seas. Perhaps she would have been better off if the King of Scots had sent her to the monastery. At least there she'd be miserable and not tempted by a man who stirred her blood every time she glanced his way.

Anya dashed out of the solar and hastened toward Rory. "Come, stroll with me atop the wall-walk, Wolfie. I need some air."

"Would ye like me to find a wee collar and lead for ye, miss?"

She shook her head, unable to engage in their saucy banter at the moment. "If Robert the Bruce had it his way, I would be the one on the end of a leash."

The guard cleared his throat and followed without saying another word. At least having Rory skulking behind her with his weapons clanking was what Anya needed to remind herself that she was not a guest at Dunyvaig. Nor was she there upon her free will. She was a prisoner and Islay was a renowned scoundrel who had been detested by her father. The next time she went weak at the knees when in his presence, she vowed she would not disregard her principles and everything she had been brought up to believe.

As the weeks passed, Angus grew increasingly agitated. Not only was the weather foul, every time he looked up, Anya O'Cahan managed to be somewhere nearby. His mother repeatedly sent her to the solar with frivolous gifts. The lassie was always in the hall when he broke his fast. And he knew she tried her damnedest not to look his way at the evening meals because he continually watched her out of the corner of his eye. Without a doubt, she tried to ignore him. Hell, he'd done his damnedest to ignore her. Except doing so had proved utterly impossible.

Frustrated beyond reason, Angus paid a visit to the chapel, finding Friar Jo alone.

"Ah, m'lord. 'Tis fine to see ye this lovely day."

Angus grumbled under his breath. "Today is as dreary as yesterday and the one afore that. In fact, the rain hasn't let up in the past fortnight."

"'Tis a good sign, I say. Spring will soon be upon us."

"If it doesn't drive the entire clan mad afore then."

"Judging by your high spirits, I take it there's something needling your craw." The friar started back to the small chamber where he kept his pallet and writing table. "Come join me for a tot of fine MacDonald whisky, blessed in this very chapel, mind ye. 'Tis the cure for foul moods, I'll guarantee."

"Mayhap this wasn't the worst idea I've had today," Angus mumbled to himself. He chose one of the two seats at the table and stretched out his legs. The chamber was cozy. He and the friar oft solved the problems of Christendom over a wee dram or ten.

"Ye've no cause to worry, m'lord," said Jo, returning with two cups in his hands. "Everyone grows a bit sore-headed by the end of winter. 'Tis why we sinful souls feel a wee bit tipsy when the weather turns—the birds are merrier, the glens greener, the hunting better, the flowers happier."

"Ye needn't tell me about bloody spring." Angus took the offered cup and raised it in toast. "This will douse the fire within."

Smirking, the old friar sat opposite. "Or turn it into a raging flame."

Angus sipped and let the amber liquid slide over his tongue. "Mm. There's no spirit finer than a peaty Islay brew."

"On that I will agree." Jo returned the toast and drank in kind. "Now tell me, what has ye scowling like an angry bull?"

"Och, give me the spray of the sea on my face and a week of sunshine and I'll be fit."

"Aye? Wait a month or two and the good Lord will provide. But I reckon ye are skirting about the cause of your consternation, m'lord. I'll wager your woes are on account of a wee Irish lassie flitting about the keep—the very lass who sits beside me at the evening meals."

"A bloody O'Cahan she is."

"But ye like her."

Angus shrugged. "I have no business liking her. I

ought to lock the chit in the wee tower chamber. She is my prisoner, after all."

"Nay, she's the king's prisoner, ye are simply her jailer."

"Och, aye, that makes me feel better. Mayhap I ought to tote around a headman's axe." Angus took another drink and savored the whisky as it burned its way down his gullet. "I wish she'd never hid in my *birlinn*."

"Is that so?" asked the friar, not sounding convinced. "I do not believe God ever puts someone in your path on mistake."

"Och, the lass made a mistake for certain. One she'll regret for the rest of her days."

"Because she was supposed to marry a man for whom she harbored no love?"

"How do ye ken? Mayhap Miss Anya was ecstatic about the prospect of marrying that cad."

"I think not." Jo rubbed his fingers over the large wooden cross he wore around his neck. "She told me herself she had never felt terribly affectionate toward her intended."

Angus eyed the holy man across the table, then blew out a guffaw. "Do ye think Miss Anya would rather bide her time here?"

"From what I've observed, I do no' believe the lass is miserable." The Friar poured himself a second tot and pushed the flagon across the board. "And it has not escaped my notice that she has eyes for ye, my friend."

Angus' heartbeat sped, thumping away as if he were a wet-eared lad. Pounding his fist on his chest, he thumped back, restoring a more moderate rhythm. "She's not mine to woo."

"Is that so?"

"Aye. Though she may not see Ireland for a time, and O'Doherty may move on, our king, mind ye, entrusted her care to me."

"'Tis a conundrum, is it no'?"

"'Tis a bloody miserable state of affairs." Angus drained his cup and refilled it. "Mayhap I ought to sail to Jura for a time."

"Because of the lass?"

"Aye."

"What will that prove? And how can ye be responsible for the woman when ye're no' here?"

"Och, the Bruce will call me to fight for the kingdom soon. I'll not be on hand to be Anya's high protector sooner or later."

"Hmm." Friar Jo patted his belly with his thick-fingered hands. "Her circumstances are tragic, the poor woman. This war could endure for a decade or more, though I stand by my beliefs. There is a reason the Lord has sent her to Islay. In time, God's plan will be revealed."

"Until then, I'll either go mad, or I'll be off fighting the wars. I cannot lose sight of the fact that the MacDonalds are the Lords of the Isles, and until there is no question of our sovereign right to rule the Hebrides, there will be no rest."

"The ambitions of men have led many astray." The friar leaned forward. "The good Lord has a plan for ye as well. But first ye must listen to your heart."

"Aye? I'll have ye ken—"

With a slice of his hand, the holy man silenced Angus. "Wheesht. Your brother and your father afore him were the same—fighting one battle after the next whilst never pausing to examine what truly matters in their hearts."

Though Friar Jo may have spoken true, his words did nothing to put Angus at ease. Scotland was at war and this was no time for any man to laze about pondering the meaning of his existence—or, worse, pining after a lass he could never have.

13

Her Ladyship had gone to the village for a change. With the morning to herself, Anya opted to spend it reading in her bedchamber rather than taking Rory to explore the crevices of the castle. To her chagrin, two mornings past, she had awaken with a nagging cough and a tender throat that hadn't yet gone away. She blew her nose as she turned the page of her book. It was too early in the season for congestion of the lungs. That dreaded misery seemed to plague her every spring when the trees bloomed.

She coughed again, a very productive cough that made the throat burn all the more. Mayhap the seasons were different in Scotland.

"Fire!" shouted someone, who sounded very much like Angus.

Anya set her book aside, headed to the window, and pulled across the fur. Indeed, down below, His Lordship wielded a bow as did a dozen MacDonald men, all shooting at targets across the way.

Dropping the fur, she blew her nose and donned her cloak. No use letting a little cough ruin an entire day, especially one where she did not have to do the bidding of the lady of the keep. She took a sip of water to bathe her throat and headed out the door.

"Good morn, Wolfie," she said, a tad hoarsely. "How's the sprouting of that tail coming along?"

He stroked his fingers down his neatly groomed beard. "Nothing as of yet. Mayhap by the end of your tenure here, I'll be wagging a nice wiry one."

"To wave goodbye?"

"Och, I reckon ye'll grow so fond of me ye'll not be able to live without me."

She started through the corridor. "Is it not the other way around? Ye are supposed to grow fond of me."

"Right again, Miss Anya," he said, following as always. "Are ye going out?"

She glanced at him over her shoulder. "I thought I'd watch archery practice."

"It might be a bit safer if ye watched from your window."

"And a great deal less entertaining." She ducked into the stairwell and started downward. "Are ye fond of archery?"

"Aye."

"Then why are you not down there practicing?"

"I think ye ken why."

"Though ye'd rather be with the men, would ye not?"

"What I want does not matter."

She stopped and faced him with her fists on her hips. "I emphatically disagree. Everyone is entitled to do what they please."

"With all due respect, miss, I have a half-holiday once a sennight when Archie guards ye. 'Tis fair."

"I disagree. Guarding me must be the most tedious task ye've ever had."

"A man can use a wee bit of tedium in his old age." He winked. "I'll never admit it to His Lordship, but our banter is amusing. I oft wonder what ye'll be dreaming up next."

Anya chuckled, but when she swallowed, her throat

burned. Continuing on her way, she decided she would be heading for her bed early this eve.

The stoop beyond the main doors looked out over the courtyard, where she stopped and rested her elbows on the balustrade.

Raising a loaded bow to his cheek, Angus stood directly below. The string twanged as he let his arrow fly. Anya muffled her cough as his shot hit an inch right of center.

"Not bad," said Raghnall who followed suit, hitting the center mark.

His Lordship grumbled and loaded his bow. This time, his arrow darted straight into the middle. He grinned at the man-at-arms. "Spot on. That makes us two-for-two. Next point wins."

Raghnall drew another arrow. "I'll be more than happy to relieve ye of your coin, m'lord." He hardly looked at the target as he drilled another dead center.

"Bloody miserable braggart," Angus growled, as he loaded his bow. Rather than haste, he stood very still, like a hunter homing in on his pray. His back as straight as a board, his feet planted wide, his gaze unwavering from his mark. Good heavens, he posed a picture of a majestic Highlander.

Anya inhaled with him as his chest expanded. With a resounding hiss, he released the arrow, shooting it through the air like a dart.

From where Anya stood, the contest was too close to call.

The two men marched forward and examined their targets while Friar Jo followed, waving a ribbon. "The only fair way to judge is with a proper measurement!"

She knew the outcome when Raghnall held out his palm. And judging by the way Angus dug in his sporran and parted with a coin, he wasn't happy with the results. But his scowl was replaced by a grin when he looked to the stoop.

Pretending her cough was a giggle, Anya waved, the motion making her head swim. "May I have a go?"

Raghnall motioned toward the soldiers, flicking his thumb over his shoulder. "I'll set to putting the men through their drills."

Angus hesitated before he held up the bow and grinned. "Why not?"

She pattered downward. "I haven't any coin with which to place a wager."

He met her at the foot of the steps and took her hand, but his gaze flickered to the friar as the older man followed the MacDonald soldiers. "I reckon we can come up with something interesting."

Anya glanced at Angus' lips before she had a chance to check herself. "Have ye anything in mind?"

"Well..." His tongue slipped to the corner of his mouth. "If I win..."

Anya's heart leapt.

"I'd like ye to draw me a picture of Dunyvaig."

The leaping was replaced by a lump in her chest. She thought for certain he'd want a kiss. Of course, Anya would have drawn a picture of his castle without even being asked. "Very well. But I cannot properly draw the castle within the walls. I will have to find a spot where I'll have some landscape to work with."

"I think that can be arranged."

She eyed him. Would he take her to find a spot, or would he assign the tedious task to Rory? And now he hadn't asked for a kiss, she must ask for something other than that which she truly wanted. "If I win, I should like to take another ride to the Oa."

His Lordship's eyebrows arched. "I believe that is fair." He handed her the bow. "Ladies first."

As she took it, a hacking cough erupted from her throat. Doing her best to recover and stop the swooning of her head, Anya patted her chest. "Good heavens, forgive me."

"Are you ill?"

"Nay, I just have a bit of a cough." She loaded an arrow and raised the bow, drawing the string to her cheek. "I think the outside air will do me good."

"Very well. Would you like a few practice shots to begin with?"

Anya should have thought to make such a request. "Thank you," she said as she released her arrow, her spirits sinking as it hit the far left of the target. "Oh dear, that was awful."

"'Tisn't a bow ye've used afore."

Though it was kind of him to say so, she wasn't accustomed to missing by such a wide margin. Swallowing against her urge to cough, she drew another arrow from the quiver. Her next shot was better, though a bout of dizziness caused the third to miss the target altogether.

"Allow me to retrieve my arrows," she said, hoping the walk might clear her head.

"I'll go."

"Nay." She held up her palm as she stared off. "I will do it."

As she approached, the throbbing in her head grew tenfold. And when she tried to yank out an arrow, Anya doubled over with coughing. The ground spun beneath her feet. She leaned on the target, trying to steady herself. "Not to worry," she mumbled. "I'll be—"

The target gave way and sent her tumbling to her knees.

ANGUS FLUNG THE QUIVER ASIDE AND RAN. "ANYA!" he shouted, sweeping his arms around the lass and helping her to her feet. "Whatever is wrong?"

She turned her head away and coughed into the crook of her elbow. "I've had a bit of a sore throat and it seems to be growing worse."

He pressed his palm to her forehead. "Och, ye're afire. Ye should be abed, not out here."

The lass looked as pale as bed linens, her eyes glassy. "But our wager."

"Oh, aye? Ye'd prefer to succumb to an ague? I'll take ye to the Oa if ye desire, wager or nay." He swept her into his arms. "I'll not hear another word. To bed with ye."

"I'm able to walk," she mumbled.

"Ye barely made it to the target. Lord kens how ye managed to make the journey through the keep."

Rory met them by the door. "Allow me to help, m'lord."

Angus eyed the guard. "Did ye ken she was ailing?"

The man stammered. "She coughed a bit but told me she was feeling fine, otherwise."

"Go fetch Lilas and Freya as well. I'll take Miss Anya to her chamber."

On the journey above stairs, the lass grumbled about being too heavy, about being a capable archer, and about it being too early in the season for congestion of the lungs.

"I'm sorry to be such a bother," she said for the tenth time as he pushed inside her bedchamber.

"Wheesht." He placed her on the bed and smoothed his hand over her forehead. She was very warm, which he didn't like at all. "Lilas will be here anon."

Groaning, Anya lay back and tried to roll the coverlet over her shoulders. "'Tis terribly cold in here."

Angus looked to the fire smoldering in the hearth. It was a mite warmer in here than it had been outside. He pulled a plaid from the end of the bed and draped it over the lass. "This will help."

Coughing, she clutched the blanket beneath her chin while he doused a cloth in the basin and placed it on her forehead.

Anya pushed it off. "Nay. 'Tis too cold."

He tried again. "Ye are afire, lass. We must cool your fever."

As she pushed it away for the second time, Lilas came in clutching her medicine bundle, with Freya in her wake. "Rory said Miss Anya has a cough," the healer said with a furrow in her careworn brow.

Angus ushered the healer toward the bed. "She's fevered as well."

Lilas set the basket on a wooden chair and leaned over the lass. "How long have ye been ailing, miss?"

As she opened her mouth, Anya was unable to staunch her coughing.

Angus found a cup of water on the table and brought it to the bedside. "Have a nip of this."

A bit splashed out of the cup as Anya sat up enough to take a sip. "Ah," she sighed. "It started with a sore throat two days past, then the cough came a rattling in my chest. And now it seems to be growing worse."

Lilas frowned as she felt Anya's cheeks and forehead. Angus stood back while the healer conducted her examination, including removing the patient's shoes and stockings and looking between her toes. Then she had the lass sit up and pressed her ear against Anya's chest.

The healer glanced to Freya. "Help the lass remove her kirtle and climb beneath the bedclothes whilst I have a word with His Lordship in the corridor."

Angus' mouth ran dry as he followed her out the door. "Is it bad?"

"It can be. The lass has winter fever, and if we do not nip it in the bud quickly, we might lose her."

"Dear God." He pounded his fist on the stone wall. Of all the people in the keep, why must it be Anya who fell ill?

"I'll leave a tincture of violets and whey for the fever, and one of black spleenwort to help with the cough. We also must apply deer's grease to her feet three times daily until the coughing ebbs. I think it would be best for someone to sit with her at least as long as her forehead is warm to the touch."

"I'll do it."

"Ye? Why not Freya?"

"Because the maid is not Miss Anya's guardian. The king entrusted her care to me." Grinding his molars, Angus paced. He'd already botched things up enough when it came to Robert the Bruce, and he had no intention of allowing this wee wisp of a woman to succumb to winter fever when in his care.

Rather than barge inside, he knocked on the door and waited for Freya to open it. "Is she settled?"

"Aye, m'lord."

Raucous coughing came from within, cutting him to the quick.

14

As evening gave way to night, Angus maintained his vigil at Anya's bedside, the chamber lit only by a candle and the peaty coals smoldering in the hearth. The sound of her raspy breathing was enough to drive a man insane with worry. God Almighty, he wanted to rouse Raghnall and spar until he was so exhausted he could no longer raise his sword.

Resolutely, he doused a cloth in the bowl. At this late hour, when he wrung it out, the droplets hit the water with resounding pings reminiscent of the trickle of a Highland burn. He'd kicked off his boots hours ago and now padded across the floor where he stood over Anya's sleeping form. Before he replaced the cloth on her forehead, he watched her for a time. Even though she was ill and coughing now and again, she posed a lovely sight. Her luminous chestnut locks sprawled across the pillows in thick waves. In the glow of the dim light, her fair skin reminded him of fresh cream. She breathed through slightly parted full lips—a mouth that had set his heart to flame more than once. Across the bridge of her red-tinged nose was a delightful splay of freckles. They expressed her saucy nature, as if to announce here is a woman who is full of mettle, whose art flows from her fingertips, and who isn't afraid to take chances.

Any man ought to admire Anya's free spirit. Though from what she'd said, she'd oft been chided for it.

Angus removed the overwarm cloth and replaced it with the cool, then kissed her cheek. In deep slumber, the lass' cough was more peaceful now than when awake. Though the rattle in her breathing made his heart twist. If only he could have fallen ill and not her.

In truth, his feelings for Miss Anya were far different than anything he'd ever experienced in his life. Even Ella.

Hmm. 'Tis interesting my recall of the vixen's gave me no pause whatsoever.

Most times a lassie would catch his eye, and he'd dally with them until he grew bored. But Angus wanted to protect this woman with every fiber of his being. He wanted to shelter her from all harm, including Robert the Bruce. Not that the king intended to do her bodily harm, but caging this dove as a political prisoner seemed a crime in itself.

Och, aye, if times were different, he might look upon her as a woman with whom he could start a family. If she weren't an O'Cahan. If she weren't aligned with the House of Ulster. If she weren't already promised to another.

Alas, Angus had naught but to persevere—rein in his lustful nature and enjoy what time he had with her.

"Nay!" she shouted, tossing her head from side to side, making the cloth drop to the mattress.

"Anya?" he whispered.

"Nay, nay, nay!"

Angus tried to replace the cloth, but she batted his hand away. "What has ye so riled?"

"I do not want to go!"

"Where?"

"This is my home," she mumbled, followed by thrashing and a string of imperceptible blathering.

Realizing she was in the midst of a night terror, Angus tried to rouse her. "Anya, ye must wake."

She flung out her arm, smacking him across the face. "Why? Why must females always be used as pawns? No one cares about what we want or how we feel!"

"Anya?" Angus tried again.

This time, an enormous sigh seemed to come from the depths of her soul. Then she coughed and curled onto her side, her body quiet again, though her breathing still rattled.

Ever so gently, he brushed the cool cloth across her cheek and forehead. "Hush, *mo leannan,* and sleep."

Moving to the foot of the bed, he exposed her feet and rubbed in the deer oil that Lilas had provided, praying it would work and that Anya would be well come morn.

Once the lass was resting peacefully, he moved back to the chair at her bedside and for some reason, he started to talk. "My mother says God blessed me with many things, but when it comes to matters of the heart, I am sorely lacking. I suppose she's right. After all, she's a female, and Lord kens I oft have no idea what women are thinking or what they might truly want, or what they may think of me."

He stretched out his legs and crossed his ankles. "I wonder what ye think of me, lass. I ken ye first saw me as Fairhair, the man with the devil's heart. But if ye take away the gossip, the title, and the feuds, and look at me as a man, am I good? Am I worthy? If things were different, would ye want...*me*?"

ANYA'S COUGH STARTLED HER AWAKE, BUT WHEN SHE swallowed, she was surprised to discover doing so didn't hurt very much at all. As she stretched out her arms, her fingers brushed over a crown of silky hair right there on her tiny little bed. Opening her eyes, she found the Lord of Islay sitting in a chair, hunched forward, and cradling his head on the mattress atop folded arms. His eyes were closed and by the slow cadence of his breathing, he was deep in slumber. She raised her hand to caress his head but, not wanting to wake him, she clenched her fist and pulled it away.

How long have I been abed?

Though she couldn't be certain, every time she'd awoken, Angus had been there. He'd relentlessly applied cold cloths to her forehead. He'd talked to her in a soft voice that was ever so soothing. Anya rolled to her side and examined his face, partially hidden by tawny hair. His beard had grown in as it had done on the Isle of Nave, but this time he didn't look like a pirate at all. He was scruffy, to be sure. But up close like this and sound asleep, he resembled a guardian angel.

She gently brushed his hair away from his face and examined a small scar at his temple. About an inch long, the puckered skin was straight as if he'd been nicked by a blade—most likely he had been.

If only he were Irish. Or even a Scot who supported the English crown.

Does it matter upon which side he stands?

As soon as the question passed through Anya's mind, she knew the answer. What truly mattered was what lay in a man's heart. *In war, are there not good people on both sides? Does God truly choose one side over another? Is it blasphemous toward my father to be smitten by the brother of the man responsible for Da's death?*

A cold chill coursed through her.

Why must everything be so complicated?

With a sputter, Angus cleared his throat, sat up and stretched. "Ye're awake."

Anya pulled herself up against the pillows, careful to keep the bedclothes beneath her chin. "I am. How long have I been ill?"

"Three days." He pressed his palm to her forehead. "Your fever has broken. How do ye feel?"

"Like I could sleep for a sennight."

"Lilas said it would take time for ye to fully recover." He scratched the stubble along his jaw. "Are ye hungry?"

The mention of food made Anya's stomach squeeze. "A bit. Perhaps some toast and cider or mead?"

"'Tis music to my ears. I was ever so worried, especially when ye refused to eat for so long. I even had to drizzle the tincture into your mouth to keep your fever from burning ye alive." Pushing to his feet, he gestured toward the door. "If ye will be all right for a time, I'll go see to it that Freya brings up a tray."

Anya grasped his hand. "Before you go, I..."

"Hmm?"

She kissed his knuckles "Thank ye. I know anyone could have tended me, but ye stayed here all along and no matter what people on the other side of this war might say about ye, I know in my heart, it is all wrong."

Angus paused for a moment, his vivid gaze studying her with a wealth of unspoken emotion. "Mayhap I should tend the sickbed of all my enemies' daughters so that their opinions might forever be altered."

Anya drew back, her mouth falling open. "I do not recommend it, my lord."

Chuckling, he gave the back of her hand a whisper of a kiss. "I jest, of course. Yours is the only sickbed beside which I care to sit, and I hope ye will live out the rest of your days in good health so it will never be necessary again."

By afternoon, Anya was ready to be up and about, but Lilas had insisted she remain in bed for another day. Evidently, the healer had the final say on the matter because Angus told Rory that should Anya try to leave her chamber, she was to be marshalled straight back inside without argument. Heavens, he reminded her more of a wolfhound every day.

Fortunately, the lord of the castle had sent up several sheets of vellum, a cutting board from the kitchen to use as a writing surface, three sharpened charcoal sticks, as well as an ink pot and quill.

Grateful for something with which to occupy her time, Anya spent the afternoon sketching like a zealot. So many ideas popped into her head, she drew faster and more vividly than she'd ever done. She drew the geese in the sweeping moor of the Oa, with Angus riding and looking as if he were the king of the Highlands. She drew the shore beneath Dùn Athad, including Angus lighting the fire. She drew a rendering of Angus in slumber, as he'd been this morn, with his head perched on the side of her bed. She couldn't bring herself to stop, drawing Angus in the tailor shop, looking on with his arms crossed and his stance wide, Angus on the Isle of Nave, hunting for crabs. Angus at the helm of his boat as they sailed into a violent storm.

Anya was about to start yet another sketch when the Dowager Lady Islay opened the door. "Lilas told me ye're much improved so I thought I'd pay a visit, if ye're feeling up to it."

Covering a cough with her hand, Anya quickly moved the drawings aside and covered them with a blank sheet of vellum. "I am honored, my lady."

"Ye had us all so very worried," she said, taking the chair where Angus had been. "It is such a relief to see ye sitting up."

Anya rose and moved to the washstand to scrub the

charcoal from her fingertips. "I am happy to be feeling better. I'd hate for anyone else to suffer winter fever."

"Have you suffered the malady afore?"

"Not exactly." She rubbed the soap between her palms. "I do get a bit wheezy in springtime, but it passes with the season."

Her Ladyship's gaze trailed to the pile of velum. "Ye do ken Angus refused to leave your side."

"I do." She pulled a drying cloth from where it hung in front of the washstand. "He feels responsible for me, though he should not."

"My son has always been duty bound. In truth, I believe he is more suited to the lordship than Alasdair was."

After drying her hands, Anya rehung the cloth and returned to the bed, sitting across from Her Ladyship. "Why do ye say that?"

"Do no' misunderstand. I loved them both equally. But Alasdair focused more on improving his own lot than that of the clan. Angus wishes to secure the Lordship of the Isles to ensure the people who count on him live happy lives, free from the yoke of tyranny."

"He desires peace, yet he's thrown in his hat with Robert the Bruce, which will ensure more fighting and bloodshed."

"Unfortunately, the battles will be fierce regardless of what side he chooses to support. Angus pledged his fealty to the Scottish king because it was the right thing to do for clan and kin. Because he believes in Scotland as a sovereign nation."

"I think I'm beginning to understand. Would it not be nice if all Scots felt the same?"

"I believe they will in time." The Dowager Lady Islay pointed to the drawings. "May I have a look at your work?"

Anya gathered the sheets of vellum and held them

against her chest. "Forgive me, but they are but mindless scratchings at the moment."

"I rather doubt that. Come, until my son marries, I am still the lady of this castle and I want to see them."

A blast of heat spread across Anya's cheeks as she passed her sketches to the woman. "When given time, I can denote much more attention to the details."

Her Ladyship pursed her lips as she studied each one. Anya sank lower on the bed, wishing she could pull the bedclothes over her head and melt into a puddle. What would Islay's mother think once she realized her son was featured in every picture? Would now be the time for Her Ladyship to decide to send her to the tiny chamber in the tower to serve out the duration of her sentence?

Anya squeezed her eyes shut. She might be bent and grey by the time this horrid war ended.

"These are quite good," said the Dowager Lady Islay, peering over the parchment. "Who taught ye to draw so well?"

One of Anya's shoulders ticked up. "I suppose I've been drawing since I first held a quill. My father had a number of books in his library, and I oft studied the pictures and tried to copy them—the shadowing and whatnot. In time, I improved, I suppose."

Her Ladyship returned the sketches. "Well, I ought to have ye draw a scene from the Oa for my next weaving project—a tapestry with the geese would be lovely, mayhap add deer. And I do believe it would make quite a statement to visitors in the great hall if my son were on horseback riding through the moor as well."

As Anya released a pent-up breath, she straightened. Perhaps she'd escaped a lonely existence in the tower yet again. Angus had requested such a drawing as well, which made the request doubly enticing. "I would definitely want to put a great deal more detail into the sketch if it were to be intended for a tapestry to adorn the hall, my lady. I'll need a larger canvas as well."

"Well then, once ye've fully recovered, I'll see to it ye have whatever size ye need. And mind ye, I want my fierce Angus Og featured in the drawing. Ye are quite skilled at capturing his likeness." Her Ladyship stood. "Mayhap a rendering with bow and arrow in hand, chasing a seven-point stag."

15

Though it was not a feast day, the tables in the hall were nearly full this eve, teeming with those who supported the MacDonald army. There were also many nearby crofters who were running low on supplies due to the end of winter. Angus had heard their tales of woe many times before. He was only glad that the castle's larder was well-stocked and his hunters brought in fresh meat daily. If he did nothing else in his tenure as lord of these lands, he would see to it no soul went hungry.

Beside him, Raghnall picked up an ewer and poured a tankard of ale for himself. "Ye can inform the king we've recruited another five hundred fighting men from Skye."

Angus tore his bread and slathered half with butter. "He'll be pleased for certain, though I want ye to send up a team of men to train them, ensure they are ready."

"I have just the men in mind."

"I would have thought no less."

"Did Miss Anya tell you I've asked her to sketch a picture of the Oa for my next tapestry?" asked Mither on his left. "She is quite talented."

Angus shifted his gaze down the table to where the lass sat beside Friar Jo, recalling he'd wagered for such a drawing, but then Anya had fallen ill and there had been no contest. "'Tis good to hear ye are keeping her occupied."

When he caught Anya's eye, she smiled, her grin bright enough to light the entire hall. Angus' heartbeat sped, yet as he returned the gesture, he told himself his reaction was because she had made a full recovery.

"Have ye seen her work?" asked his mother.

"Hmm?"

"Anya's charcoals. Have you seen them?"

"Aye, she drew a picture when we were on the Isle of Nave. It was a very realistic rendering."

"Indeed?" Mither sipped her ale. "Then I believe ye'd be doubly impressed to see the wee sketches she made whilst she was convalescing."

"I'm certain they're good." As Angus watched Anya, his mother's voice faded into oblivion. At first, he had placed the Irish lass at the end of the table near the friar for two reasons. She was nobly born, and thus it was apt for her to sit at the high table. But she was not a guest. In effect, she had invited herself to Dunyvaig by stowing away on his *birlinn*. Thus, since she was also under Angus' supervision, he felt it important not to be seen as growing too fond of the woman.

Except the seating arrangement hadn't helped him to distance himself in the least. His heart had a mind of its own, and Anya O'Cahan might as well be seated beside him.

But such a thing simply wasn't done. Her Ladyship's chair would be occupied by Mither as long as Angus remained unwed. And the man-at-arms always sat on his right. There were certain conventions that absolutely must not be overruled, even by the lord and master of the keep.

By the stars, the lass looked radiant this evening. The color had returned to her face and her eyes shone like emeralds in a crown. She laughed at something Friar Jo said, then hid her grin behind her tankard as she raised it to her lips. While she drank, her gaze flickered to Angus.

Sitting taller, he smiled.

She looked away, her face growing apple red.

Good God, he felt like a wet-eared lad playing googly eyes. As the servants began clearing the table, Angus picked up his tankard and stood. "If ye will please excuse me, I mean to have a word with the artist."

Mither gave a knowing nod as if she'd been planning for Angus to move all along. Bless it, he liked Anya, but he knew as well as anyone that a match between the pair of them was absolutely out of the question. The king would have Angus hanged if he even considered courting the lass, then what good would he be to her?

As he approached, Friar Jo stood. "'Tis time I headed for my pallet, m'lord."

"But it is so early," said Anya, gesturing to a lutist tuning his instrument up on the gallery. "It appears we will have music to enjoy this eve."

"I do enjoy a wee tune now and again, however I've some reading awaiting me in the Good Book and the Lord waits for no one." The stout little man bowed. "Good night, miss."

Angus gave Friar Jo a nod of thanks and took the empty seat. "How fare ye this eve? Feeling well, I hope?"

"Much better, thank ye. I do believe I'll have to ask Lilas for her violets and whey tincture recipe. I'm certain it helped immensely."

"Not the deer's grease?" he asked with a lilt of humor. It had always puzzled Angus as to why rubbing the feet helped cure a cough. But who was he to judge? Lilas had been born into healing and had studied herbal lore all her life.

Anya chuckled. "I daresay the calluses on my heels have softened considerably."

"I wouldn't boast about that to Lilas."

"I shan't, though I must admit my cough has been cured. Nonetheless, I have an inkling the black spleenwort helped far more than the grease." Anya made a sour face. "But I swear it is the foulest tasting tincture that has ever passed my lips."

"My mother always said the worse it tastes, the better the cure."

"Then I'm ever so grateful Her Ladyship did not mix the black spleenwort, else I may not have been able to keep it down."

"Let us hope ye'll no' need the tincture ever again." Angus silenced himself by swilling his ale. He wanted to tell her how worried he'd been, how he'd prayed over her sickbed, how he'd sat night upon night, tirelessly cooling her forehead. But doing so would be folly.

Anya turned to watch the lutist as he began to strum. "Have ye received word from the Bruce?" she asked as casually as if she were inquiring about the fare for tomorrow's evening meal.

"Not of late, but now the weather is turning for the better, I reckon it will not be long afore I am summoned."

Did a bit of disappointment flash through her eyes? Angus watched intently but Anya quickly averted her gaze to her hands. "Such is the lot of men. Always off to battle."

"Aye. It seems so." He plucked away one of her hands and rubbed it between his palms. "Would ye miss me overmuch?"

She rolled a coy shoulder and gave him a teasing arch of her brows. "Nay, not overmuch."

"A little?"

"Perhaps a little." Pushing to her feet, Anya tugged him up. "Come. The clansmen and women are dancing. 'Tis nigh time I kicked up my heels."

"Aye, so it is the lassie's choice, is it?"

"It is when ye start mumbling blather about missing ye after marching off to war—fighting on the wrong side, mind ye."

Oh, how he adored her saucy Irish lilt. Still, Angus rolled his eyes to the rafters as he let her pull him down the dais steps. Here he was trying his damnedest not to be smitten with the woman and utterly failing. Thank God she reminded him exactly why with her "fighting on the wrong side" comment, even though the reason for keeping his distance was never far from his mind. Especially when he moved into line across from her. And when he took her hand and skipped in a circle. And when she smiled and laughed like she hadn't a care, the joyous sound surrounding him like bells on Christmas morn.

Anya made him want to throw his head back and croon. She made him want to dance all night as long as he could dance only with her and she promised to hold his hand with those soft, lithe fingers.

To his chagrin, partway through a turn, the music came to an abrupt stop.

A sentry marched across the floor, his expression grim. "I've a missive from the king."

"So soon?" Anya whispered, the doom in her tone increasing the size of the stony lump in the pit of Angus' stomach.

"Thank ye." He took the letter from the messenger and gestured aft. "Ye'll find food and drink in the kitchens, friend."

Raghnall move in beside them. "What does it say?"

Angus gripped the missive in his fist and shifted his gaze to the dais where Mither watched like an expectant hen. Anya, too, had lost all color in her face. Angus reckoned everyone knew what the king wanted without breaking the seal. Regardless, the contents were confidential. "I shall read it in my solar. Join me there anon."

Angus signaled to Rory before he bowed to the lass. "Ye'd best go above stairs for the night."

Throwing her shoulders back like a lass born to nobility, Anya shook her head. "But I'd like to know what the missive says as well."

"I'm certain ye would, but must I remind ye of your standing whilst residing at Dunyvaig? Ye cannot ever be a party to the king's correspondence."

As the words left his lips, Angus had never regretted uttering such drivel in all his life. And by Anya's bereft expression with tears welling in her eyes, he had wounded her deeply. Damnation, he didn't want to hurt the lass, but she was the absolute last person on the Isle of Islay to be apprised of the contents of a confidential message from Robert the Bruce.

And the state of her claim on his heart had no bearing on the matter.

What if she succeeded in flagging an English ship? What if she told Longshank's men what the Bruce was planning? Angus didn't want to mistrust her, but she'd signaled a ship once before, who knew if she might try it again?

Hell, she is a prisoner of the crown. By rights, she should not be making merry in the hall. And I should not be hopelessly flirting with her either.

Forcing himself to ignore the woman's shocked and wounded stare, Angus marched for the stairs and didn't look back. He fumed all the way up to his solar and slammed the door.

"Damn it all to bloody hell!"

Bless it, he had no right to be angry. In truth, it was surprising it took this long for the king's summons to arrive. No matter what he wanted, Angus could not allow a slip of a lass to addle his mind to the point where he lost his sense of duty. He was the Lord of Islay and the Kingdom of Scotland was looking to him to help regain sovereignty from a heartless tyrant who had named himself as the kingdom's overlord.

Clenching his teeth, he strode directly toward his chair, lit a candle from the embers in the hearth, then examined the seal in the light. Sure enough, the wax bore an imprint of the king's signet ring. Angus slid his finger beneath the hardened blob, shook open the calfskin vellum, and read while a lead rock sank to his toes.

Not only had Angus been ordered to sail a dozen *birlinns* into the Bay of Turnberry, he was to first escort Miss Anya O'Cahan to Orkney and deliver her into the care of the monks at Eynhallow Monastery. The king's reason? He believed if Angus was not at Dunyvaig to watch over the lass, an escape was more likely.

God on the bloody cross, did the Bruce not trust Angus to appoint a suitable guard?

For that matter, once he sailed to the mainland with his army, Dunyvaig would be left with but a small force of older soldiers to defend the keep. Robert didn't say it in his letter, but when Angus left the fortress with his fighting men, there was a greater chance of an English attack. Though the odds were unlikely, Angus understood Robert's caution.

The problem?

He wasn't about to ferry Anya to Eynhallow. Not now. Not ever.

ANYA PACED IN HER CHAMBER, WHILE HER FACE burned hot. She'd been treated so well at Dunyvaig, she had almost forgotten what it was like to be imprisoned against her will.

"Argh!" she shouted, pounding her fists on the bed.

Fairhair had sat beside her sickbed for days. Aye, he could have appointed anyone in the castle to the task but he, the Lord of Islay, had worried over her. On more than one occasion he had kissed her...though once she had initiated the kissing, he'd truly seemed to enjoy it. What of all the glances of longing they'd shared? What of his kindness?

Was it all an act?

Why? Why would he go to so much trouble to feign to be smitten when she was but a mere woman? He never had to give her free rein of the keep. Aside from Rory being attached to her flank, she could go anywhere she pleased. She could even pay a visit to the village.

Oh yes, she mustn't overlook their jaunt to the Oa where Angus had shown her the magnificent moor of which he was clearly proud. He had taken her to the tailor and more!

And now a letter from Robert the Bruce arrives and he sends me above stairs as if I am not to be trusted?

If Islay didn't realize how much her opinion had changed since she'd flagged the English cog on Nave, then he was blind. Anya didn't kiss a man and pretend it had never happened. Bless it, she'd opened her heart to him, and yet he still didn't trust her a whit.

She rifled through the drawings she'd sketched in her sickbed. Every last one of them contained a picture of His Lordship. If that didn't prove the man was ever-present in her thoughts, nothing would. How could she betray someone who cared enough to remain beside her sickbed for nights on end?

Anya rolled the vellum and slapped it in her palm. *If he doesn't think I love him, then these will prove it!*

She marched to the door and flung it open. "I demand you take me to the lord's solar at once."

Rubbing his eyes, Rory lumbered to his feet. "Beg your pardon, but His Lordship told ye to retire for the evening, miss."

"He told me to go above stairs for the night. Is not his solar above stairs?"

"Aye, but I do not reckon paying him a visit is what he had in mind."

Anya poked the guard in the chest with her pointer finger. "If ye do not wish for me to go, then ye'll be forced to restrain me. And I'll say here and now, I can make one hellacious racket when I have a mind to."

"Very well. But if he grows cross, remember I told ye so." Rory gestured along the corridor. "Except I'll most likely be the one to bear the brunt of his ire."

"Ye will not," Anya said with more conviction than she felt. She marched toward the steps and descended until she reached the landing leading to the solar. "If Angus balks, I'll...I'll..."

"Ye'll what?" asked the guard.

"I shall give him a piece of my mind."

"Bloody good that'll do," Rory mumbled, though Anya ignored him.

Once they reached the door, she raised her fist to knock, but with a spike of rage, she instead grabbed the latch and thrust it open. "I need to speak to ye at once, my lord."

Angus, Raghnall, and two of the MacDonald elders gaped at her.

Perhaps she shouldn't have been quite so forward. Perhaps a little knock would have been appropriate. But now that she was standing there with her cheeks afire, she wasn't about to back down. Anya held up her roll of vellum. "I only need a moment."

Angus stood. "Gentlemen, I believe we have a solid plan. Ye are dismissed."

Anya released a pent-up breath and gave Rory a nod. She hadn't been chastised. At least not yet. After the men left, she stepped inside, making sure the door closed behind her.

Angus did not offer her a seat, but folded his arms and knitted his eyebrows. "Did I not tell ye to retire for the eve?"

"I did—I mean, you did, and I was unable to sleep."

He moved to the sideboard and poured a dram of whisky, then held up the flagon. "Would ye care for a tot? There's no greater sleeping elixir than MacDonald brew."

Anya slid into the chair at the corner of the table. "Perhaps a thimble full. I'm not terribly fond of whisky."

"I'm surprised to hear ye've tried it."

"Finovola and I stole into Papa's solar years ago and we each helped ourselves to a nip. It burned something fierce."

Angus chuckled as he returned to the table with two cups—his half full, hers a quarter. "It seems ye have a knack for slipping into places ye shouldn't be."

"Good heavens, ye would say such a thing." Refusing to allow his slight to dissuade her, Anya set the roll of drawings on the table and took a tiny sip. No matter how much she tried to remain impassive, her nose scrunched and her eyes watered as the liquor burned all the way down her throat. She fanned her face "I have no idea why men like whisky so much."

"One grows accustomed to the fire."

"That explains it." She sipped again, this time proving him right. It didn't burn as much the second time.

"I'm certain ye did not come here for a wee dram and a chat," he said, tapping the scroll. "What is on your mind?"

He asked the question so casually, as if he hadn't cut her with his remarks in the great hall. But Anya wasn't one to forget so quickly. "Well..." Exactly how did a female manage to tell a man she cared for him?

"Yes?"

Just out with it, ye daft Irishwoman. Anya unrolled the vellum. "Ye were rather blunt with me in the hall and it set me to thinking."

Angus glanced at the first drawing—the one she'd sketched of him at the helm of his boat.

Anya covered his rendering with her palm. "Ye made me feel as if ye cannot trust me."

He bit his lip. "I—"

"Allow me to finish, please." Beneath the table, she flexed her toes.

His brows arched as he raised his cup. "By all means, miss."

"Ye see, after I recovered enough to draw, and ye were so kind as to send up the parchment and whatnot, I set to sketching that which has been consuming my mind ever since ye pulled away the tarpaulin and discovered me in the midst of the storm."

Anya showed him the drawings one after one. Aye, she might have depicted cliffs of Dùn Athad, but Angus was front and center on his horse, and lighting the fire. He was front and center of it all. She had even captured the beauty of his smile. "Do ye realize no man should ever be so captivating? I ought to hate ye to my very bones, but I do not. My lord, the only reason I believe ye to be the greatest pirate on the seas is because ye have stolen my heart and I am powerless to claim it back."

16

Unable to speak, Angus stared at Anya with his mouth agape. If only he could drown himself in the cup of whisky sitting before him rather than look this woman in the eye.

She drew a trembling hand to her chest. "Have ye nothing to say?"

"I...ah..." Angus glanced to the folded missive from the king sitting at his right. Damnation, he'd never felt like such a heel. And yet, when it came to Anya, he had never practiced so much restraint. Most times when he wanted a woman, he wooed her, bedded her, and moved on. But everything had been different with this Irish rose.

He felt different when he was with her. Aye, he wanted her to his very bones. He ached for her. Yet she had never been his to woo.

And now she'd gone and pledged her affection. Uttered the very words that had been on the tip of his tongue for weeks.

He mustn't lose sight of the fact that Anya O'Cahan had planned to wed another before she was torn away from her life. And heaven knew she hadn't been gone so long Lord O'Doherty would have moved on.

Angus swiped a hand across his mouth. He needed

to tell the truth. He owed her at least that, and there was no gentler way than to have out with it. "I have been ordered to take ye to live at the monastery in the north."

The hand at her chest slid to her throat as an expression of stunned disbelief filled her eyes. "Nay."

"On that we are agreed." Angus thrust to his feet, turned away and braced his hands on the mantel. He was incapable of taking her to Orkney, yet the woman could no longer remain at Dunyvaig. If the English laid siege to the fortress because of her, he would never hear the end of it.

And he hadn't forgotten the war, nor had he forgotten the promises he'd made to the King of Scots and his duty to the kingdom as well as his clan, his kin, and the brother who had given his life to protect the lordship.

"I beg your pardon?" Anya whispered. "Ye would subvert an order from your king?"

Little did she know that the war trumped all, even an order to ship her to Eynhallow. Aye, it was a risk to take her to Carrickfergus, and doing so would surely have its repercussions, but a slight disobedience would most likely be overlooked if Angus proved his worth on the battlefield. "It is I who must face Robert in due course. But I have made my decision. It is time for ye to return to the life ye had afore ye stowed away on my boat. Ye must go now, whilst there's still time to pick up where ye left off."

The silence filling the air was enough to slay him.

Angus faced her and set his jaw. He was no stranger to delivering bad news. He was no stranger to pain and suffering, but what he was about to say had his gut tied in knots and his heart crushed in an iron vise. "Our destinies are at odds, lass. No matter how well we may get along, ye are promised to another. Ye must return to the life ye were meant to live."

"Oh," she whispered, as a scarlet flush spread across her entire face. "I-I have been so utterly foolish. Ye must think me nothing but a silly goose!"

As she stood and dashed for the door, her chair clattered to the floorboards.

"Anya." Angus hastened after her, tripping over the blasted chair. "Wait!"

"Leave me alone," she shouted, slamming the door in his face.

Stopping abruptly, Angus stared at the timbers, wanting to run after her but knowing he must not. He was damned to hell no matter what, and Lord knew the Bruce would also take his pound of flesh. But as far as Anya O'Cahan was concerned, she did not deserve to spend the prime of her life laboring in a monastery, barely surviving on a meager diet of gruel and broth.

And so be it. Angus had made his decision. He would face his king and bear the Bruce's ire, knowing the lass was safe and content. Anya would marry and raise bairns that would be as spontaneous and imaginative as their mother. She deserved to be happy. She deserved to be worshipped and loved.

With a love I cannot possibly give.

Aye, Angus had just been ordered to sail into battle. And this time he would lead the charge. There was every chance he would not live through this year. How could he be so selfish as to pledge his adoration when his days were numbered?

He knew his time was nigh. His father was killed in battle, as was his brother.

The vise clamping his heart tightened enough to make the appendage bleed. Angus staggered to his chair and guzzled the remaining whisky. Then he turned and threw the cup at the hearth, making the pottery shatter.

He gritted his teeth against his urge to bellow. Through the blur of the water in his eyes, Anya's drawing danced as if the charcoaled lines were swimming. Angus grabbed the flask and took a healthy swig before he paged through the rest.

God. On the bloody. Cross.

Not only were they beautifully rendered, she had captured the essence of his expressions in every last one. It was as if he were looking into a mirror.

Heaven help him, if he traveled to the corners of Christendom, he would never find another woman as astonishing as this Irish rose.

THE SUN SHONE LOW IN THE WESTERN SKY AS ANYA shaded her eyes and stared at the horizon, dreading her first sight of her beloved Ireland's verdant shore. It wouldn't be long now, though the MacDonald crew were waiting for dark before they sailed within sight of Carrickfergus Bay.

During the voyage, Anya had remained in the bow of the *birlinn*, unable to bring herself to look at Angus while he manned the tiller. She had foolishly bared her soul to him, thinking he returned her feelings in kind. But she had been ever so incredibly naïve. She'd thought him kind and generous. He'd made her believe he was not the monster her kin had reputed him to be.

How wrong could she have been? Fairhair was as black-hearted as the self-proclaimed king who had imprisoned her in the first place. And now she rued the day she had stolen into his boat.

I wish I'd never seen his face or allowed him to give me comfort on the Isle of Nave. I wish I hadn't gone to the Oa with him or awakened to find him beside my bed when I suffered from winter fever.

I am nothing but a fool! I opened my heart to a man who is incapable of love. A man who chooses battle over all else. Worse, the very brother of the scoundrel who killed my father!

By the time darkness fell and Islay gave the order to tack into the harbor, Anya was in such a lather, she wanted to leap into the icy sea and swim for the pier. But doubtless, His Lordship would dive in after her in a display of ill-begotten heroism.

The castle loomed against the moonlit sky, growing more ominous as the *birlinn* approached, cutting through the waves with a gentle rush.

"Furl the sail and take up the oars," Angus ordered, his tone commanding but no louder than necessary.

Anya wrapped her arms across her midriff and waited in silence until they reached the pier. One of the men hopped out and secured a rope around a mooring cleat. Angus disembarked, strode to the bow, and offered his hand. "Allow me to assist ye."

"I am perfectly able to alight on my own," she said, climbing onto the bench.

His meaty hand secured her elbow. "That may be so, but I would be no gentleman if I stood idle and watched."

Such was the lot of women. Men were able to do whatever they pleased, but the poor females were seen as weak and unable to help themselves. Anya stepped onto the pier and started off, but Angus didn't release his grip on her arm. "Ye're not thinking of leaving without bidding me farewell?"

Hadn't enough words already been exchanged?

"Come, where the men won't hear," he said, urging her along the pier.

When he stopped, she cast her gaze to the center of his chest. "Do ye expect me to thank ye for keeping me captive for two months?"

"Nay," he said, his voice gravelly. "I fear I was insensitive last eve and I've hurt ye."

"'Tis for the best. Our destinies are at odds. Is that not what you said?"

"I should not have been so brash. I... Damn," he

cursed. "I am not good at making amends, but I want ye to ken I wish for your happiness, and I would face an army of archers afore I let ye waste your youth in a poor monastery, working your fingers to the bone."

God help her, Anya looked into his eyes. Shaded by moonglow, he appeared dark and dangerous and far too fetching. Before her knees turned to mushy peas, and before she humiliated herself by grasping his hands to her breast and begging him to take her away to a land where they could start anew, she shook her head. "Then I am grateful to be home, my lord. Fare thee well."

"Anya," he whispered, gripping her fingers between his palms. "I do not want to part with hostilities between us."

Her eyes stung as the Lord of Islay dropped to a knee and kissed the back of her hand. "I wish we had met in a different place in a different time, *mo leannan*. I do care deeply for ye."

As a tear dibbled onto her cheek, Angus released her and strode back to the boat. Unable to move while she held in the sobs wracking her body, she forced herself not to call after him. Not to declare her love. If only she were able to put her charcoal to work and draw the anger she'd built on the voyage across the sea. But Fairhair had utterly disarmed her with a mere kiss applied to the back of her hand. Those blasted lips had taken her ire and turned it into ash floating about in her soul.

As she watched the men row away from the pier, Angus stood beside his tiller, his hand raised as he bid farewell.

Forever.

Oh God in heaven, why must it hurt so badly to say goodbye?

When the boat was but a dot in the black abyss of the sea, Anya wiped her face and looked to the tower. No, Carrickfergus was not her home, but she had lived there for seven years. It was unusually odd to return, akin to being a stranger in a place that was once familiar. What ought she say to the earl? What will he think after all this time? She'd been so upset with Angus, she hadn't thought as to what might happen next.

Gathering her wits, Anya walked toward the sea gate. "Guards!" she shouted. "'Tis Anya O'Cahan, returned from the grip of Robert the Bruce."

MARSHALLED INTO THE HALL BY A RETINUE OF guards, the warmth inside blasted her face as if someone were holding a torch close enough to burn. The noise from the crowd ebbed to a low murmur as they escorted her along the aisle and toward the dais steps.

At one end of the high table, Finovola caught Anya's eye first. Her sister gasped, then exchanged glances with Lord Chahir O'Doherty, who sat beside her.

Anya's mind raced. She hadn't expected to see His Lordship. Had he remained at Carrickfergus since Saint Valentine's Day? Surely, everyone had thought the worst. Even as Anya continued forward, she felt as if she'd returned from the dead. Bucking up her courage, she painted on a feigned smile, giving her sister a nod as she approached the lord and lady of the castle.

"Praises to Mother Mary and Joseph," said the countess.

"Anya?" asked Ulster. "We thought we'd lost ye forever, child."

She sank into a deep curtsey. "I fear I was in the wrong place at the wrong time. The day Robert the Bruce came to ask for your assistance, I was beyond the sea gate. Upon hearing the battle, I sought refuge in what I thought was a fisherman's boat—"

"And there was a fierce storm that eve," said the

earl. "When my search parties turned up with no news, we feared ye had fallen victim to the tempest."

"Forgive me. There was no opportunity to send word. I was held as a prisoner—intended to be used as collateral for negotiations in Elizabeth's return."

"Did ye escape?" asked Her Ladyship.

Anya bit down on her lip. "I was released."

"Released? That seems rather odd." The earl rested his eating knife on his plate. "Ye were released by whom?"

"Angus Og MacDonald, Lord of Islay."

Along the table, Finovola again gasped.

Ulster sprang to his feet. "Is Fairhair here? Guards!"

"Nay. His Lordship's *birlinn* is long gone," Anya said, stepping forward. Unless she explained everything, her guardian might set sail and attack Dunyvaig come dawn. Steeling her resolve, she told them about the shipwreck, omitting the incident when she flagged the English ship. She told them about Robert the Bruce declaring her a political prisoner and his plans to send her to a monastery somewhere in the north of Scotland. She explained that it had been the Dowager Lady Islay's idea for her to remain at the castle, yet she said nothing of Angus, or of the kind treatment she'd received.

"Thank the good Lord ye have been returned to us at last. We shall discuss these matters further come the morrow," said Ulster, gesturing toward Finovola's side of the table. "Sit. Eat."

Anya's stomach was tied in so many knots, the last thing she wanted to do was eat. "Thank ye, my lord, but I would rather retire for the evening if you please."

"I'll go with you," said Finovola.

As she began to rise, Lord O'Doherty quickly hopped to his feet and held the lass' chair. "Miss Anya, allow me to say it brings me much comfort to see ye are well."

She curtsied politely, wondering if he would want to

recommence negotiations for their betrothal, though trying not to care. "Thank you, my lord."

When her sister wrapped her hands around Anya's arm, it was the first time she allowed herself to take a deep breath.

"I am so relieved to see ye safely home," said Finovola. "I cannot tell ye how many nights I cried myself to sleep."

"I'm so very sorry. I had no way of sending ye the letters I wrote." Anya leaned into the lass as they ascended the stairs. "I knew ye would worry the most."

When she opened the door to the chamber the sisters shared, everything on her side was in its place as she remembered it, yet moving inside was surreal, as if she belonged there no more. "And how have ye fared, my dearest?"

"Aside from worrying about ye, things..." Finovola picked up a doll from Anya's bed and toyed with the lace on the collar. "Things have changed little."

"I figured ye would have told Ulster about my alcove."

"How could I not? That was the first place we looked."

"I dropped the key and was unable to enter through the cellar gate."

"Aye, we found it. Needless to say, our guardian has replaced the lock with something far sturdier."

"Unfortunate."

"Do not tell me after your ordeal ye would deign to slip beyond the castle walls ever again."

No, Anya's sister would never do anything to subvert their guardian's authority, but even after everything that had happened, Anya could not imagine always being trapped inside. And though she had been guarded by Rory, her ever-present wolfhound, she hadn't really felt trapped at Dunyvaig. "I suppose not."

"Ye seem overtired, my pet." Finovola sat on the

bed, hugging the doll. "Will ye ever recover from being absconded by the vile MacDonald scourge?"

Anya's nostrils flared as she clenched her fists so tightly, her nails dug into her palms. "Don't say that. Never again refer to Islay thus."

"I beg your pardon? Ye are referring to Angus Og, are ye not? Fairhair the Terrible with the heart of a devil? The very brother of the scoundrel who killed Da?"

Turning away, Anya didn't want her sister to see her face. True, only hours ago the same thought had crossed her mind, but that had been when she was at the pinnacle of anger. "He's nothing like his brother. Even his mother agrees."

"What are ye saying?"

"I don't know." Anya buried her face in her palms. "The Lord of Islay showed me unexpected kindness. If he had not, I would now be laboring in a monastery for the duration of this war, working my fingers to the bone until I was no longer of marriageable age."

Good heavens, had she just repeated Angus' words? Had he truly been thinking only of her welfare when he chose to take her home? It had hurt so badly to know she'd never see him again, Anya had been unable to look beyond her own pain to see the goodness in his intentions.

Why had she stood on the pier and said nothing when, on bended knee, he'd so passionately kissed her hand? Why had she let him sail away?

17

It was nearly dawn by the time Angus and his men dragged the *birlinn* onto the shore at Dunyvaig Castle. "Let us go inside and break our fast. I intend to set sail for Turnberry by the hour of terce."

"No time to sleep?" asked Raghnall.

Angus gestured to the half-dozen clansmen who'd sailed to Ireland with him. "We will have enough men aboard each boat for ye to close your eyes whilst sailing to the mainland if need be."

No one uttered a word as Angus led the way into the hall. It was a good thing they'd all kept mum. At the moment, there was nothing he'd like more than to bury his fist into someone's face. And why the bloody hell had saying goodbye to Anya nearly sent him to Hades? Dammit all, he had made his decision and that was the end of it.

After helping himself to a bannock, he left his men in the hall and headed up to his chamber to splash some water on his face and clean his teeth, but before he reached the door, Mither stepped into the passageway. "It is done, then?"

A tic twitched in his jaw as he gripped the pommel of the dirk he wore on his belt. "Aye. Anya O'Cahan has been returned to her home. Where she ought to be, mind ye."

"If ye believe that, then ye are a fool."

"Thank ye, Mither. 'Tis nice to ken what ye truly think of me."

"Bless it, son, I've said it afore, and I'll repeat it now. Ye are stronger than both your father and your elder brother in brawn and your mind is keener, but I do believe God gave ye the short end of the stick when it came to your heart."

"Mayhap that's why I feel as if the worthless organ has been ripped from my chest and thrown to the briny deep," he growled, pushing into this chamber and letting the door swing closed behind him.

He stormed to the bowl, and splashed his face, the brisk water providing enough of a shock to clear his muddled mind. After cleaning his teeth and changing his shirt, Angus started below stairs. Stopping at the landing that led to Anya's chamber, her door caught his eye. Rory no longer occupied the chair she'd placed in the passageway. Angus detoured and grabbed the chair, intending to return it to its place at the small table but once he stepped inside the empty chamber, the onslaught of memories arrested him.

Leaving the chair in the center of the room, he strode to the bed and gazed upon the coverlet, neatly tucked into the mattress, appearing as if it hadn't been used in ages. But he knew differently. Not long ago, he'd sat at this bedside for hours, praying for Anya's fever to break.

He picked up the pillow, drew it to his nose, and closed his eyes. Heaven help him, Anya's scent lingered. As he hugged the cushion to his chest, he imagined holding her in his arms, watching her laugh, watching her draw with a charcoal, watching her chat animatedly with Friar Jo every eve at the far end of the high table.

But it was time to turn his attention to the duty at

hand. Angus was the leader of a powerful clan and if the king didn't send him to the gallows for disobedience, there lay a great many battles ahead. As he moved to replace the pillow, a scroll of vellum tucked under the bedclothes caught his eye. He plucked it from its hiding place and unrolled it.

Good Lord, Anya had drawn a picture of herself atop the wall-walk, gazing out to sea—gazing toward Ireland. She'd caught every detail from the wind picking up her hair to the satiny texture of her skin. Angus could almost smell the salty water, feel the breeze cut through his linen shirt. Most of all, he imagined caressing her cheek with his knuckle, then turning her face up to his and kissing those inviting lips.

"Damnation!" he cursed, slamming the pillow back in its place. He rolled the blasted scroll and shoved it into his sporran. Did she have no idea what leaving such a picture would do to his worthless heart?

Blast it all, his mother was wrong. When it came to his heart, God had made his too large for his chest and too easily broken. Angus could not afford to pine and wallow in misery. That is exactly why he had not allowed himself to fall in love since Ella, and it was exactly why he must buck up now and forget Anya O'Cahan had ever entered his life.

HAVING GONE WITHOUT CLOSING HIS EYES FOR TOO long, Angus felt as if his head was filled with flax tow as he and his men strode through the gates of Turnberry Castle.

"What are ye planning to tell the Bruce about the lass?" asked Raghnall.

Angus thumped the man-at-arm's helm. "I'll wager that question has been needling at ye since I decided to take Miss Anya back to Carrickfergus."

"Aye. And so it should do. 'Tis no' as if ye have a seasoned heir waiting in the wings when the king sends ye to the gallows."

Angus ground his molars as he adjusted his sword belt. "I aim to tell the bloody truth."

Raghnall rolled his eyes skyward. "God save us."

"Wheesht," Angus growled. "Oh, ye of little faith."

"I happen to like my faith, as well as my skin," Raghnall mumbled under his breath.

Arthur Campbell approached and extended his hand. "'Tis good to see ye, Islay. It seems ye've arrived in time to face the English yet again."

Angus clasped the knight's forearm in a show of solidarity. "When do we march?"

"Soon." Campbell led the way into the keep. "Spies have reported the English are readying to move northward."

"We need a victory."

"Aye, we need a parcel of them."

"The Lord of Islay," boomed the steward as Angus stepped into the great hall.

The walls were festooned with tapestries in rich reds and verdant greens. Behind the dais stood a fireplace, spanning the entire width from wall to wall.

Robert the Bruce looked to Angus, as all heads turned. Many a powerful men sat at the board with the king—Lennox, Boyd, Douglas, and Keith, to name a few.

"Greetings, m'lord," said the king. "Ye must have had a favorable wind to sail to Orkney and back in such a short time."

Angus didn't flinch, though he expected a fair bit more banter before revealing his disobedience. "I must have a word."

"Then say it." Robert gestured to the men at the table. "There are no secrets between us."

A bead of sweat trickled from beneath Angus' helm.

He removed it, wiped the perspiration away with the tips of his fingers, and tucked his helmet in the crook of his arm. "With all due respect, sire, Miss Anya O'Cahan does not deserve to spend the years of her prime cloistered in a dank monastery working like a common crofter. She's only a maid—of marriageable age, mind ye. To deliver her into the hands of the monks would be sealing her fate to a life of misery."

The color drained from the king's face. "A life of piousness, mind ye."

"Aye."

"So that is why ye arrived so soon? The lass is still at Dunyvaig with your mother?"

"Nay, Your Grace." The muscles in Angus' abdomen constricted, readying himself for a blow. "She is at Carrickfergus with your father-in-law."

"What's this?" the king boomed with spittle shooting from his lips, his eyes ablaze. "I give ye an explicit order and ye defy me? Moreover, ye have the nerve to stand here afore me with helm in hand? Exactly what makes ye think I'll spare ye from a climb up the Turnberry gallows steps?"

"Forgive me." Angus bowed.

"Forgive? Have ye forgotten the Queen of Scotland is imprisoned in some godforsaken stronghold in England? Is my young wife not in *her* prime? Doubtless, your cock has marred your judgement."

The king's ire merely served to strengthen Angus' resolve. The one thing keeping him from spending the rest of his days in a miserable pit was his numbers. Robert Bruce needed him as an ally. At least for now, and that might purchase enough time for Angus to exonerate himself. "Hear me afore ye pass judgement, sire. Upon our next battle, I give my solemn oath I will capture a bevy of high-ranking English—men of far more value to Edward than the mere daughter of an Irish lord."

Robert drummed he fingers, but it was Sir Douglas who sat forward and cleared his throat. "He's right. An English nobleman is worth three of O'Cahan's daughters."

"But I will not be defied!" The king pounded his fist on the table. "For this misdeed, I want a solid victory and a cache of prisoners. Dammit all, the MacDonald army will lead the charge and every last man will be the first to face the cold steel of Longshank's knights. And if by some miraculous stroke of God ye survive and do present me with English nobles with whom I can barter, I *may*...I repeat...I *may* no' choose to sever your cods from your ill-begotten loins."

"That is only fair," Angus replied, his tone pitched a tad higher, sweat rolling from his temples. "My men are ready, sire."

Robert glowered. "They had best be."

18

As the door to her chamber opened, Anya hid her drawing of Angus under the mattress.

The countess entered, her expression dour while Finovola followed wringing her hands, her brow pinched. Behind them came the midwife who delivered all the local women's babes.

"Is all well?" Anya asked, while her back shot to rigid. In seven years, Anya couldn't recall Her Ladyship ever visiting her bedchamber. The woman always sent a messenger.

"I truly hope it will be." The countess gestured to the midwife. "Ye have been in the company of a rogue and, as your guardians, Ulster and I must ensure ye have not been compromised."

Finovola hid her face in her palms and lamented, "Oh, dear."

"Compromised?" Anya clutched her arms across her midriff. "How could ye think me capable of such a disgrace?"

"I will accept not a word of your insolence. It is our duty to ensure your maidenhead remains intact."

Anya scooted away. "I have assured ye with my word. I am untouched."

"So say you." Her Ladyship thrust her finger toward

the bed. "Lie upon your back now, unless ye want me to call upon the guards and make this more unpleasant that it needs to be."

Anya glanced to her sister, who stood aghast as if this humiliation were being bestowed upon her. But she had no choice. It was already mortifying enough to have such an examination with only women present. She might die of embarrassment if guards were brought in. Heaving an enormous sigh, she climbed onto the bed and lay on her back, her every sinew as taut as harp strings.

The midwife moved beside Anya and gave her shoulder a gentle pat. "Not to worry, miss. Ye ought not feel a bit of pain. All I need is a wee peek and the unpleasantness will be over."

Pressing the heels of her hands against her eyes, Anya cringed. "Just be done with it."

"I'll need ye to spread your knees."

Merciful heavens, a fire burned within her breast. How dare they doubt her word? As the woman raised her skirts and peered into the most secret place on Anya's body, she wanted to scream. She wanted to tell the countess how much she'd enjoyed being a lady-in-waiting for the Dowager Lady of Islay. If only Anya could tell this shrew how wonderfully she'd been treated.

True to her word, the midwife did not linger and quickly covered Anya's legs. "She remains untouched."

"Thank heavens," said the countess. "I'm quite astonished, truth be told, given the Lord of Islay's reputation."

A tear slipped from the corner of Anya's eye. Her Ladyship would never understand the sense of honor and duty that lay in the heart of Angus Og MacDonald.

Her Ladyship snapped her fingers. "Come. Both of ye attend me in my solar."

During her years at the castle, Anya had interacted with the countess far more than Ulster, who was not only the most powerful man in Ireland, he had a way of making everyone around him uneasy. Though it was a rare occasion to be summoned to the great hall by her guardian, not long after her humiliating examination, Anya was not surprised when the sentry came to the lady's solar and requested she follow him at once.

When she stepped into the hall, she hesitated, taking in a few breaths to slow the beating of her heart. After her ordeal with the midwife, she wasn't yet ready to face His Lordship who, to her chagrin, was seated beside Lord O'Doherty. By the somber expressions on both men's faces, something was amiss, for certain.

"Haste ye, lass," demanded her guardian. "We haven't all day."

Anya quickened her pace, pattered up to the dais, and curtseyed. "My lords. Is all well?" Out of the corner of her eye, she spotted Finovola exit the door from the kitchen, carrying a tray with the countess' tonic.

Lord O'Doherty's gaze flickered to her sister. When again he regarded Anya, he lowered his chin to his chest, his expression vacant.

Ulster adjusted the earl's medallion he wore suspended from shoulder to shoulder whenever he held court. "Might I remind ye that the negotiations for your betrothal were to be sealed on Saint Valentine's Day?"

"Aye. I have not forgotten." Anya pursed her lips. She had hoped her guardian would allow her some time to recover from her ordeal before he broached the subject of her nuptials.

"I am sure ye will be happy to learn the terms have been agreed and ye will marry Lord Chahir O'Doherty a fortnight hence."

Gasping, Anya clapped a hand over her mouth. Simultaneously, Finovola dropped the tray, shattering the cup, spilling tincture across the floorboards.

Lord O'Doherty started to rise, but the earl grabbed his forearm. "Sit."

"Must we wed so soon?" Anya asked, while her sister dashed through the hall and fled to the stairs.

"'Tis time for ye to cast aside your foolishness. This is a good match. And mark me, after your misadventure with the Scots, I was forced to augment your dowry to obtain His Lordship's agreement. Thank God your virtue is still intact, else there would have been no hope for ye whatsoever."

Her face burned as she kept her gaze lowered. So this was to be her fate? "Aye, my lord."

"Furthermore, I have decided that ye must remain in your chamber until your wedding day. I cannot have ye slipping beyond the castle walls yet again."

"What of Finovola?" Anya asked. "Is she to be imprisoned as well?"

"I've given the guards instructions to allow your sister to come and go so that she may continue her service to the countess. But ye, my dear, will nay be given such leave. If ye should disappear again, Lord O'Doherty has informed me he will not renew his offer."

Anya dared glance at the man she was to marry. His eyes immediately shifted away. He did not smile, nor did he offer any expression to make her believe he derived any satisfaction in the arrangement. "Is this what you desire, my lord?"

Though her question was directed at Lord O'Doherty, her guardian answered, "Indeed, the contract has been signed. Now off with ye. I've many supplications to hear this day."

With a snap of Ulster's fingers, Anya was joined by two guards who led her away. As she climbed the stairs, her forehead beaded with sweat. She did not know Lord

O'Doherty well but was quite certain the man had been coerced into agreeing to the marriage, the proof being the increase to her dower funds. His Lordship no more wanted her as his wife than she wanted him as a husband.

But Angus Og MacDonald had gone for good. Anya closed her eyes only to have an image of Islay consume her mind as if he were standing in front of her now. Oh, how much she had relished their time together—strolling atop Dunyvaig's wall-walk with him. Gazing out over the sea. Being in his arms. Kissing him. Dear Lord, what she wouldn't give to kiss him again. If only Robert the Bruce had let matters lie, she might still be on Islay, working on the tapestry drawing for Her Ladyship, and teasing Rory as he followed her about. Aye, Angus had posted a guard outside her door, but otherwise she had been free to come and go as she wished. Now, her guardian had decreed she was to be locked in her bedchamber for a fortnight until her wedding day.

Alas, most highborn marriages were arranged without giving consideration to love. Many brides did not meet their husbands before the ceremony. Though Chahir O'Doherty had been known to Anya for years, in all that time, they had exchanged merely a handful of words. She did not know him as she knew Angus. She did not love him as she loved Angus. And now she was to join in holy matrimony with a man she was quite certain harbored no fondness for her whatsoever.

So flummoxed by this state of affairs, Anya did not remember her journey above stairs, standing dazed as the guard opened the door to her chamber and gestured inside. "Miss."

Still unable to believe her lot, she held her chin high and strode inside. Anya's heart might be torn to shreds, but she was not about to act the victim. Especially not when everyone in the castle thought the match was favorable.

"Not to worry," said the second guard. "A fortnight will pass in no time, and then ye will be Lady O'-Doherty."

As the door closed behind her, across the room, Finovola lay with her face buried in a pillow, her body wracked with muffled sobs.

Immediately shedding her own woes, Anya dashed to her sister. "Whatever is the matter?"

The lass turned toward the wall, hugging her arms across her body. "I cannot say!"

"Nay, lass, ye mustn't hold your woes inside." Climbing onto the bed, Anya mirrored her sister and wrapped her arm around her shoulders. "Have we ever harbored any secrets between us?"

"This one is unforgivable. If I dare utter it, I fear ye never will be able to look me in the face again."

"Oh aye? Is your secret as abhorrent as me developing a fondness for the Lord of Islay?"

Finovola hiccupped with her cry. "F-fondness?"

"Merely a wee bit of affection, I'd call it. I could not help myself." Now Anya was telling tall tales. The first time she'd set eyes on Angus, he'd taken her breath away. But that was not the issue at hand. She sat upright and urged her sister beside her, holding her in an embrace and rocking gently. "Come now, my pet, tell me what has ye out of sorts."

Finovola had been crying so intensely, she could barely catch her breath. "I—am—too ashamed to utter it."

In the hall, Anya had been rather surprised at Finovola's reaction to the earl's news. And the night before, she had also noticed her sister sitting beside Chahir at the high table. "Have ye a care for Lord O'-Doherty?"

"Oh, if only what I felt in my heart were merely a care." Finovola buried her face in her hands. "I cannot help myself. I love him."

"Oh," Anya said, while a stone sank to the pit of her stomach.

"I'm so ashamed," Finovola wailed. "I have always loved him, from the very first time he visited the castle. But I swear we did not act upon our affection until after..."

"After?"

"After the men Ulster sent to find ye returned emptyhanded." Finovola rocked to and fro. "I was bereft with grief and, God save me, I found comfort in His Lordship's a-a-arms," she cried, launching into another hiccupping bout of sobs.

Anya was not unfamiliar with finding solace in a man's arms. And she'd felt plenty guilty about it as well. But her own sister loved the man she was contracted to marry? It seemed familial betrayal was rife between them. How could life be so cruel as to deny Finovola of the love she craved, forcing Anya to wed the same lord? How could she possibly go through with the wedding ceremony now?

The lass sucked in a gasping breath. "H-he promised to ask for my hand, but then ye returned. And ye know how persuasive Ulster is. Chahir pays fealty to Ulster. Going against the earl's wishes would ruin him."

"I'll wager Lord O'Doherty tried to back out of the agreement. Our guardian told me he was forced to add to my dowry."

"It is hopeless! Ye know there is no chance Ulster would allow me to marry first. Ye are the eldest and I cannot ruin your prospects."

"Hush." Anya swirled her palm around her sister's back. "If ye love him, then His Lordship ought to face the earl and speak the truth."

"He cannot! Not when the agreement is already signed."

"I beg your pardon, but the marriage vows have not yet been spoken."

"A plea to Ulster will not work, I swear it." Finovola grasped Anya's arm and squeezed, her expression filled with suffering, her eyes swollen and red. "And ye do not understand the extent of my sin. I am *ruined*."

"Och, nay," Anya whispered, hugging her sister tightly.

But as they sat clinging to each other with Finovola's sobs filling the chamber, the condemning significance of her sister's words sank in. "*Ruined* did ye say?"

"Have mercy on my soul," the lass cried. "W-we pledged our love. Chahir told me he could wait no longer—that he wanted *me*. And I was too weak to resist. I am nothing but a wretched jezebel!"

Scarcely able to breathe, Anya released her arms while Finovola curled over, and cried all the more.

"Is this why Lord O'Doherty is still in attendance at Carrickfergus so long after Saint Valentine's Day?"

Gasping for air, the lass nodded while tears spilled from her eyes. Of course, the lordling had not stayed to assist Ulster's efforts to find Anya. The man had stayed to woo Finovola. If Angus had waited to take her home, her sister might have received the proposal which she so desperately desired.

So many warring emotions coursed through her, and not all of them kind. By the rood, Anya had only been gone for a couple of months and yet in that time, her husband-to-be had courted her sister.

Had he mourned?

No.

His Lordship most likely never gave a fig about Anya's whereabouts. And then he'd been so obsessed with wooing Finovola, he'd bedded her. A sickly feeling swirled in Anya's stomach. Chahir O'Doherty had stolen her sister's maidenhead without giving care to Anya's plight. Adding insult to injury, the cur had never once tried to kiss Anya or hold her hand. At the countess' insistence, they had once taken a stroll together atop the wall-walk and they'd barely spoken.

Yet the man had readily pledged his affection to her lovely, winsome sister.

After all, Finovola was prettier, lither, more gifted with embroidery, and, as far as Lady Ulster was concerned, was exceedingly more suitable to be the wife of a nobleman.

Anya hopped off the bed and paced, clutching her fists against her stomach. "I cannot marry the man ye love. Good heavens, ye could be impregnated with his child."

Finovola responded with a heart-wrenching wail. "Nay, nay, nay! Ye deserve him far more than I."

"But I do not want him," Anya spat.

"How can ye say that? He is the sun and the moon and the stars."

Anya stopped her pacing and stamped her foot. "I do not love him. I *never* wanted to marry him."

With Anya's every word, it grew harder and harder to breathe. She needed to leave this chamber and think. To clear her head, she needed the wind on her face. If only she could run for her alcove. Marching across the floor, she jerked on the latch but the door didn't budge.

How the devil was she going to help her sister and wheedle herself out of this disaster when she was trapped inside this godforsaken room?

19

After days of meetings with the Bruce and his knights, spies finally arrived announcing Lord Aymer de Valence was marching his English forces to Stirling—exactly what Angus needed to win the king's favor. Together with six hundred soldiers, the Scots hastened to Loudoun Hill, where it took three days for Angus and his men to dig trenches in the boggy marshland before the pass. Ever since Longshanks first invaded, the English cavalry had dominated most battlefields, making it nearly impossible for the Scots to defend. The Bruce's army was still so poor they had no cavalry and their army of foot was lightly armored at best. Angus had seen for himself brave Scottish solders trodden to death under the hooves of the horses of English knights. And he wasn't about to allow such barbarism to happen again.

"Dig it deeper," Angus hollered, inspecting the third trench. "It will be *your* throat cut if we cannot stop their cavalry."

Covered with mud, Raghnall hopped out of the hole. "With the thicket to the east and the enormous rock on the right, we'll stop them."

"Never allow overconfidence to mar your judgement," said Angus, looking up the craggy hill that presided over the pass that led to the north. Loudoun Hill was a landmark, the top of which could be seen for miles to the south.

At the top, a soldier blew a ram's horn. "The enemy is less than three miles out."

"Cover the trenches with brush," barked Angus, picking up an armload of rushes they'd cut to camouflage the ditches.

"Are they deep enough?" asked a sentry.

"They'll have to be."

James Douglas approached, riding one of the few warhorses in the king's retinue. "Did ye hear?"

"Aye, and as soon as we have the trenches covered, we will stand in plain view as agreed."

"After ye have words with de Valence, Campbell's archers will fire from the hill and take out as many front men as possible. Once ye engage, I'll lead the second regiment of foot and attack their flank."

"We will be ready."

Angus belted the orders for his army of nearly three hundred men to take their places behind the trap, Douglas and his army hid from sight, as did the archers above. If de Valence sensed the possibility of a quick victory, he would be more likely to give the order for his cavalry to surge forward with a head-on attack.

At least that was their plan.

Marching across the line of men, Angus thrust his sword above his head. "At last, this is the day for Scotland to reign victorious. We have favorable ground, men. We will render their horses useless and put their knights under our blades. Nay, not all of us will survive this day, but we will die knowing that the blood we shed was not lost in vain. God save the king!"

"God save he king!" boomed the men, thumping their targes and raising a hellacious racket.

As Angus stood ready with a sword in one hand and a dirk in the other, the thunder of the English approach shook the ground. On the wind, the boom of the enemy's drums reached him before the sun glistened off the first soldier's helm.

But all too soon, the enemy's numbers multiplied until countless horse and foot stopped but fifty paces from the trenches.

"I am Angus Og MacDonald," he bellowed, standing front and center. If these were to be his last words, he wanted to be damned sure everyone heard. "In the name of Robert the Bruce, the true King of Scots, I bid ye turn back now or face your doom."

"MacDonald, is it?" De Valence walked his steed forward, first glancing to the top of the hill and then to Angus. "Another traitor come to take on the greatest army in Christendom. We will be happy to slay ye and your lot of bedraggled miscreants."

With the slight, laughter resounded from the enemy ranks—laughter that served to make Angus hate them all the more. "Suit yourself but let no one say I did not give ye fair warning."

Angus signaled to the only archer in sight atop the hill while de Valence gave the order for his cavalry to prepare arms.

"Look at them," moaned a sentry no more than five paces away. "They outnumber us at least three to one."

Facing his men, Angus again thrust his sword into the air. "We are the sons of the MacDonald of the Isles, of Somerled, and his clan. The blood of the most powerful men ever to call Scotland home thrums through our blood. I swear by all that is holy, we will make these *sassanach* bastards tremble in their boots. This is *our* day and we will not fail!"

The ranks erupted with a tumultuous battle cry while the English cavalry thundered forward.

"Hold!" Angus shouted.

The horses charged head-on into the trap, horses falling into the boggy trenches with nowhere to go. The men atop the hill barraged the English with an onslaught of arrows sailing toward the flailing knights. Only then did Angus slice his sword through the air and lead the charge. "Advance!"

Confused and already bloodied, the English stood knee-deep in mud as the Scots bore down upon them. The heinous sounds of battle swelled around him as pikes pierced through flesh and the clang of swords clattered. Shrieks and groans of the wounded and dying rose louder as Angus pressed forward with Raghnall at his side, both men fighting as if Satan himself were blowing fire up their backsides.

By the time Aymer de Valence gave the order to retreat, the English had suffered countless losses. Angus and his men surrounded a half-dozen well-armored knights, knee-deep in mud, standing back-to-back, so exhausted they were scarcely able to raise their swords.

"Throw down now and we'll spare ye," Angus shouted. "I give my word, no harm will befall a one of ye."

"I'd rather finish them," growled Raghnall.

"The king needs these bastards alive. Relieve them of their weapons and bind their wrists." Angus leapt onto the high ground and faced the king's army. "Sons of Scotland, God has looked upon us with favor this day. Let it be known that Robert the Bruce will hide no more!"

AFTER THE BATTLE, THE BONE-WEARY SCOTS CAMPED with the Trinitarian monks at Fail Monastery. By the next day, their energy was once again restored on the march to Turnberry, where they were met with a feast of the king's venison and casks of ale.

Angus opted not to dine at the high table and made merry with his men. "Ye all proved your worth and instilled the fear of the MacDonald in the hearts of the English."

They raised their tankards and bellowed their Gaelic war cry, "*Fraoch eilean.*"

"Let us march on Sterling!" shouted one.

"Aye, afore the bastards have time to regroup!"

"I commend your spirit," Angus replied, though he knew they did not yet have the numbers for a successful march on the stronghold known as the gateway to the Highlands. Nonetheless, this was no minor victory and, with the news, the king and his nobles were already bringing in fresh recruits. But they needed tens of thousands more to end this war.

Angus swilled his ale and chuckled as he watched his men celebrate. After the loss at Loch Ryan, it felt good to be triumphant at long last. Mayhap he had even redeemed himself with the Bruce. At least he prayed his efforts at Loudoun Hill were enough to regain a modicum of favor.

Raghnall grabbed the ewer and poured himself another pint. "What is next, m'lord?"

Angus released a long breath as he stared into his frothing ale. "I need to right a wrong."

"I beg your pardon?"

He finished his drink and climbed off the bench.

"Where are ye off to?" asked the man-at-arms.

"Off to cut my own throat, I reckon."

"Then I'd best go with ye."

Raghnall started to rise, but Angus grasped his shoulder and urged him to stay put. "I've something I must do. Remain here and if the king doesn't sever my cods, I'll return anon."

Though he ought to be inflated with the frenzy of a victor's mirth, Angus headed for the high table with a heart as heavy as a five-stone rock. Even the roar of the crowd ebbed to his ears, replaced by the thumping in his chest and the rush of every breath.

Robert gave him a nod. "Come join us, Islay."

"My thanks," he said, taking a seat across.

The king leaned forward on his elbows. "Why do I perceive ye want to talk?"

"Because I've something to say that cannot wait."

"Ye have made up for your blunder with the O'Cahan lass, though I..."

"Nay, I have made amends for nothing."

Robert sat back and stroked his beard. "Go on."

"It is true, I greatly desire favor in your eyes. I pledged my men and my sword to ye and Scotland. I provided ye with a safe haven through the winter. I also supplied men and boats more than once and will do so any day at any time for any reason. And though my losses are not as great as yours, my brother fell to the MacDougall and for that I will not rest until the Lord of Lorn is in his grave. Aye, I am the first to admit I have made mistakes, but my biggest blunder was saying goodbye to Miss Anya O'Cahan."

The king snorted. "'Tis a wee bit late to realize that now."

"Aye, but it is no' too late to beg for forgiveness."

"Och, but I have already forgiven ye, lad."

"Nay, 'tis the lass who must forgive me, and then I wish for nothing more than to marry her."

"The daughter of an O'Cahan?" asked the Bruce, with a belly laugh. "Are ye in your cups?"

"I've had but two pints of ale this night and I'm as sober as a lark on a chilly Highland morn."

When a serving wench landed in his lap, Angus promptly set her on her feet, then met the king's steely-eyed gaze. "Sire, I beg your leave come dawn."

"My leave? Are ye telling me ye intend to confront Ulster?"

"Under the flag of parley—and this time without men-at-arms behind me. Not even Ulster would dishonor the black flag waved without threat."

The king drummed his fingers on the handle of his tankard. "Very well, I shall grant ye leave. But have a care. My father-in-law has been quite clear as to where his loyalties lie."

"Aye, and that is exactly why I'm going alone with no army to provoke him."

20

Angus set sail beneath an overcast dawn sky but with a favorable breeze. But by the time his *birlinn* passed the Isle of Rathlin, the north wind had kicked up her ire, bringing rain, and making the voyage perilous. When the square sail collapsed and flapped like wet bed linens, Angus tied the tiller in place before he lunged for the boom's rope, whipping through the air.

As it slashed across his face, the boat listed starboard and sent him crashing to his back, but by some miracle, he managed to catch the rogue rope in his fist. Grunting as he stood, Angus adjusted the boom's angle until the sail again billowed, making the boat shoot through the white-capped waves like a dart.

Before the wind overpowered him, he wrapped the rope around a cleat and secured it with a knot. Only then did he return to the tiller, setting a course for Carrickfergus.

Battling the storm not only sapped his strength, it took the lion's share of the day, but by the grace of God, Angus sailed into the protection of the harbor before dark. He tied the *birlinn* to the pier and splashed some water on his face and then made his way to the sea gate, which, unlike his last visit, was closed and heavily guarded.

"Who goes there?" asked a sentry, peering through a barred viewing panel.

"Angus Og MacDonald, Lord of Islay." He held up the black flag. "I've come alone and in good faith to request an audience with His Lordship."

The viewing panel shut and great deal of shuffling sounded beyond the gate. When it opened, Angus faced a dozen men with pikes leveled at his heart.

He spread his arms. "I come in peace under the truce of the flag of parley."

"Relieve him of his weapons," barked the man-at-arms.

Angus had hoped to be shown a courtesy by arriving alone. Nonetheless, he surrendered to the inspection of a nervous wastrel who skittered forward and removed his sword and dirk.

"I'll be wanting those back," Angus growled.

"Not so fast," said the leader. "Take the knives in his flashes and search him."

Biting the inside of his cheek, he endured the search while the little weasel took both of his *sgian dubhs*. Bless it, the bastard even removed the eating knife from his sleeve. It was good for them, they did not frisk his loins, or bother inspecting the contents of his sporran where he kept the charcoal picture Anya had drawn of herself.

Only then did the man-at-arms give a nod. "Diamond formation men. Pikes at the ready and if he takes one step out of line, skewer him."

"I appreciate your kind hospitality," Angus grumbled as the blunt end of a pike jabbed him in the back.

Inside, music grew louder while they moved through a passageway. Blinking rapidly, Angus fought to adjust his vision to the dim light when ahead the leader signaled for the retinue to stop in the archway of the hall. Beyond, an ensemble of minstrels performed with lute, flute, drum, and voice.

The earl and his countess watched the performance from their high-backed thrones. Flanking them were knights and high-ranking officials, and a skinny lass with blonde hair peeking out from under her veil. Angus craned his neck and searched for Anya, but she was not to be seen.

The guards waited until the song concluded to polite applause.

"My lord," said the man-at-arms, motioning for the retinue to march forward. "The Lord of Islay has arrived alone, requesting an audience under the terms of parley. Ought we throw him in your gaol?"

Ulster chuckled. "The gaol might be too good for the likes of him."

"I bid ye hear me, m'lord," boomed Angus, trying to step forward, only to be stopped by the sharp point of a pike leveled with his eyeball.

The earl leaned back and crossed his arms. "Ye have nerve coming here, that I'll say. After your exploits at Loudoun Hill, I doubt I need to tell ye it is too late to pledge fealty to Edward."

A stabbing pain needled Agnus' back. He hadn't expected the news of the battle to travel so quickly. "I've come neither for political gain, nor for political ruin. I am without arms or army, facing ye as a man, wishing for an audience, one man to another."

"Ye'll never have an audience alone with His Lordship," growled the guard.

Ulster stroked his beard. "Why would ye risk coming here?"

Angus shifted his feet. It would be a great deal easier to say his piece without a crowd, but come what may, he'd have out with it. "I come to ask for the hand of Anya O'Cahan."

The blonde lass gasped, clasping a hand over her mouth.

The earl leaned forward. "What games are ye playing? Ye had the lass in your clutches for months. If ye wanted to wed my ward, then why did ye bring her back?"

"'Twas my mistake."

"Come now, Islay. Ye may be a lot of things, but daft is not one of them. Ye expect me to believe ye did not intend to return Anya into my care?"

Angus looked to the rafters. He only had one chance at this and he could not afford to shove his boot into his mouth. "Robert the Bruce ordered me to move Miss Anya to a monastery so that he could use her for negotiations in exchange for his wife—your daughter, mind ye."

The earl snorted. "The fallacies grow more convoluted by the moment. So, my lord, ye willfully disobeyed an order from the King of the May?"

Good God, on any other day, he'd challenge the bastard to a duel of swords for such a scathing slight. "I did."

"And I'll reckon he has no idea ye are standing here now, begging to wed my ward."

"This time I have his blessing."

"Unbelievable." Ulster examined his fingernails. "Regrettably, ye are too late. Her union with Lord O'Doherty has already been set."

"My lord," said the blonde lass. "I think—"

"If I wanted to hear your thoughts I would have asked," clipped the earl before returning his attention to Angus. "Ye, sir, have committed treason of the highest order. Ye are an outlaw, and I'll see to it your lands will be forfeit to the English crown."

"I have come in peace under the flag of parley. Where is she? I bid ye grant me due respect—"

"Ye lost your right of respect when ye took up arms

with my treasonous son-in-law." Ulster thrust his finger forward. "Angus Og MacDonald, ye will be flogged and suffer the hospitality of my prison guard. And I am quite certain Edward will be all too happy to parade ye through the Traitors' Gate beneath the Tower of London. Ye made a grave error by coming here, an error that will cost ye your life! Remove him from my sight!"

Angus grabbed the nearest man's pike, wrenched it from his hands, and jabbed him in the throat with the blunt end, using the momentum to drive the spear into the guard's chest behind. Spinning in place, he cut down two more before a blow to the back of his head sent him face-first to the floor.

The iron taste of blood filled Angus' mouth as the point of a sword cut into his cheek.

"Take him to the post!"

THE DOOR OF THE BEDCHAMBER FLEW OPEN AND Finovola hastened inside and dashed across the room. Cupping her hands around her mouth, she shouted in a whisper, "Ye will never believe what just happened in the hall!"

Anya set her book aside. "Tell me now."

Being ever the dramatic one, the lass clapped her palm to her forehead and gasped. "The Lord of Islay arrived under the flag of parley and asked for your hand."

By the stricken expression on her sister's face, it took a moment for the news to sink in. "Please say ye are not jesting!"

"'Tis true, but it is awful! Ulster refused to honor the code of parley and called Islay a traitor." Finovola grasped Anya's hand and tugged her toward the window as shouts rose from the courtyard below. "He demanded the guard to seize him and now they're taking him to the courtyard to be flogged."

"No!" Anya pulled aside the furs.

Finovola thrust her finger toward the courtyard. "There he is."

Anya's knees buckled as guards muscled Angus to the post at the far wall. "Stop!" she shouted, her plea falling on deaf ears. She searched the faces and recognized no MacDonald kin. "Where are his men? Where is Raghnall?"

"He came alone, without a single man-at-arms."

"God, no." Anya winced as they tore the shirt from Angus' flesh. "Why would he do such a thing?"

"Because he loves ye." Finovola's voice sounded haunted as she turned away and hid her eyes. "I cannot watch."

The whip hissed through the air and made a red stripe across Angus' back.

"No!" Anya shouted so loudly, her voice grated, but the roar of the hecklers below swallowed her plea. How could they be so callous when he came alone and under the accord of parley?

Filled with horror, she watched as they turned His Lordship's back into minced meat, until Angus' legs gave out from under him, yet he uttered not a sound, his silence sending an eerie message that he would not be broken. "Mercy," she cried, while the crowd repeated in kind.

Once it was done, Ulster appeared in the courtyard with Lord O'Doherty on his flank. Though she couldn't hear what was being said, guards dragged Angus away—and there was no doubt they were taking him to the filthy prison below the main gates.

"How dare they treat him like a common criminal." Anya's stomach convulsed. "He'll die down there."

Anya grasped Finovola's shoulders. "I must see him!"

"Aye? And exactly how do ye intend to do that? Not only is there a guard at our door, there's no chance anyone can slip past the men guarding Ulster's gaol. And then..."

"Then? What is the earl planning?"

"He mentioned taking Angus to the Tower."

"Of London? When?"

"He didn't say."

Anya paced. "Soon?"

"I know not, though I would suppose soon. The longer Islay remains here, the greater the chance of a MacDonald attack."

There was one person who would know, one soul who might help. Anya grasped Finovola's shoulder and looked her in the eyes. "Did ye speak true? Ye are in love with Chahir O'Doherty?"

"What the blazes does that have to do with things now?"

"Do ye love him?"

"Aye."

"And he returns your love?"

Finovola nodded emphatically. "He said he did."

"Then bring him to me."

"Up here? The countess will flay me."

"Nay, 'tis me she will flay. Nonetheless, to ensure the guards do not suspect anything, ye will act as my chaperone."

"I don't know if he'll come." The lass bit down on her fingernail. "What should I say?"

"Tell him I need to speak to him." Anya slammed her fist into her palm. "Tell him it is a matter of life and death. Go at once!"

21

Ever since she watched the horrors in the courtyard, Anya had been at her wits' end, furiously knotting her bed linens. How dare Ulster treat the Lord of Islay like a common criminal? Not only was Angus of noble birth, he had come to Carrickfergus in good faith, to ask for her hand of all things! And he'd been punished severely for it. Worse, the torture had only begun.

Anya felt as if she could jump out of her skin. And if she didn't act swiftly, Angus' fate would be sealed.

Because of me.

When the latch clicked, Anya startled. Hopping to her feet, she held her breath as Finovola led Lord O'Doherty inside.

"Ye'd best be quick, else His Lordship will hear about this," barked the guard in the passageway.

"Ye cannot deny the lass a chance to see her betrothed even if she is restricted to quarters," Finovola replied, her words like honey flowing from a spigot.

After kicking her work beneath her bed, Anya smoothed trembling hands over her hair. "Thank ye for coming."

Lord O'Doherty and Finovola exchanged glances

before the man regarded Anya with a frown. "This is very untoward."

"Forgive me, but it could not be avoided given my *imprisonment*." Anya led them away from the door and to the bench seats in the window embrasure, where they could speak without being overheard. "I have a plan to benefit us all. If the two of ye indeed want to marry, I must have your help, my lord."

Her eyes dancing as if filled with sunshine, Finovola clasped her hands, though Chahir appeared to be about as comfortable as a man sitting in a bed of nettles. "Ye are aware that Ulster is my overlord. I cannot and will not agree to anything that might put the earl or his men at risk."

"Ye will not. I swear it. The only favor I ask is for ye to take me to Dunyvaig...tonight."

Finovola gasped. "But ye cannot leave this chamber, let alone set foot outside the castle."

"With all due respect, I have been slipping beyond these walls for seven years. Do ye think I cannot spirit past a guard or two?" Sounding far more self-assured than she felt, Anya looked to His Lordship. "Tell me, when is Ulster planning to take Islay to London?"

"He hasn't said for certain, but the morrow is Sunday, and I do not reckon he'll set ships to sea on the sabbath. Did ye know his plans are to send Islay to Carlisle and have the Lord Warden take him to London?"

"Ulster is not accompanying him to the Tower himself?"

Chahir cringed, his gaze shifting to the woman he truly loved. "Not with our wedding coming so soon. He insists the ceremony cannot be delayed."

"Well, it will not be *my* wedding. On that ye have my solemn vow."

"Once ye leave, what should I tell the countess?" asked Finovola.

"Nothing. And she'll never know. The only time Her Ladyship has ever visited this chamber was when she brought the midwife. Am I wrong?"

"Nay...but she could come all the same."

"She will not. I swear she will not." Anya tiptoed to her bed and pulled out the rope of bed linens she'd hastily made, then returned to her perch in the embrasure, addressing her sister with a somber stare. "To purchase time for my plan to run its course, after the Lord of Islay has been gone for two days, ye are to report that I was not in my bed when ye awoke that morn. Tell the countess ye slept sound and did not wake."

"Wait two whole days?"

"'Tis the only surefire way Lord O'Doherty will not be suspected of intervention." She shook the rope. "We'll pile pillows under the coverlet so it looks as if I'm abed. If anyone asks, say I'm suffering a bout of melancholy. Then, once time has passed, tell the countess ye found my mode of escape and show her my makeshift rope. Let them form their own conclusions. Meanwhile, my lord, ye will be safely tucked away in your keep and none the wiser. After ye return ready to take your vows, and discover I have once again disappeared, ye will be free to demand Finovola's hand in place of mine."

"But my plan is to remain here until the wedding," said Lord O'Doherty.

Sitting straighter, Anya tightened her grip around the rope. "For the love of all that is holy, ye have a castle to run—lands and enemies. I do believe ye are able to conjure something that requires your immediate attention—requires ye to set sail for home this very night. With the promise to return for the wedding, of course."

Chahir brushed his fingers over the O'Doherty crest embroidered in the center of his surcoat. "Providing I agree to this, what is your plan? Fairhair is an outlaw.

Not only that, he's an enemy of your kin. My kin as well."

Anya blinked. No wonder Angus thought the man dull. He had no imagination whatsoever. "Do ye want to marry me or my sister? Think of your future, my lord. With whom do ye want to share a bed for the rest of your days?" Anya drew in a deep, calming breath. "I am nay destined to be your wife any more than ye are destined to be my husband, and the Earl of Ulster has been using us as his pawns for far too long. Are ye a man or a puppet?"

Finovola squeezed His Lordship's hand. "Please."

Anya stood. "I'll meet ye in the courtyard near the sea gate when the tower bell rings for the change of guard."

"But ye will be seen," said Finovola.

"Nay. At the change, the soldiers convene at the gate house—for a few moments, they will not be in view of this window. I'll wear a dark cloak with my hair hidden beneath the hood. No one will know 'tis me, let alone a woman."

"'Tis a grave risk," said Lord O'Doherty.

"One I'm willing to bear." Pursing her lips, she eyed him. "The question is, are ye?"

The man stood and offered a curt bow. "I will make my excuses as ye asked, but if ye are not there upon the change of the guard, I will sail without ye."

ATOP A PALLET OF MUSTY HAY, ANGUS CURLED ON HIS side. Every time he moved, hot pain seared his flesh as if he were being whipped anew.

Tap. Tap. Tap.

What the hell was the tapping? It rang out through the cavern of the dungeon cell and rattled in Angus' head, making it throb.

Where was Anya?

The fair-haired lass in the hall had to be Finovola. He'd spotted O'Doherty as well, but what had become of his Irish rose? Had he risked all for naught?

By the saints, if Angus knew Anya O'Cahan, she would move heaven and hell to see him. Would she not? Or was she still angry?

They hadn't parted on the best of terms, but he knew in his heart if he were allowed to face her and pledge eternal love, she would realize he meant every word. Except her guardian had proven as trustworthy as a gnat. There were unspoken rules between the nobility. Tying a nobleman to a whipping post in a public courtyard and issuing twenty lashes was unforgiveable. Especially when Angus had clearly arrived under the protection of the laws of parley.

Tap. Tap. Tap.

The high-pitched pounding was enough to drive a man to madness. Angus raised his chin ever so slightly and peered through the slits of eyes.

"The great Fairhair lives," growled a black-bearded cur, sitting on the other side of iron bars with his filthy hands gripping the picture of Anya that had been in his sporran.

"That's mine," Angus said, dropping his head back to the musty hay.

The man grinned, displaying a row of brown teeth. "'Tis mine now."

"I'll be wanting it returned."

"Ye'll not need it where ye are heading."

"And where is that?"

"Ye'll die in the Tower, mark me. And Longshanks will send the pieces of your body throughout Scotland just like he did with William Wallace."

Angus tried to swallow, but there was no moisture in his mouth. "Water."

Tap. Tap. Tap. The arse relentlessly kicked the bars

with an iron-tipped boot. "The lad will bring a ladle around...eventually." The guard examined the drawing. "Who knew the pirate with the devil's heart would lose it to an Irish lass?"

In a single move that made the flesh on his back sear with pain, Angus rolled to his knees and thrust his face through the iron bars. "Where is she?"

Jolting away, the man howled with an ugly laugh. "Ye may as well forget Anya O'Cahan. By the time ye arrive in London, she'll be married."

DRESSED IN HER BLACK SEALSKIN CLOAK AND wearing a kirtle of charcoal grey, Anya waited beside the window while her sister sat in the embrasure, then stood, then paced with her palms pressed to her temples. "This is never going to work."

"Stop!" Setting aside her makeshift rope, Anya tugged up her black leather gloves, grasped Finovola by the shoulders, and gave her a firm shake. "I cannot listen to a naysayer at the moment. The only way I will be successful is if we play our parts. Heaven's stars, all ye must do is mind guards and insist I refuse to allow anyone inside—for but two days. Can ye not do that for me?"

Finovola huffed. "Aye. I can."

"There's a good lass. And when this is all over, ye will be in the arms of the man ye love."

"But what if Ulster discovers our ruse?"

"As long as ye allow no one in this chamber, he will not." Anya took her sister's hand and led her back to the window. "When the sun rises, Sunday will be upon us, then all ye must do is wait one more day. When ye wake on Tuesday morn, tell the countess I've gone missing and show her the rope. They'll be none the wiser."

"Ugh!" Finovola threw her arms about Anya's shoulders. "I hope ye are right."

"I am right." Anya kissed her sister's cheek. "Furthermore, Ulster will curse me to hell for disappearing again. He'll not be able to deny your happiness, especially when Lord O'Doherty demands your hand in place of mine."

"Oh, bless it. Why does everything have to be so difficult?"

"Heavens, I'm the one risking my neck. All ye must do is bide your time—embroider and act like the winsome, compliant lass Her Ladyship adores."

The tower bell sounded, announcing the change of the guard. "I must go." Anya already had one end of the rope secured to the iron tieback on the wall. She peered out the window and scanned the wall-walk to ensure the guards had all moved toward the main gate.

Taking one last moment, she clasped Finovola's cheeks between her palms. "Never forget I love ye with all my heart. Ye are my blood and all these years, ye have been my confidant and my closest friend. I wish ye every happiness that ye deserve."

"Don't go," she whispered, a tear dribbling down her cheek. "We shall work it out somehow."

"I must make haste." Anya threw her rope out the window, gathered her cloak tightly about her body and climbed out. "As soon as ye see slack, pull it in as fast as ye can."

"But it isn't long enough."

Anya clutched the rope tightly. "It will get me close to the ground and allow me to jump without injury."

Without another word, she started on her way. But her gloves didn't grip well at all. Slipping, she darted downward far faster than she'd intended. By the time she reached the end, there was no stopping. Gritting her teeth, she swallowed her urge to scream while she dropped to the cobblestones, her knees jarring as she landed.

"Oof," she grunted while stars darted through her vision with the searing pain. With no time to spare, she drew in a deep breath. Above, the rope began to disappear, bless her sister's heart. The pain ebbed as Anya hugged the wall and tiptoed through the shadows, making her way to the sea gate. About halfway, footsteps clattered from the wall-walk and she chanced an upward glance to her window. A flash of white caught her eye as did the veiled amber from the candlelight within. Finovola must have dropped the fur because all at once the light snuffed.

Anya hesitated for a moment as the guard's march continued. Confident she hadn't been seen, she hastened through the shadows.

"There ye are," whispered Lord O'Doherty, grasping her elbow.

"The gate is open?" she whispered.

"For the moment. The earl knows of my departure. I informed him I'd received word of unrest." He hastened forward. "Now hush."

True to his word, the sea gate had been opened.

By the time they reached the pier, Lord O'Doherty's men had already hoisted the galley's sail, but Angus' *birlinn* caught Anya's eye. "A moment," she said, hastening toward Islay's boat.

"We haven't time," called His Lordship in a loud whisper.

But Anya ignored him, stretched for the MacDonald pennant, and raced back. "We might need this."

His Lordship offered his hand. "Sit in the bow and keep your head covered."

She gripped his fingers and allowed him to assist her to alight. "Thank you."

Chahir gave her a thin-lipped nod before he turned his attention to the crew. "Cast off."

22

Raghnall did not usually sleep soundly, but when the sentry banged on his door, a fog filled his head as if he'd been asleep for a week. As he forced his eyes open, the pounding came again. "Why the devil will ye no' leave me be?" he barked.

"An Irish galley is approaching."

Instantly awake, Raghnall sat bolt upright and shoved his feet into this boots. "Is it Fairhair?"

"Nay, but I swear there's a woman standing in the bow waving the MacDonald pennant as if her life depended on it."

Raghnall flung open the door. "How far out?"

"Close enough to cause trouble," said Gael, his eyes wide. "Shall we allow them to run aground?"

"Aye. Order the archers at the ready upon the wall. Ye said 'tis only one boat?"

"Only one. No other vessels in sight."

"Good lord, I pray Islay has not met with an untimely end." Raghnall belted on his sword and slung his cloak about his shoulders and started for the stairs of the guardhouse while his stomach roiled. If there was an Irish woman approaching, waving MacDonald colors, it could only be one female who'd risk her life to sail into the bay. "Assemble a retinue of twenty men on the shore."

Raghnall took two steps at a time while Gael followed. "Where are the archers?" he bellowed.

"Already waiting above the postern gate, sir."

"Good. No one fires unless I give the order."

"Understood."

By the time Raghnall's boots crunched over the stony beach, the galley was near enough for him to make out Anya's chestnut locks whipping against the dawn sky.

"They must have sailed all night," said Gael.

"Aye." Raghnall hailed the lass with a wave as the crew prepared to pull the boat ashore. But his gut sank to his toes when he made out the worry in her expression.

An armored Irishman hopped over the side and carried Miss Anya toward the beach.

"Raghnall!" she shouted while the man splashed through the surf. "Ulster has imprisoned the Lord of Islay. We must leave at once."

The Irishman placed the lass on her feet. "I've fulfilled my promise," he said, looking none too happy.

Anya curtseyed. "Thank ye, my lord. Be kind to my sister."

"Do ye require food, friend?" asked Raghnall.

"Nay, I only ask that my identity be forgotten. I was never here, understood?"

Raghnall gave a curt bow. "Understood."

Anya tapped his elbow. "This gentleman was kind enough to transport me here, though no one at Carrickfergus knows I'm gone."

"Ye took great risk to come."

"'Twas the only thing I could think of to do. Ulster intends to take Angus to London to stand trial—by way of Carlisle. We must leave at once."

"We?" Raghnall asked, watching the crew in the Irish galley man their oars and head back out to sea.

"Aye, Lord O'...I mean, the man who brought me here said Ulster would not set sail until after the sabbath. He plans to deliver Islay into the Lord Warden's hands at Carlisle and from there transport him to the Tower of London." Anya grasped Raghnall's arm, her grip surprisingly strong for such a wee woman. "And just yesterday they issued him twenty lashes. I'm afraid he's in no shape to fight, no shape at all."

"My God."

She gestured toward the moored MacDonald *birlinns*. "Come, sir. We must go."

"Perhaps, but ships and crew first need to be appointed and provisioned." Raghnall inclined his head toward the path to the keep. "I'm sure ye are tired after sailing all night, I bid ye go break your fast and take some rest."

"How can I rest when Islay's life is hanging on a precipice?"

To that, Raghnall had no response. Nonetheless, one thing was for certain, a rescue mission was no place for a female, even if she had risked life and limb to bring the news.

SINCE LEAVING CARRICKFERGUS, ANYA HAD FOCUSED on one thought—to free Angus from the clutches of her guardian and anyone else who saw fit to imprison him. But by the time she had entered the Dunyvaig by way of the kitchen, her purpose became even clearer.

"Miss Anya," said Cook. "I just heard the news."

"'Tis dreadful. Please tell me, how long will it take to provision the ships?"

"No more than an hour or two."

"Thank ye. I must find Lilas at once."

"At this early hour, she's most likely in her cottage."

It took but a moment to reach the dwelling, just beyond the castle gates. Anya rapped on the door. "Lilas, are ye within?"

"A moment," came the reply before the door cracked open. "Miss Anya? Something has happened."

"Indeed it has," she said as the healer stepped back and gestured inside, wearing a shift with a blanket wrapped about her shoulders. Drying herbs hung above, making the cottage smell like an autumn garden. Anya quickly explained all that had transpired. "I need a medicine bundle to take along. I'm afraid His Lordship's wounds are grave."

"Ye were right to come here. I'll prepare a salve for the welts and a tincture to ward off fever."

"Thank ye. I'd like to bring along rolls of bandages as well. Will ye be preparing the violets and whey tincture?"

"Aye." Lilas took a vial from a shelf lined with stoppered pots and the like. "But ye'll need this more. 'Tis the oil of avens. There is nothing better to treat open wounds. I only pray they have not already started to fester."

Anya left the healer's cottage with a basket filled with everything she ought to need to tend Angus' wounds. At least she prayed it would be enough.

From there, she made her way to the armory and found a bow. She tested the string for strength, then slung a quiver of arrows over her shoulder.

"What, pray tell, are ye doing, miss?"

Anya stopped short as if she'd been caught red-handed stealing weapons. With a huff, she stood taller and regained her composure. "Hello, Raghnall. I am preparing for the voyage, much the same as ye, I'd surmise."

"Did I no' make myself clear? Ye are *no'* sailing with us."

"With all due respect, you need me."

"Nay, if I were to allow ye to come, ye would sorely hinder our progress."

"Why? Because I am a woman?"

"Exactly. This is no' a game. We won't be firing arrows at targets, and I cannot be responsible for your well-being. Asides, Islay will have my hide if I allow ye to climb aboard one of those *birlinns*."

"And I will not stand for it if ye force me to stay behind." Anya held up the basket. "He needs me as much as he needs you. I'm prepared to treat his wounds."

"Are ye prepared to die? Because once we leave the security of the barbican walls, that is very well what may happen. There's no telling how long we'll have to lay in wait, or if we'll face a sea battle or will be forced to march inland. We could be gone for sennights—perhaps months."

"Which is exactly why I must go along." Anya picked up another quiver of arrows and slung it over her shoulder as well. "The Lord of Islay traveled to Carrickfergus to ask for *my* hand, did he not?"

Raghnall crossed his arms and jutted out his chin. "Aye, against my better judgement, and look where it got him."

Pushing past the man-at-arms, Anya marched on. "I will not be dissuaded on this...and if ye try to stop me, I'll...I'll..."

"Ye will what?"

"I will find another way, even if I have to sail a boat on my own."

"On the North Sea? Ye'll drown."

"Precisely, and what would the Lord of Islay say about that when he discovers I died because ye would not allow me sail in a MacDonald *birlinn*?"

When the man grew red-faced, Anya beckoned him.

"There's no use arguing the point. And I promise to tow my own weight without complaint. I am nay the daughter of Guy O'Cahan for naught."

Raghnall grabbed the remaining arrows and followed. "Lord save us all."

23

When they marched Angus out to the pier, he squinted to shade his eyes from the blinding daylight. How long had he been imprisoned in the dank shadows of the dungeon? Two days? Three? Wallowing in a constant state of darkness made it impossible to know.

The Earl of Ulster stood at the end of the pier where three galleys prepared to set sail, yet Angus' boat remained were he'd left it tied to a mooring cleat. He eyed the cur. "Three ships for one man? Are ye expecting a fight?"

"Where are your men, Islay? Rutting in the Highlands with my wayward son-in-law?"

Angus damn well hoped they were nearby. Except he had not expected the earl's wrath. Certainly, when Robert had paid a visit with an armada of armed men, there might have been cause for a battle, but when a highborn man came alone with his heart on his sleeve, it was against every chivalric convention to imprison him.

"Tie Fairhair to the anchor. If the MacDonald attack, throw the bastard overboard and let him sink."

The earl's hospitality grew more hideous by the moment.

Pushed from behind, Angus stumbled forward and climbed into one of the boats. He was immediately forced to sit while a beef-witted brute secured the damned anchor to Angus' wrists.

"Anyone who tries to hoist me over the side will be joining me," he growled, looking the behemoth in the eye.

The man squeezed Angus' arm. "They say ye have the heart of a devil, but I reckon your arms are as feeble as a newborn babe's."

"Aye." Angus tightened his muscle. "Would ye like to go a few rounds afore we set sail? Mayhap a swim in the bay will do ye some good."

Rewarded with a backhand across his mouth, the man laughed. "I'd like nothing more than to rearrange that bonny face of yours."

Angus licked the iron-tasting blood at the corner of his mouth, making a show of being unruffled. After the guard finished ensuring the anchor was secured, Angus feigned exhaustion. Leaning forward, he stealthily slipped a hand beneath his kilt and wrapped his finger around the *sgian dubh* hidden beside his loins. Dammit all, if they decided to throw him overboard, he wasn't about to be pulled to the depths by Ulster's anchor.

As the armada set to sea on an easterly heading, Angus masked his movement, ever so slowly sawing his knife through the rough-hewn rope.

From across the hull, a sentry glowered at him. "Ye have the look of a starved dog."

Angus stilled his hand while agonizing prickles tortured his back. "A few days wallowing in hell will do that to a man."

"Ye'd best grow accustomed to it."

God on the cross, he prayed it wouldn't be so. But he'd stupidly given Raghnall orders to come looking for him after a fortnight. Not enough time had passed. If Angus harbored any doubts about the sense of honor of those loyal to Edward, he certainly did not now. The Earl of Ulster was as much a backstabber as the king he served. If Angus made it out of this mess alive, it would be nothing short of a miracle.

With a favorable wind, it didn't take but a half day to sail into the Firth of Solway. On the northern side of the water lay Scottish lands with England to the south. Angus was so close to being home, if he shouted, a man might hear him on the shore. But he had no friends here, neither on water nor land.

"Where do ye aim to drop anchor?" he asked, knowing full well the earl's galleys were too large to navigate the River Eden and sail all the way to Carlisle. Not only would the crew be rowing upstream, they'd most likely run aground. Doubtless, the army would be marching to the city gates.

"Shut your gob," the behemoth replied to his question.

On a sigh, Angus returned his *sgian dubh* to its hiding place. The journey on foot might be a good place for an ambush. If only he had a retinue lying in wait—a dozen bowmen would do. As they sailed deeper into the firth, a pair of Scottish *birlinns* rounded the headland at Southerness.

Angus quickly averted his gaze. Did he dare hope?

It was midday on Sunday when the MacDonalds sailed four *birlinns* into the Firth of Solway. At the mouth of the River Eden, Raghnall and a small crew had taken the smallest boat upstream to scout about Carlisle and verify that the Earl of Ulster and his party had not yet arrived. It would be exciting news to march the Lord of Islay through the city gates in chains—and every man and woman in the shire would be talking about it.

Of course, there was no chance the man-at-arms would allow Anya to sail in the boat that went to Carlisle. But at least she had been allowed on this voyage, her boat commanded by Gael. Last night, their *birlinn* and one other had moored hidden in a cove off Southerness and lain in wait until morn. On high alert, even Anya had taken a turn at guard duty, watching the waters for approaching ships, be them Ulster's or otherwise.

True to Lord O'Doherty's word, no galleys bearing Ulster's colors were spotted until midday on Monday. The square sails of three of her guardian's ships billowed with a strong westerly wind, heading directly for the outlet of the River Eden.

As the MacDonald ships got underway, Anya shaded her eyes, trying to catch a glimpse of Angus, but they were too far away to make out anyone.

He's there. I can feel his presence in my soul.

"Do ye know what Raghnall has planned?" Anya asked one of the oarsmen.

"No idea, though our chances of nabbing His Lordship are far greater if we head off those ships afore they disembark."

"Then why are we staying so far away?"

"Because we do no' want them to ken we're following."

Anya checked her bow as well as her arrows. "But we're out of range."

"Aye."

"Unless we sail nearer, we'll be of no use at all."

"Patience, miss."

"Ugh." Anya wanted to pace, wanted to pick up an oar and row, wanted to do anything except sit on the uncomfortably hard bench and wait. She'd already bided her time long enough. They could have headed off Ulster's ships at the mouth of the firth. They could have attacked directly with an onslaught of arrows. But all this waiting was enough to drive her mad.

She thrust her finger in the direction of the boats. "Look, they're tacking southward. If we do not stop them now, they'll reach the English shore!"

As soon as the words left her mouth, Raghnall's ship and the other two MacDonald *birlinns* sailed out from a bluff on a direct heading for Ulster's lead boat. With the shifting of sails, the three Irish galleys started an abrupt turn toward the English shore.

"There he is," Anya shouted, spotting Angus sitting midship, his light hair whipped by the wind.

Raghnall's boat headed directly for the lead galley—aiming to ram them for certain.

Anya held her breath as the Scottish *birlinn* picked up speed.

"Archers!" shouted Gael.

With her bow in her fist, Anya planted her feet, letting her knees bend with the rocking of the waves. She drew an arrow from its quiver, aiming for the third boat, one not carrying Angus. And though it was near impossible to steady her bow, she didn't fire. What if she actually hit someone? What if she took a life of someone familiar? Good heavens, she hadn't thought about that.

A thunderous boom resounded across the white-capped surf as Raghnall's *birlinn* broadsided the lead galley. Water jetted high into the air while splinters shot out like darts.

As the Scottish ships encircled the Irish, an arrow hissed past Anya's ear.

A sailor yanked her sleeve. "Get down!"

She dipped behind the hull, peeking over the edge with her bow at the ready. If it came to life and death, she mustn't hesitate to use it. Ahead, another MacDonald *birlinn* broadsided the ship with Angus in another enormous spray of water. As the ship began to sink, two of Ulster's men grabbed Angus by the elbows.

"Dear God, they have him tied to an anchor!" Anya shouted.

"Man the oars," bellowed Gael from the tiller.

In Ulster's galley, Angus sprang to his feet and smacked a guard in the head with the anchor. As the second man reached for his sword, Angus hurled the anchor into the blackguard's gut.

Gael howled with a resounding laugh. "Leave it to Fairhair to use an eight-stone anchor as a weapon."

But Islay's plight was not humorous in the least. Anya thrust her arrow toward the sinking ship. "Row faster! The galley is taking on water."

As Ulster's men futilely set to bailing, the Lord of Islay bellowed a hellacious war cry and launched himself backward into the surf.

"No!" Anya screamed as men from the converging boats dove in after him. "Quickly, we must move closer."

As the sailors fought to cut through sea, she watched the mayhem with men diving and resurfacing while Ulster's galley disappeared beneath the waves.

"There he is," bellowed Gael from the tiller.

Anya's heart stuck in her throat as she scanned the surf, spotting a form swimming directly toward them. "Angus?" Could she hope?

With powerful strokes, the swimmer came nearer, while two men leaned over the side, stretched out their hands, and pulled him in.

"Angus!" Anya cried, tripping over rowing benches until she reached him and flung her arms around his neck. "Praises be, 'tis you!"

Laughing and crying all at once, she smothered his face with kisses.

His teeth chattered as he cupped her cheek and gazed into her eyes. "I returned to Carrickfergus to ask for your hand and met only with Ulster's ire. How did ye come to be here?"

"She's a tenacious lady, sir," said Gael, gripping Angus' arm with a Highland welcome, "I'll say for certain."

A giggle puffed through Anya's nose as she realized all eyes had turned her way while she'd flung herself into the Lord of Islay's arms—very soggy arms. "'Tis a long story."

"Come, men, we'd best set a course for Dunyvaig straightaway, afore any other wayward swimmers attempt to climb aboard," said Gael, circling his hand over his head.

As the sailors set to shifting the boom, changing tack, and taking up the oars, Anya explained about being imprisoned in her chamber, her escape, and her frantic dash for the Isle of Islay. "It turns out my sister is madly in love with Lord O'Doherty and he with her. Better yet, Ulster will never know His Lordship helped me. When Finovola reveals that I have disappeared on my own accord, Ulster will have no reason not to allow her to marry the man of her dreams."

Angus tucked a lock of Anya's hair behind her ear. "Nearly betrothed, no longer?" he asked, his teeth chattering.

"Good heavens, ye are freezing." Anya pulled off her cloak, but when she started to drape it over his shoulders, he stilled her hand.

"Nay, lass. I'll not be having ye catch your death."

"But—"

"No arguments."

"How are the wounds on your back?" She pointed to the medicine basket. "I've brought a salve from Lilas."

Hissing, he leaned forward. Fresh blood from the welts had seeped through the wet linen.

"Remove your shirt at once, my lord. There's not a moment to spare." Anya retrieved her bundle. "I cannot believe Ulster's poor treatment of ye. He ought to be flayed."

Angus rested his elbows on his knees while Anya carefully applied the soothing ointment. "One day he'll pay. But at the moment, there's nowhere I'd rather be than right here beside ye, *mo leannan*."

24

Once they reached Dunyvaig, Angus insisted on disembarking from the boat without allowing anyone to assist him, including the lass whose doting affection he'd immensely enjoyed on the voyage home. Only when his feet were firmly on Islay's soil, did he allow Anya to take his arm as they made their way into the castle. He never again wanted his woman to be out of his reach.

"Send up a pail of warm water, and tell Lilas His Lordship has arrived," she said, taking charge as if she were already the lady of the keep.

Angus liked her fortitude, but after enduring the lashes and the misery of the dungeon, the only person he wanted in his chamber was Anya. "Nay, no' Lilas. I will only allow ye to tend me. And I want a bath filled with piping hot water."

"But Lilas is a healer."

"I assure ye, it is no' healing I require."

"I—" Anya took one look at his face and held her tongue. "It will be an honor to tend ye, my lord."

Together they passed through the hall, greeting the worried clansmen and women as they made their way to the stairwell.

"Everyone is so happy to see ye," whispered Anya. "Ought ye announce a feast?"

"Later," he growled, needing her to himself. As soon as they arrived at his bedchamber, he pulled her inside, he kicked the door closed, and wrapped her in his arms.

Within the beat of his heart, he claimed her mouth, their kiss more impassioned, more deliberate, more intense than ever before. Every fiber in his body came alive as he tasted her, showing this woman exactly how much she had come to mean to him.

Angus' hands kneaded her back, urging her against his body, wishing she could remain in his arms for the rest of their days. "I never should have let ye go."

"I've chided myself over and over because I did not plead with ye allow me to stay."

"Can ye find it in your heart to forgive me?"

"After all ye have done? Angus Og MacDonald, I love ye from the depths of my heart. And if ye ever try to send me away again, I swear I'll skewer ye to within an inch of your life."

A knock came at the door. "I've the warm water, m'lord."

He let the servants in. "Place the tub beside the hearth, pour the water in, then let it be known I am not to be bothered."

Freya entered as well with a trencher laden with food. "I thought ye might care for a wee bite to eat."

"My thanks," Anya replied, blushing and giving the maid a friendly smile.

On her way out, Freya grasped the lass' hands. "It is ever so good to have ye back, miss."

Angus chuckled to himself. With what he was planning, by dawn the lass would no longer be referred to as miss.

When the servants had taken their leave, he locked the latch to ensure they would not be bothered. "I have the stench of Ulster's gaol upon my person."

"'Tisn't so bad after your swim in the Firth of Solway." The lass stepped forward and tapped the brooch at his shoulder. "Nonetheless, my mother always said there is nothing as refreshing as a tub, especially after a hard day's work or, in your case, a horrific ordeal." She scraped her teeth over her bottom lip as she glanced toward the door. "Shall I take my leave?"

Unable to help himself, he pulled her into his embrace. "I never want ye to leave my side again."

Anya wrapped her arms around him, placing her hands on his back, but when he drew in a sharp breath, she hopped away. "Goodness! Forgive me."

Sauntering toward her, he tugged her back into his arms. "There is nothing to forgive. When your hands are upon me, I barely feel a thing."

Lowering his lips to hers, he once again claimed her mouth, taking time to savor her.

Sighing, Anya caressed his cheek. "Ye'd best bathe whilst the water is still warm. Did ye not say piping hot?"

"Perhaps, but there's something I must do first."

"Oh?"

Taking her hand between his palms, Angus lowered himself to one knee. "I went to Carrickfergus to ask for your hand and was told I was too late. In that moment, I thought I'd lost ye forever. It was the darkest hour of my life. Ulster may have ordered the lash to be taken to my hide, but I did not feel the pain because my heart was bleeding for you and only you."

Tears welled in Anya's eyes.

"I love ye more than I love anything of this earth and I wish for ye to marry me here and now in the Highland way, between us, with God as our witness."

Anya squeezed his hand, her bottom lip trembling while a tear glistened, streaming down her cheek. "Yes, I will marry ye, Angus. I'm here because Finovola told me of your declaration of love in the hall. Nothing in this world would have stopped me from finding your arms."

Pulling him up, she again held him, this time careful to keep her hands away from his wounds. "I'm so happy."

Angus brushed his lips across her forehead as he unfastened her cloak, sending it to the floorboards with a swoosh.

Anya drew her fists beneath her chin as if bashful. "Truly, I should step out and allow ye to wash, my lord."

"I rather hoped ye would..." He unfastened his brooch and slid the brechan from his shoulder.

The lass turned scarlet as her gaze meandered to the tub of steaming water. "I would...?"

"Stay."

Anya's tongue slipped to the corner of her mouth. "But will ye not need to disrobe?"

"Aye," he replied in a low growl. "I want to see ye bare as well."

"Me?"

"Do ye ken what happens in a Highland marriage, lass?"

"I-I think so."

"Allow me to explain." Angus released his belt and let his brechan drop. "I intend to take ye as my wife, to bed ye, and do my best to plant a bairn in your belly."

"I-I-I reckoned that was what ye meant. Ah...but what will Friar Jo say?"

"He's ordained as a deacon and will want to marry us in the chapel."

"He will not banish us?"

"Och, lass, if he banished everyone who invoked a Highland bond first, there would be but a handful of parishioners attending his Sunday mass."

Her gaze raked down his body as she slowly untied the bow securing her bodice laces. "Well then, what would ye have me do?"

"I reckon the tub is large enough for the both of us."

"Both?"

"Aye," he said, his voice cracking as he pushed the kirtle from her shoulders. Angus wanted her so badly, he didn't know if he'd be able to wait. But then again, he did not want to claim his bride until he washed away all the lingering remnants of that damned rat-infested gaol. "Please?"

With a nod, Anya tugged up the hem of her shift and exposed her ankles.

Angus' breath caught as upward it went, giving him an eyeful of shapely calves, of silky knees, of feminine thighs plump enough to make her soft as down-filled pillows. "Take it completely off."

The adorable imp waggled her eyebrows. "Now?"

"Aye."

In one motion, she whisked the linen garment over her head and sent it sailing. Seeming to realize she was naked, Anya crouched and crossed her arms over her breasts, though not before Angus spied pure perfection. Untouched by the sun, her skin was like fresh cream, her breasts tipped by pink roses, the arc of her waist incredibly small, flaring into glorious hips.

Instantly hard, he removed his shirt and grasped her wrists, tugging her arms away ever so gently. "Ye must never hide from me, for in my eyes ye are the bonniest woman in all of Christendom."

Again, she raked her gaze down his body, gasping when she saw him standing as erect as a stallion. "Astonishing," she whispered.

"This is what ye do to me, lass."

In a heartbeat, he drew her into his body and kissed her. God on the cross, she felt so heavenly he never wanted to release this woman. Unable to drink in enough of his Anya, he slid his hands downward, pulling those luscious hips against his cock.

"Mm." With a womanly sigh that aroused him to the point of boiling, she moved in a swirling rhythm. "Angus...ought we bathe, my love?"

"Aye." With a trembling hand, he led her to the tub.

"Are ye certain the friction will not hurt your back overmuch?"

"Having ye in my arms, I can barely feel the wounds now."

Angus stepped into the water first, then urged her to join him. In each other's arms they sank into the tub, the fit so snug, Anya had not but to straddle him.

One of the servants had left a pile of drying cloths and a cake of soap beside the bath. Anya took the bar and drew it to her nose. "'Tis as fragrant as a lea of wildflowers."

She dipped it into the water and lathered his body. If it weren't for his wounds, Angus would have leaned back and closed his eyes and given himself over to her ministrations, but that didn't detract from the delight he felt from her gentle touch. Nor did it detract from the anticipation of making her his wife. He wanted this woman clear to the depths of his soul. He would worship her, love her, adore her and, if the odds were stacked against them, he would die for her.

"NOW YOU," ANGUS SAID, SLIPPING THE CAKE OF SOAP from Anya's fingers.

"Ye mean to wash me as well?"

His eyes grew dark as his gaze meandered to her bare breasts. "I desire to place my hands on ye, lass."

Never in all her days had Anya thought being naked with a man would make her so indescribably wanton. Though a bashful voice at the back of her head told her to cross her arms, she knew he didn't want her to do so. She grasped the sides of the tub and tipped up her chin, opening herself to whatever he willed. "I trust ye."

And oh, his touch felt so incredibly divine. The soap made his fingers slick, and he kneaded her flesh with those strong, yet soothing fingers. Anya's breathing became labored as he cleansed her breasts as if they were as delicate as butterfly wings. Downward he continued, missing nothing, until he stopped at her sex.

"This is where I want to be," he growled like a devil —a very kind-hearted devil.

As he slid his finger into the most sacred place on her body, Anya's eyes flashed open with her sharp gasp.

"Relax," he whispered, covering her mouth with a kiss that left her with no doubt as to his affection.

He touched her with a swirling motion, so erotic, her head swam. "I think I am going to swoon."

"Simply having my hands upon ye makes me ravenous."

Anya grasped his shoulders and looked him straight in the eye. "Then take me. Take me to the bed and show me how a woman pleasures a man. Take me to the bed and make me your wife for all of eternity."

The corner of his sensual mouth lifted lazily, his eyes growing dark. "Ye have no idea how much your words stir the fire within me."

By the burning want swirling throughout Anya's body, she must have some idea what it felt like for him.

Together they stepped out of the tub, hastily drying each other with the cloths until Angus swept her into his arms.

"Oh my," Anya exclaimed. "Does the burden of my weight not hurt your back?"

He chuckled as he carried her to the bed and lowered her to the mattress. "I am no' holding ye against my back, *mo leannan*."

Anya reached for him, but he took her fingers and kissed them. "Allow me to gaze upon perfection."

No matter how much she wanted to cover her nudity, his words made a yearning pool in her loins, while a hot, swirling pulse of awareness thrummed through her blood. What he mightn't realize, was by stepping back, Angus gave Anya a gift, allowing her to drink him in. For all that was holy, the Lord of Islay posed a picture of unmitigated manhood. Gazing upon him made her wild with desire, made her want, need, hunger to lie with him. Made her crave the rough pads of his fingertips upon her flesh.

Taking a stuttered breath, her eyes devoured every inch of the only man Anya had ever loved. His sculpted chest, the rippled muscles in his abdomen that tapered to sturdy, masculine hips. Her tongue swept across her top lip and her breathing arrested when her gaze meandered to the blond curls surrounding his erect manhood. A flood of awareness surged between her legs as it had done when he'd touched her in the one place reserved only for him. Only for her *husband*.

With a deep chuckle, Angus lifted her chin with his pointer finger. "If ye continue to stare at my cock, I'll come undone." A feral growl rumbled from his throat as he took a step nearer and smoothed a finger across her lips, making them tingle. "God help me, ye make me want to do wicked things with your body."

Anya scooted over and patted the bed beside her. "Then do not delay."

Angus grinned and joined her, cupping her breast, greedily kissing her mouth. His hand worked magic as if he knew exactly what she wanted. He teased her nipple, and Anya replied in kind, kissing him, smoothing her fingers down his taut abdomen. But she craved more, needed closeness, needed all of him joined with her. She inched closer until she pressed her body against his, showing him how much she wanted him to make love to her.

The feel of his skin and the heat of his body made

her inner hunger rage. As if Angus read her thoughts, he kneeled over her, nuzzling into her neck, then trailing kisses down to her breasts. Anya gasped when his tongue circled the tip, so sensitive, a flame deep inside ignited as if fed by a gale-force wind. She arched her back and sighed as he caressed and suckled her.

"Your every touch intensifies the passion deep within me," she whispered, nearly breathless.

"'Tis only the start of the magic to come." Angus raised his lashes and met her gaze with a smoldering glint in his eyes.

Shuddering, Anya sank her fingers into his shoulders. The man who would make her his wife this night was virile, masculine, so incredibly desirable. Her tongue slipped to the corner of her lips. "I want ye to show me how a man makes love to a woman."

"Growing impatient are ye?" He grinned, this smile even more seductive than the last. "Not to worry, lass. It is all I can do not to ravish ye afore ye are truly ready."

Without another word, his kisses continued downward. Gooseflesh rose across her skin when he swirled his tongue in her navel.

With a rumbling growl, he combed his fingers through her sacred curls, his touch nearly driving her into madness. "I've dreamed of kissing you here."

"Kiss?" Anya's thighs quivered with his wicked wink. The memory of his finger teasing her in the bath made her desire stir like wildfire.

"Open your knees for me, lass." He grazed his teeth over his bottom lip, looking like sin and temptation served on a silvery platter. "Since the day we met, I've dreamed about this moment." Inhaling deeply, he coaxed her legs wider with his shoulders.

Mercy, with one lap of his tongue the passion inside her grew nearly to the point of bursting. A shrill gasp pealed from her throat. Again he licked. Unable to control herself, Anya rocked and swirled her hips, tossing her head from side to side.

Oh God, he slid his finger to her opening and circled it—yet another new sensation that sent her mind into a maelstrom of hot, driving need. His finger slid in and out while his tongue worked magic. Higher and higher her driving need soared until all at once her entire body went taut, hanging upon the precipice of pure ecstasy. A cry caught in the back of her throat. With her next gasp, the entire world shattered into pulsing bursts of euphoria.

When, finally, Anya regained her senses, she reached down and urged him atop her. "What happened to me?"

He nuzzled into her hair, his thick member pressing between her legs. "I gave ye a sample of what it will be like when I'm inside ye, *mo leannan*."

As she shifted her hips, his manhood brushed her, instantly rekindling the craving desire. She turned her lips toward his ear. "Show me how to bring ye the same pleasure."

AT THE SOUND OF ANYA'S VOICE, A SPIKE OF DESIRE hit Angus low and hard, making his ballocks squeeze. God save him, he was on the brink of losing his seed. Needing to contain his fervor, he rolled beside her and gazed into her eyes—intoxicating emerald orbs able to hypnotize and bring a man to his knees. "Do ye truly want me, lass?"

She nodded, her gaze drifting to his manhood. "More than I've ever wanted anything in all my days."

Having her eyes on him made a wee bit of seed dribble from his tip. He ran his finger around her nipple, aching to be inside her. "It might hurt. But I want our joining to be a memory ye will treasure in your heart."

She kissed him, her lithe fingers reaching down. "It will be. Joining with you will be akin to heaven." When her fingers lightly brushed the tip of his cock, Angus sucked in a ragged breath.

Gasping, she snapped her hand away. "Did I hurt ye?"

"Nay," he managed to croak. With a feral growl, he again rolled atop her, this time positioning his member between her legs.

She cupped his face in her hands. "Have I ever told ye how fine ye are to me?"

Angus kissed her, remembering how at first he believed she didn't care for him. "I'm glad of it." He moved his cock against her, his thighs shuddering as her steamy moisture spilled over him.

Anya arched and caught the tip of his member at her entrance. Angus could scarcely breathe as her moisture brimmed around him. God on the cross, he could spill in this very moment. But he wanted to make this the most memorable night of her life, show her exactly what she'd been missing. "I'll try to be gentle."

She nodded, her hips continuing their seductive swirling rhythm. Merciful saints, Angus was supposed to be the one seducing Anya, but without a lick of schooling, she proved an expert. Slowly, he pushed inside until she gasped.

He froze. "Is the pain too great?" he asked, easing the pressure. "If ye want to stop..."

Her fingers sank into his buttocks. "Nay." With a firm tug, she urged him deeper. God, he adored this woman. Ever so slowly, he slid into the length of her, and when he reached a wall, he gazed into her sultry eyes full-well aware he'd arrived in heaven.

"Is all well?" he whispered, nuzzling into her neck.

She moved beneath him. "Astounding."

Angus rocked his hips. "With this act, I am making ye my wife, Anya O'Cahan. Will ye have me as your husband, never to part?"

"Aye. I will be your wife and cherish ye and our children forever."

Forcing himself to wait, his eyes nearly crossed with his need to thrust. "Ye are my wife, and I am your husband in the Highland way and nary a soul can part us."

"I love ye."

"And I love ye as well, m'lady."

With his pledge, Angus could hold back no longer. A frenzy of passion claimed his mind. While Anya's fingers gripped his backside, he lost all control, his need growing while her breathing sped. Stars flashed through his vision.

Faster and faster he thrust. Anya cried out, clinging to him for dear life. His heart hammered, as a feral roar burst from his throat. Blessed euphoria pulsed through his blood while, with one last thrust, he crashed into a sea of glorious release.

Angus held himself over her, his head dropping forward as he fought to catch his breath. "Lord have mercy," he growled, while the rhythm of his heart began to steady.

Pushing up on his elbows, he raised himself high enough to clearly see his wife's face. Her lips swollen and slightly parted, her heavy-lidded gaze, silken hair sprawling in a mass of tangle, framing her darling face with its splay of saucy freckles. God save him, she defined the epitome of feminine beauty.

With a satiated sigh, he kissed those freckles he so dearly adored. "Was it good for you, lass?"

She swirled her hips beneath him, stirring the passion again. "So wonderfully astonishing, there are no words to describe it."

"Ye are the world to me." Breathing deeply, he rolled

to his side and pulled Anya flush against his body. "Ye ken I adore ye with all my heart."

She rested her head on his chest. "And I you, *husband*."

Oh, how her words warmed his heart. Angus combed his fingers through her hair, cherishing the softness of it. The woman in his arms made his chest swell with pride—made him want to be a better man. In Anya's arms he was, not a lord, not a chieftain. He was merely a man who adored this woman to the depths of his soul. And he fully intended to revel in her love until the sun rose on the morrow.

25

While Angus lay on his stomach, Anya applied the avens oil to his wounds. "I reckon Lilas works miracles because these nasty welts look better than they did yesterday."

His Lordship grunted. "I wish they felt better."

She coughed out a wee laugh. "I thought ye said ye feel no pain when ye're in my arms."

He twisted his head enough to give her a devilish waggle of his eyebrows. "Then crawl back into bed and I shall be healed."

Anya hummed as she worked in the oil, careful not to let it run onto the bedclothes. After a night filled with ravenous passion, she was a bit sore. "But ye told me we must go to the hall and announce our nuptials." In truth, she was in no hurry. Everyone in the castle must know what had happened between them last eve. And though she would have things no other way, looking the clansmen and women in the eye was not going to be easy.

"We do, though ye cannot fault a man for trying."

She brushed his hair away from his face and kissed his cheek. "Will ye have such an insatiable appetite forever?"

He tugged her downward and nibbled her ear.

"When it comes to my bonny wife, yes, most definitely."

How on earth was he able to render her utterly smitten with a whisper?

With a sigh, he sat up, pulled on his shirt, and tucked it into the waist of his brechan. "No matter how much I want to stay and while away the day with ye in my arms, we'd best venture below stairs afore my mother sends a search party."

Anya squeezed his hand while her stomach did the same. "I suppose we cannot put it off any longer."

"Are ye nervous?"

"Terribly so."

He cupped her cheeks between his palms. "Do not be. Always remember ye are the Lady of Islay and the woman I have chosen to be at my side."

"Yes, my lord," Anya said, pulling his plaid across his shoulder and securing it with the chieftain's brooch.

He offered his elbow. "M'lady."

It was a relief to have Angus at her side, but as soon as they stepped into the hall, everything grew deathly quiet. All heads turned their way before the benches scraped the floorboards while everyone shot to their feet.

"Mercy," Anya whispered under her breath.

"Smile," he replied, starting down the long aisle to the dais, where the Dowager Lady of Islay sat in the seat that rightfully now should be Anya's. Fortunately, the woman was smiling. Friar Jo, however, appeared as if he'd just swallowed a bitter tonic.

As they approached, Her Ladyship stood and greeted them at the top of the stairs. "Son, I pray ye have tidings of good news this morn."

Angus said nothing as he kept Anya at his side and turned to face the crowd. "I have invoked the Highland vow of marriage and claimed this woman as my wife. Welcome the Lady of Islay to the clan!"

"Oh, rapture!" cried Her Ladyship as the hall erupted in a resounding applause.

"Let us break our fasts," said Angus before he led Anya to the table and gestured to the lady's chair.

She hesitated and glanced to the dowager.

"Nay, lass. Your place is at your husband's side. I've always prayed this day would arrive."

"I beg your pardon, m'lord," said Friar Jo, wringing his hands. "This pagan custom ye have invoked is quite unfounded."

Angus plucked a goblet from the table and signaled for a servant to fill it. "Have ye a solution?"

"Ye must marry in the chapel straightaway. Ye cannot wait. I shall deliver your vows this very day to ensure your souls do not end up in purgatory for the rest of your days."

Anya clapped a hand to her chest. "This day?"

"There can be no exceptions."

Angus gave her arm a nudge. "The friar has spoken."

"If it must be today, then there is no time to spare." Her Ladyship clapped her hands. "Send a tray to my chamber for the Lady of Islay and tell Freya to join us there straightaway."

As Anya was about to take a bite of porridge, Angus' mother grasped the spoon, set it aside, and pulled Anya to her feet. "Come with me."

She looked longingly at her food. "Now?"

"Ye can eat above stairs." Her Ladyship smiled to the friar and then to her son. "We shall arrive at the chapel following the midday meal."

With that, Anya found herself whisked into her mother-in-law's bedchamber. "We've much to do if ye are to be properly married this day."

Smoothing her hands over her hair, Anya moved farther inside. "I haven't brought anything to wear. I did, after all, jump out of my window with nothing but the clothes on my person and my cloak."

"And that is exactly why I hastened to bring ye up here." At the foot of her bed, the lady opened an ornately carved cedar trunk, pulled out a dress, and shook it. "I wore this when I married Angus' father."

Anya stepped in and examined the fabric, taking note of the intricate embroidery around the neckline. "Is this silk?"

"It is."

"Oh, my, 'tis ever so soft and the embroidery is exquisite. I love the birds...all different sorts and colors, aren't they?"

"Aye. It is difficult to believe the colors haven't faded after all this time."

"Did ye do the stitching yourself?"

"I did."

"I see ye were quite talented even back then."

"I suppose I had a good teacher."

"Your ma?"

"I began under her tutelage, but when I showed a wee bit of promise, she sent me to the master weaver in our village. He was renowned throughout the kingdom —even made tapestries for the king."

Anya had no doubt as a young lass, the dowager had shown more than a wee bit of promise. "And ye were allowed to be apprenticed, even though ye are a woman?"

"The weaver didn't like the idea at first, but one does not grouse overmuch when one is given a directive by the lord and lady who control the lands upon which one's shop was built."

"Ye were most fortunate."

A knock came at the door. "I've a tray for your ladyships."

"Come," said the Dowager Lady Islay.

Freya stepped inside. "I figured since I had been summoned, I'd bring the food ye requested."

Anya plucked an apple and took a bite. "'Tis ever so

good to see ye again, and I'm glad ye will be tending me."

Freya set the tray on the table. "I've missed ye as well, m'lady. I hope ye don't mind, but I took the liberty of clipping some bluebells from the garden. I thought ye might like a crown of blooms on your wedding day."

Anya bent down to sample the fragrance. "These are perfect, thank ye for thinking of me."

"Have ye considered who might give ye away?" asked Her Ladyship.

Straightening, Anya drew her hand over her heart. If only her father were still alive. She couldn't ask Friar Jo because he'd be conducting the ceremony. Raghnall was a possibility. After all, he was shipwrecked on the Isle of Nave with her and Angus. "Rory," she blurted.

"The guard?"

"Whyever not? He spent a great deal of time watching over me during my *imprisonment*."

"Well, then, I have no doubt he will be honored."

ANGUS PACED AT THE FRONT OF THE CHAPEL WHILE Raghnall looked on with his arms crossed. But it was well after the noon meal. The welts on his back needled him to the point where his temper was on edge. He barely felt the pain when Anya was near, but as soon as Mither had taken her above stairs, the agony had set in. "We sent a messenger hours ago."

Raghnall tapped his boot on the flagstone. "I do no' believe the bell has rung since. That means an hour has no' yet passed."

Angus panned his gaze across the crowd of clansmen and women who had amassed for his wedding. "Ever the practical one," he growled under his breath. "It feels as if eons have passed."

"Good Lord, I do no' believe I've ever seen ye so

overwrought in all my days of serving ye, m'lord, and all on account of a wee Irish lassie."

"My wife, mind ye. The ceremony is merely a formality."

The man-at-arms crossed himself. "Oh, ye of little faith."

Angus rolled his eyes to the cross atop the altar. "Wheesht." Perhaps the order of his marriage had been a bit back to front, but considering one sundown to another, everything was perfectly executed, or it would be if his bride would make an appearance.

The door swung open and young Fenn burst through. "Her Ladyship is approaching!"

"Thank heavens for small mercies," said Raghnall, moving beside him. "I was afraid ye'd wear a hole through the flagstone."

Choosing to ignore the man's remark, Angus watched the steward lead his mother to the front pew. Her smile couldn't have been broader as she gave him a nod. But his attention was soon drawn away by the gasps of awe from the crowd.

Anya stepped inside on the arm of her guard, Rory, who appeared to be as happy and as proud as a father giving his daughter away to a king. The bride looked a tad nervous until her gaze met Angus'. In that moment, as she strode forward, all the onlookers seemed to vanish, making it seem as if they were the only two people on the entire Isle of Islay. His bride wore a flowing gown of silk, which fit snugly enough to give him a glimpse of the shapely form beneath its folds. In her hands she carried a bouquet of spring bluebells, the same blooms encircling a sheer veil atop her head.

Aye, he'd thought her the most radiant woman he'd ever beheld this morning, but as she approached, there was absolutely no doubt in his mind that no one surpassed this amazing woman in anything. They were perfectly matched. What lass would fashion a rope out of bedclothes, climb out a window of her guardian's keep, and convince her intended to ferry her to Islay in order for her to raise an army to rescue the man she loved? If Anya hadn't done it, no one in all of Christendom would have believed it possible.

As she stepped beside him, he forced himself not to pull her into his arms. "Ye are stunning, m'lady."

Her gaze meandered down his body, making him feel like a god. "And ye look like a Highland king, my lord."

Friar Jo cleared his throat and began chanting the Latin mass while Angus stood staring into his bride's eyes. He must be the luckiest man in all of Scotland to be marrying a woman who not only could fulfill is dreams, she was a force to be reckoned with, his equal in the eyes of God.

"Give me your hands," said the friar, switching to English. When had he completed the rites? Angus had been so absorbed in his thoughts, the delivery of the rites had passed in a blur.

Anya smiled and held out her right hand while Angus offered his left. Friar Jo bound the two together with a stole. Angus gripped her fingers, so slight and delicate compared to his. She had the inner strength of a queen, yet she was no taller than the center of his chest. By all that was holy, he would love and cherish this gift for the rest of his days.

The friar placed his hand atop the bindings. "With the fashioning of this knot, all the desires, dreams, love, and happiness wished in your hearts shall merge. In the joining of hands, so are your lives now bound to one another, woven like the ever growing and intertwining limbs of a great oak. By the joining of hands, ye are now and forevermore bound to your marriage vows to love, honor, obey, and protect one another. This knot shall remain tied in your hearts for as long as ye both shall live."

Friar Jo made the sign of the cross atop their joined hands. "May this cord draw your hands together in love, never to be used in anger. May the vows you have spoken never grow bitter in your mouths. The knot creates the symbol of partnership and union. As your hands are bound by this cord, so is your partnership held by the symbol of this knot. Two entwined in love, bound by commitment and fear, sadness and joy, by hardship and victory, anger and reconciliation, all of which brings strength to this union. Always hold tight to one another through good times and bad, whilst ye watch as the strength of your bond grows."

Drawing their hands up above their heads, he recited a Latin blessing. "I shall now remove the cords."

The cool air chilled Angus' skin as the bounds fell away, though he did not release Anya's hand. "I never want to let go," he whispered.

She blessed him with a smile. "Nor do I, my love."

26

Enjoying the longer days of midsummer, Anya and Angus rode side by side as they returned from a journey to the Oa. There, Anya had completed her drawing for Mither's tapestry. "I'm ever so excited to show it to her."

"You mean to tell me, she didn't convince ye to show her your progress?"

"Oh, no. I never allow anyone to see my work afore it is complete. At least I try not to do so."

"Unbelievable, I say. Had I been the artist, my blessed mother would have found a way to snoop for certain."

"That is because ye cannot refuse her."

"I beg your pardon, I am the lord of these lands, I can refuse anyone when I so choose."

"Except her."

Flicking his reins, Angus coughed out a guffaw as they rode through the village of Lagavulin.

"Ye may say no at first, but she's your ma," Anya continued. "I'll wager she has been capable of twisting your arm throughout your entire life."

"Aye? Well, it is a lot easier to give her what she wants than to endure her ire. Have ye suffered her silent treatment?"

"Not as of yet."

"'Tis like death. I recommend avoiding it whenever possible."

Turning her mount onto the path leading to Dunyvaig's main gate, Anya tapped her heels and requested a trot. "I shall keep that in mind."

Atop the wall-walk, the ram's horn sounded with three consecutive blasts, announcing visitors were approaching by sea. Anya exchanged glances with her husband. "Whoever could it be?"

Angus' jaw tensed. "Go on to the stables. I'll meet ye in the hall after I've found out whether 'tis friend or foe."

Anya tightened her grip around her reins. "Surely Raghnall would have sent someone to fetch ye if there was trouble."

"Just do as I say," he said, though when he caught a glimpse of her pointed frown, he added, "Please, m'lady. I wouldn't want ye to be harmed."

Groaning, she gave in. "Very well, oh master protector."

"'Tis music to my ears to hear ye refer to me thus."

"Do not grow accustomed to it," she whispered under her breath, sure he couldn't hear her above the growing shouts from atop the curtain.

After parting from Angus, she hastened to the stables and was met by one of the grooms straightaway. "Have ye heard whose ship is on the approach?" she asked.

"The only news is the pennant is Irish."

Anya dismounted while the hair on her nape stood on end. "Is it the Earl of Ulster?"

"Not certain, m'lady. Would ye like me to go investigate?"

"Nay, please attend my horse and give him an extra ration of oats. He has earned it this day."

In a time of war such as this, Anya knew better than

to dash across the courtyard to the sea gate. Aside from inviting Angus' ire, she might put herself in harm's way. And if the visitor was Ulster, the earl might very well try to put her in irons. She hastened to the nearest corner turret, ducked inside, and pattered up the stairs. But when she reached the top, the view of the beach was blocked by a stony promontory.

"Blast," she cursed, hastening toward a row of bowmen. "Whose colors are they flying?"

"Not certain, m'lady, but..."

"But what?" she asked, stopping beside him and looking out to sea.

"I reckon since there are only two boats, they've come on friendly terms. Though in wartime, one can never be certain."

As the boats approached, there was no mistaking the long blond tresses billowing from beneath a woman's veil.

Gasping, Anya ran toward the north tower. "Stand down, I say! 'Tis my sister!"

Her toes barely touched the steps as she descended through the narrow, winding stairwell. "Angus!" she cried. "Angus!"

Raghnall met her as she dashed through the sea gate. "M'lady, 'tis not safe."

"But my sister is in one of those boats." Her gaze darted to the crowd of MacDonald guards, but she was so short, all she saw was mail-clad backs. "Angus, 'tis Finovola!"

Raghnall clutched her arm. "He already kens, but ye are to remain here until he is certain it isn't a trap."

With a tsk of her tongue, Anya strained for a glimpse at the approaching galleys, but still could not see a thing. "For the love of Moses, there is no chance any boat bearing my sister would approach meaning to do us harm."

"Ye are most likely right, but His Lordship would

skewer me if I allowed ye to race to the shore. Just give it a moment, m'lady."

A moment seemed like forever as shouts were exchanged, imperceptible over the roar of the surf. "What's happening?" she asked, ready to force her way through the men.

"Angus has confirmed the party has come in peace. He's allowing them to step ashore."

"May I go now?"

Raghnall held up his palm. "A bit longer."

"By the rood, 'tis my only sister who has come to call."

"Look there." The man-at-arms pointed.

"Look where? Given my height, all I can see is soldiers."

"Angus has given me the signal of all clear," he said, moving forward. "Make way, men!"

Unable to wait a moment longer, Anya pushed her way to her husband's side. "Did ye see, my dearest? 'Tis Finovola."

He offered his elbow. "And Lord O'Doherty. It seems the man has become accustomed to ferrying O'Cahan sisters to my island."

"Anya!" Finovola called while His Lordship carried her ashore.

Goodness, it was wonderful to see her sister, especially after fearing she might never be in her company again. Laughing aloud, Anya waved. "Whatever brings ye to Dunyvaig this fine day?"

When His Lordship set Finovola on her feet, she fell into Anya's outstretched arms. "Oh, sister mine, we happened to be sailing past..."

"Truly?" Anya asked, unable to release her embrace.

"In a word, I suppose, though we've come bearing a message from the earl." Finovola kissed her cheek. "Now tell me true, are ye happy?"

"Ever so happy, thanks to you and Lord O'Doherty."

Anya grasped her sister's hand. "And ye? How have things been these past weeks?"

Finovola blushed as she looked to His Lordship. "Well, Chahir and I married in the chapel at Carrickfergus and are sailing home to Buncrana Castle."

Anya's eyes widened. "'Tis wonderful news. Did ye hear, husband? My sister has married Lord O'Doherty. We must hold a feast this night in their honor."

"Agreed and congratulations," said Angus, shaking the Irish lord's hand.

"My thanks." Lord O'Doherty glanced to the women. "Would ye mind if we had a word, my lord? Perhaps in your solar?"

"Very well." Angus gestured up the path. "That is, if your bride can bear to be out of your presence for a spell."

Anya led her sister toward the keep. "I think we will be quite all right in the lady's solar. I cannot wait to hear the news."

They chatted animatedly while they made their way above stairs and behind the closed door of the solar, where Anya was relieved to find her mother-in-law elsewhere. She tugged Finovola to the settee in front of the fire. "Oh, my goodness, it appears as though all your dreams have come true."

"They did, though I worried that the earl would forbid our marriage."

"Oh? But Chahir left well before ye reported me missing, correct?"

"Aye, all proceeded as planned, but ye know His Lordship. He was suspicious all the same. After I showed your rope to the countess, I was summoned by the earl and...and..."

"Yes?"

"Well, by that time, the MacDonalds had attacked Ulster's galleys in the Firth of Solway and he was convinced Chahir had been involved."

"Ye didn't tell him I escaped with Lord O'Doherty, did ye?"

"Fortunately, I was never asked if I knew who had helped ye, or exactly when ye went missing."

"Ye stayed with our plan, did ye not?"

"I did, though it wasn't easy. I confided that ye had fallen in love with the Lord of Islay, and that ye wouldn't be happy until ye were in his arms. In truth, I think the earl blamed everyone who had visited Carrickfergus that week with Chahir high up on the list. Ulster was so angry. He denounced his association with ye, and nearly booted me out as well."

"Oh, heavens, I'm so sorry."

"I believe I would have been completely on my own had Chahir not arrived and convinced the earl of his innocence. And just as ye suggested, His Lordship turned the tables and pretended to be irate that ye had disappeared from the earl's care and yet again he was left without a bride."

"Did he demand your hand?"

"Aye, and Ulster told him to rot in hell."

"No...but ye are married."

"That is only because Chahir remained at Carrickfergus, as an uninvited guest, mind ye, and slept in the courtyard. For an entire sennight, he sang ballads below my window. And below the earl's solar, he shouted curses of how he had been wronged and how the Earl of Ulster would not honor his word."

"Good heavens, I never would have believed biddable Lord O'Doherty capable of such outlandish behavior. 'Tis a wonder our guardian didn't have him expelled from the gates."

"Aye, I think he wanted to. But, in truth, Ulster had no true evidence against him."

"Thank heavens."

"Except..."

"There's more?"

"His Lordship allowed me to marry Chahir providing he agree to bring a missive to Islay threatening an all-out war."

Anya gripped her hands atop her stomach. "Are we not already at war?"

"Aye, but this one is between the House of Ulster and the House of MacDonald."

"Do ye think he will attack Dunyvaig, or Dunaverty for that matter?"

"Well, I overheard him talking, and he said the MacDonald fortresses are too well fortified for a sea attack, just as Carrickfergus is. But if Ulster ever meets your husband on the battlefield, he has threatened to run him through."

Throwing her head back with an unfettered laugh, Anya slapped her hand on the seat. "Such a thing would be a sight to see. Angus is ten times the swordsman, not to mention a score of years younger."

Finovola picked up the dowager's embroidery and traced her finger over the precise stitching. "Tis all posturing if ye ask me. He's angry because ye not only usurped him, ye marshalled the MacDonald army, who then attacked his ships and stole an important political prisoner. King Edward will be quite upset that he wasn't granted the opportunity to have Islay hanged, drawn, and quartered."

With a shudder, Anya patted her sister's hand. "My heavens, perish the thought. Would ye not do the same if it were Lord O'Doherty en route to meet his end after declaring his undying affection?"

"I would sell my soul to save my one true love."

"Then we are of like minds."

ANGUS NEVER DREAMED HE'D BE SHARING A DRAM OF whisky with Chahir O'Doherty in his solar, but destiny had a way of unfolding unpredictably. He held his cup aloft. "I'm glad ye're here, m'lord."

O'Doherty mirrored the toast. "Oh, why?"

"Because it gives me a chance to thank ye for returning Anya to Islay."

The Irish lord sipped and licked his lips. "She's quite cunning, your wife. But truth be told, if she hadn't come to me with such a compelling argument, hell would have frozen over afore I helped ye, as inadvertently as it may have been."

Now that sounded more apt. "I take it ye'll be leaving come morn, then?"

"Aye." O'Doherty pulled a missive out from inside his doublet and placed it near Angus' hand. "The Earl of Ulster asked me to deliver this on his behalf."

"I don't suppose it contains congratulations for my recent nuptials."

"No."

Angus reflected for a moment. The man sitting beside him had been present when Ulster had refused to acknowledge the rules of parley and had put Angus in chains. O'Doherty also paid fealty to the earl and, by the missive sitting on the board, Ulster still trusted him. But Angus needed allies far more than he needed enemies. "What say you to a truce?"

The lordling knit his brows. "Truce?"

"Ye ken what I'm on about. Our wives are sisters. And I need allies in Ireland. Of course, it doesn't mean we're fast friends, but I'd think an accord not to raise arms against one another is in order. Agreed?"

"I think I can concur, providing ye have no plans to launch an attack on Carrickfergus."

"Such a fortress is impenetrable, 'tis well known. How thick are her walls? Fifteen feet?"

"I would surmise they are."

Angus stood and offered his hand. "Then it is

agreed. The House of MacDonald and the House of O'-Doherty are at peace."

Standing as well, Chahir accepted his hand with a firm grip. "At peace."

When the ram's horn announced the evening meal, Angus' gaze trailed to the missive. "Would ye mind leaving me for a moment? I'd best read this lest it contain something which may need my immediate attention."

"Very well, my lord. I'll see ye anon."

Once he was alone, Angus slid his finger under the seal and shook open the letter. And though it did not immediately call him out for a fight to the death, it contained scathing prose, insisting that one day Ulster intended to run Angus through. But what really stuck in his craw was the earl's damning of Anya and insisting she was to be banished from Ireland for the rest of her days.

Angus crumpled the vellum in his fist and pounded it atop the table. *The pox on him. The bastard is too arrogant to help his own daughter let alone anyone else.*

He tossed the missive into the fire. "Burn in hell, for I will think on ye no more."

He watch the calfskin turn the color of the ink while the fire consumed the bile spewed upon it. And once the letter turned to ash, Angus finished his whisky and headed to the hall to feast with his wife and celebrate her sister's nuptials. He mightn't see eye to eye with Chahir O'Doherty, but the man had been instrumental in saving his neck and was now kin. For that, a feast with music and dancing was in order.

27

Anya sat in her place at her husband's side as naturally as if she had been destined to occupy the seat of the Lady of Islay from the day she'd been born. Because distinctive guests were in attendance, the pecking order around the table had been rearranged a tad with Finovola gracing Anya's left and Lord O'Doherty taking Raghnall's seat on Angus' right. Needless to say, she was over the moon to entertain her sister in the great hall where music played in the gallery, the ale flowed, and joints of roasted venison and lamb graced the tables aplenty.

Anya nudged Angus' leg with her knee and leaned in. "Finovola tells me Ulster sent a missive. I hope it was cordial."

Her husband snorted. "It was rude and unfeeling. Moreover, the arse never once offered his congratulations for our marriage."

"I can imagine. He hasn't called ye out to do battle, has he?"

Angus raised his tankard to his lips. "Not in so many words, but it is unlikely we'll ever be allies."

"Unfortunate."

"However, I have agreed on a truce with Lord O'-Doherty, for what it is worth."

"Marvelous. At least that leaves the door open to visit my sister."

"Perhaps it would be better if she visited us. I think all parties involved would be more likely to keep their heads attached to their necks."

"Oh, dear. My guardian's missive must have been truly dreadful."

"Aye, and it has been reduced to ash where it should be."

Finovola reached for the bread and broke off a piece. "I never would have guessed the MacDonald hall would be so festive."

Anya gestured toward the tables, so proud of being a MacDonald. "There's a great deal ye wouldn't have guessed about my clan. I'm afraid our da's alliance with the MacDougall was, perhaps, misguided as was his opinion of my husband."

"Rest Da's soul."

Anya crossed herself. "If only he knew what I know now."

"And ye reckon Robert the Bruce's claim to the Scottish throne is founded?"

"I reckon he is the best man...the *only* man strong enough to wear the king's mantle and stand up to Edward. After all, the King of England is the one who declared himself overlord and invaded. He needs to remove his army from Scotland and leave us be."

"Listen to that." Finovola kissed Anya's cheek. "Ye have completely changed your alliances."

"Mayhap I have, but my eyes are opened. Not that I wish for the war. Every night I pray for a peaceful resolution."

"Ye mean ye pray for a miracle."

"I do."

Angus stabbed his eating knife into a bit of lamb. "If only the English saw it Her Ladyship's way, picked up their arms, and headed for their hearths, we'd all be at peace."

Everyone at the table laughed. Of course, it was too idealistic to believe peace would come so simply, but Anya would still pray for it. After all, her brother, Lord O'Cahan, still paid fealty to Ulster and Edward. As did the House of O'Doherty. Whatever truce had been agreed between the sisters' husbands would dangle on the precipice of fragility until the war ended.

"We've spent far too much time speaking of politics. Where are the minstrels?" Anya asked. "I believe I'm in the mood for dancing!"

With her pronouncement, the tables were pushed to the sides and the musicians took their places on the gallery.

Angus offered his hand. "If the Lady of Islay is hankering to kick up her heels, then by all means, let us do so with a country dance."

"Agreed!" said Chahir as he stood and bowed to his wife. "Shall we?"

Filled with contentment, Anya laughed and danced long into the night...until Angus drew her into his arms and whispered into her ear, "Shall we go above stairs, wife, and continue our dancing in the sanctity of our chamber?"

EPILOGUE

SEVEN YEARS LATER

Anya sat in the window embrasure of the nursery and watched as her three children dashed about in their fine clothing, playing a game of tag. Eoin, now a young man of six, was a natural born leader, always dominating his younger sisters, Marie and Aine.

"Come, Master Eoin," said Freya, wielding a comb. The maid had volunteered to become the nursemaid with Anya's firstborn. "Ye cannot meet the king with your tresses looking as if ye've been rolling in the hay loft."

The lad had his father's blond hair and looks. Marie took after Angus as well, though Aine was the spitting image of her mother with freckles across the bridge of her nose.

"Och, why must I meet the king?" asked Eoin. "I want to go ride my pony."

"Ye can ride for days to come, but the king's visit is of utmost importance to your father. And mark me, one day ye will be lord of these lands. And ye'd best learn now, even if ye are lord, duty comes first. Always and forevermore."

The lad stopped and jutted out his bottom lip.

"Does this mean Da will be home for good?" asked

Marie, aged four, as she climbed up on the bench beside Anya.

Anya sighed as she stooped to pick up Aine and balanced the lass of two on her lap. It seemed the wars would never end. "I wish it would be so, except the King of England invaded and we've naught but to defend our borders."

"But our keep is secure," said Eoin.

"That is because our walls cannot be breached. But we owe fealty to Scotland and to Robert the Bruce, and the MacDonald forces are some of the best fighting men in the kingdom."

"I like it when Da's home," said Marie.

"I do as well," said Anya.

The babe pulled on Anya's kirtle laces. "Da, Da!"

"Even the wee one loves her father," said Freya, raking the comb through Eoin's hair, yet having no success at taming the lad's wild locks.

Trumpets sounded from the courtyard. Anya stood with the babe in her arms. "Come, children, we must go to the great hall to attend the ceremony. And remember, ye must remain quiet."

A month ago, Angus had returned from Bannockburn where Angus and the MacDonald army fought in an enormous battle with thousands of men. After the death of Edward the Longshanks, Anya had prayed that the wars would end, but nay. His son, Edward II maintained the same ill-begotten opinion that he should be overlord of Scotland, and invaded a year past.

By the grace of God, the Scots had been victorious at Bannockburn, and Robert the Bruce's favor had grown mightily. He was loved by his subjects and young men flocked to his side, eager to take up arms for the kingdom.

This was a day for pride. For so long, her husband had felt as if the king did not appreciate him as he did many of the other nobles, though the tides had turned at Bannockburn. By the show of might from Clan MacDonald, any misgivings Robert the Bruce may have had were wiped away and gone for good.

Anya and the children pattered down to the hall, which was packed elbow to elbow with clansmen and women. Raghnall met them at the entry from the stairwell and led them to a table in front of the dais beside the Dowager Lady Islay.

"All rise and behold Robert the Bruce, King of Scots!" bellowed the High Steward, who had accompanied the king on this visit.

Benches scraped across the floor. Trumpets on the gallery heralded a fanfare.

Holding her daughter on her hip, Anya craned her neck to witness the king's approach. All this time had passed, yet his wife and daughter were still imprisoned in England. It made her think of how fortunate she had been that Angus had chosen not to take her to the monastery.

As the king approached in his fine velvet robes, Anya dipped into a curtsey, checking behind her skirts to ensure Marie did the same while Eoin bowed. Bless Raghnall, he reminded the lad of his manners.

The king took his place on the dais, followed by his knights Boyd, Campbell, and Douglas. "This is a day of celebration in recognition of the might of Clan MacDonald!" the Bruce boomed, thrusting out his arms to a raucous cheer.

"Come forward, Angus Og MacDonald, Lord of Islay."

Anya's heart hammered as she watched her husband approach through the aisle. Standing tall and broad-shouldered, he posed a magnificent picture of a braw and mighty Highlander.

Aine thrust out her chubby finger. "Da, Da!"

"Shh," Anya hushed the child, grasping her hand and kissing it.

Eoin clung to his mother's skirts as Angus climbed the stairs and kneeled.

The king raised his bejeweled scepter. "In recognition of the MacDonald prowess on the battlefield at Bannockburn, I hereby grant ye the lands in Lochaber, Ardnamurchan, Morven Duror, Glencoe, and Mull. And henceforth, ye shall be known as Angus Og MacDonald, Lord of the Isles!"

As the crowd cheered, Anya's heart took flight, watching her husband receive that which he had desired, that which he had fought for all of his life. And though only the king's men were allowed on the dais this night, as soon as Angus shook the hands of the knights, he immediately came down and joined his family. Lifting Marie and Eoin onto his hips, he kissed them both.

Anya curtseyed. "Congratulations, my love."

"Con-lations, Da!" Eoin echoed.

Grinning, Angus reached out with a single finger and tugged his wife and youngest into an intimate circle, though it was Anya's lips he kissed, his gaze focused only on her. "Och, none of this would have mattered if ye were no' at my side, wife. I love ye more than life itself."

Both clung to their mother's legs as Angus climbed the stairs and knelt.

The King raised his bejeweled scepter. "In recognition of the MacDonald prowess on the battlefield at Bannockburn, I hereby grant ye the lands in Lochaber, Ardnamurchan, Morvern, Duror, Glencoe, and Mull. And henceforth, ye shall be known as Angus Og MacDonald, Lord of the Isles."

As the crowd cheered, Anya's heart swelled, [illegible] watching her husband receive that which he had desired, that which he had fought for all of his life. And though only the knights were allowed on the dais this night, as soon as Angus shook the hands of the knights, he immediately came down and joined his family. Lifting Marie and Robin onto his hips, he kissed them both.

Anya curtseyed. "Congratulations, my love."

"Congratulations, Da," Robin echoed.

Grinning, Angus reached out with a single finger and tugged his wife and youngest into an intimate circle. Though it was Anya's lips he kissed, his gaze focused only on her. "Och, none of this would have mattered if ye were not at my side, wife. I love ye more than life itself."

AUTHOR'S NOTE

Thank you for joining me for *Highland Raider*. I have always loved this time in history and have been excited to finally write about it. Though this is a work of fiction, I did fashion the story around Angus Og MacDonald, Lord of Islay. There are many spellings of his name. Some ancient references refer to Aonghus Óg of Clann Dubhghaill. Of course, there were few spelling conventions at the time and I used the more modern spelling of the clan name since the Dubhghaills eventually became the MacDonalds. It is also possible that the Lordship of the Isles was granted to Angus' son, Eoin. However, I found more than one reference referring to Angus himself as Lord of the Isles and thus wove the grant of the title into the story. It is true that Robert the Bruce had his misgivings about Angus early on in his kingship, but after the MacDonalds proved their might in the Battle of Loudon Hill and then again in the Battle of Bannockburn, Angus gained favor with the king.

Angus married Aine O'Cahan (or O'Cathan as some records show). One reference said she had a sister named Finovola, another said Fingola. Aine was the daughter of Lord Guy O'Cahan, who held the Lordship of Keenaght. The O'Cahan seat was Dunseverick

Castle in County Antrim, Northern Ireland. The feud between the clans and the girls' tenure at Carrickfergus is pure fiction, but it made for quite a twisted feud.

I hope you enjoyed the story and will consider leaving a review. Next in the series, Arthur Campbell will have his romance in *Highland Beast*. I hope you will join in the fun!

Hugs - *Amy*

ALSO BY AMY JARECKI

The King's Outlaws

Highland Warlord

Highland Raider

Highland Beast

Highland Defender

The Valiant Highlander

The Fearless Highlander

The Highlander's Iron Will

Highland Force:

Captured by the Pirate Laird

The Highland Henchman

Beauty and the Barbarian

Return of the Highland Laird

Guardian of Scotland

Rise of a Legend

In the Kingdom's Name

The Time Traveler's Destiny

Highland Dynasty

Knight in Highland Armor

A Highland Knight's Desire

A Highland Knight to Remember

Highland Knight of Rapture

Highland Knight of Dreams

Devilish Dukes

The Duke's Fallen Angel

The Duke's Untamed Desire

ICE

Hunt for Evil

Body Shot

Mach One

Celtic Fire

Rescued by the Celtic Warrior

Deceived by the Celtic Spy

Lords of the Highlands series:

The Highland Duke

The Highland Commander

The Highland Guardian

The Highland Chieftain

The Highland Renegade

The Highland Earl

The Highland Rogue

The Highland Laird

The Chihuahua Affair

Virtue: A Cruise Dancer Romance

Boy Man Chief

Time Warriors

ABOUT THE AUTHOR

Known for her action-packed, passionate historical romances, Amy Jarecki has received reader and critical praise throughout her writing career. She won the prestigious 2018 RT Reviewers' Choice award for *The Highland Duke* and the 2016 RONE award from InD'tale Magazine for Best Time Travel for her novel *Rise of a Legend*. In addition, she hit Amazon's Top 100 Bestseller List, the Apple, Barnes & Noble, and Bookscan Bestseller lists, in addition to earning the designation as an Amazon All Star Author. Readers also chose her Scottish historical romance, *A Highland Knight's Desire,* as the winning title through Amazon's Kindle Scout Program. Amy holds an MBA from Heriot-Watt University in Edinburgh, Scotland and now resides in Southwest Utah with her husband where she writes immersive historical romances. Learn more on Amy's website. Or sign up to receive Amy's newsletter.

Lightning Source UK Ltd.
Milton Keynes UK
UKHW040722170321
380478UK00001B/162